D0201884

POINT
DOOM

POINT DOOM

A MYSTERY

DAN FANTE

BOURBON
STREET
BOOKS

An Imprint of HarperCollinsPublishers
www.harpercollins.com

HarperCollins books may be purchased for educational, business, or sales promotional use. For information, please e-mail the Special Markets Department at SPsales@harpercollins.com.

FIRST EDITION

Designed by Renato Stanisic

Library of Congress Cataloging-in-Publication Data is available upon request.

ISBN 978-0-06-222901-4

13 14 15 16 17   OV/RRD   10 9 8 7 6 5 4 3 2 1

The idea for this book came from my mother,
Joyce Fante, whose love and delight for the diabolical
remained unquenchable for ninety-one years.

POINT
DOOM

PROLOGUE

I t was cold in the Austrian winter of 1940. For the entire month of December the temperature never rose above fifteen degrees Fahrenheit. All inmates from the thirty-two barracks were awakened at 5:15 A.M. each morning. They would work until 7:00 P.M. The boy was ten. Aribert Heim himself had selected him from a group of his laboring peers in the yard because of his height, apparent unusual strength, and blond hair. Dr. Heim always wore a heavily starched white smock befitting his rank and extensive education. The boy, who had been a good student until he and his parents were taken three months earlier at their flat, thought the doctor's face casual but his eyes menacing, like those in a Charles Dickens novel he had once read. One of Dr. Heim's chief assistants was called Oskar, a big Nazi serviceman with sandy hair and thick, wire-rimmed spectacles. Oskar would be the one selected by Dr. Heim to personally train and oversee the boy. He was a strict taskmaster. The sessions would begin at seven o'clock every morning when the first of the subjects would be brought in, and continue until lunchtime, then resume again at 2:00 P.M., then end when the supper siren sounded or before, if the subject they were working on was now dead. Oskar's instructions were that the boy never deviate from what he was being taught and never question an order.

When the boy did make a mistake or hesitate, his punishments were immediate and painful. Years later, when he became a man and tried to erase these memories with drugs and hypnotherapy, he would relive it all, again and again, vividly. After one session with his Beverly Hills therapist, in a rage the boy, now a forty-year-old man, would terminate his treatment with his doctor by crushing the man's head with a glass globe paperweight from a nearby desk. From the age of ten the boy would never sleep through the night. In the procedure room at Mauthausen Concentration Camp there was a long, flat oak table with belts and straps fixed to the sides and the ends. When they arrived in the morning, the subjects would be stripped of their dirty prison uniform, then strapped to the table, naked, by Oskar. The boy's very first instruction from Oskar, who, in the beginning, only spoke to him to give orders, was to place the rag in the mouth of the subject. Over time—over the two years he would continue his work with Oskar and Dr. Heim—the boy himself would become the one to do the stripping and binding and, eventually, the other duties as well.

The boy was fed normally with the prison staff and was permitted to dine in the restricted mess hall with Dr. Heim and Oskar, the other medical personnel, and ranking soldiers. As time went by the boy would gain weight and began to fill out. He would never be permitted to speak to any German soldier other than Oskar and Dr. Heim, but his blond hair made him a favorite among the staff and jokes were often directed toward him at supper. The staff nicknamed him Corporal Jewboy with smiles and affection. Oskar's primary assignment from Doctor Heim, who was infrequently present in the room, was to test— while inflicting injury—the pain endurance of their subjects. These procedures gave the Nazi high command insight into their soldiers' survival ability on the field of battle, after being wounded. The procedures would often go on for hours, sometimes longer, until the subject lost consciousness and could not easily be revived, or simply

died. On Corporal Jewboy's first day Oskar called the boy to his side.
"We begin now," Oskar had barked. "Watch and learn." He would then
start with the subject's left hand. "Watch me!" Oskar commanded.
"Learn how to do it." He would then break each finger of the subject's
left hand by sharply twisting its joint back with a thick wooden tool
resembling pliers until a snapping sound could be heard. Following
that, Oskar would break the wrist, then the elbow, and end with the
shoulder on that side of the body. This sometimes took several hours
because observing the subject's reactions and documenting them was
essential to the process. After both arms were done, the boy's task
would be to remove the straps and mouth gag. Oskar would instruct
the subject that he or she would be given whiskey with water if they
answered questions about their pain. Invariably, the subjects would
agree, if they were still conscious. Oskar would say, "Can you move
your arm?" If the subject could move the arm, he or she would be
given a teaspoon or two of the whiskey and water mixture. If they
were not conscious and could not be revived, Oskar would place the
thick, brown canvas bag that was kept under the table over the head
of the subject. The bag had one purpose: to prevent blood and brain
material from soiling the table and the room. Oskar would then shoot
the subject with his pistol by placing the barrel of the gun under the
subject's chin and firing twice, upward into the head. Oskar's gun
was a small-bore German automatic and only rarely would a bullet
exit the subject's skull and penetrate the canvas bag and travel into
the wall of the room. The noise of the gun was loud in the room
and frightening to the boy in the beginning, so Oskar would come
to the habit of permitting him to cover his ears before firing his
pistol. When the breaking of each appendage was complete, Oskar
would make sure that appendage had been twisted a hundred eighty
degrees and was facing in exactly the opposite direction from its
original position.

It was discovered that Corporal Jewboy was a quick learner and
Dr. Heim himself considered it a benefit that he could read and write.
Filling out a report during and after each procedure on the clipboard
became one of Corporal Jewboy's primary duties. Time passed until
the boy was big enough and strong enough to do the cracking himself.
For the first few sessions Oskar allowed his charge to start off on
specially selected subjects—women and a few children, those of
a smaller body type. Often, if a female subject had ample breasts,
Oskar would demand that Corporal Jewboy touch her breasts before
he began cracking. "Rub her tits with your hands," Oskar would
command. After this was done, Oskar would often go further: "Now
stick your fingers into her! In her cunt. Deep inside." At first the boy
showed hesitation to this specific instruction, and would receive a
hard backhanded slap from Oskar, but in short order his resistance
to cooperation had been pacified. Over their time together Oskar and
Corporal Jewboy conducted in excess of two hundred procedures.
Eventually, the last third of these would be administered by Corporal
Jewboy himself, with Oskar observing. His superior would sit in the
only chair in the room, sipping from the bottle of whiskey.

Mauthausen camp invariably had an overpopulation problem.
In the evenings, after their sessions that day, Oskar would stand
outside the small three-room wooden conjoined building with the
boy. They would watch as several dozen prisoners were marched to a
chalk line twenty paces from a nearby barbed wire fence. The fence
was electrified with lethal voltage and no one could survive contact
with it. Three at a time the prisoners were given a choice: to be shot
immediately or to walk the twenty paces across the chalk line into the
electrified barbed wire fence. Often, many were too weak to decide,
or obstinate. They would be shot immediately for not obeying the
command by one of the three rifle squad members attending them.
The others, usually about two-thirds of the group, would be marched

three abreast, several feet apart, into the fence. The smell of burning hair and flesh would haunt Corporal Jewboy for the rest of his life. At the electrocutions Oskar would not permit the boy to look away but would often light an extra cigarette and hand it to him. The boy found that inhaling the tobacco helped reduce the stink.

Two or three times per week, before the first subject of the day was brought into the procedure room, Oskar would lower his military trousers and, on an order, the boy would then suck his cock.

ONE

Sometimes I think that if everyone was dead around me I might be able to hear what my own mind is screaming.

It was ten minutes before the start of the meeting. I was sitting in the corner, at a right angle to the speaker's podium, far enough away so I could not be noticed. The daily Point Dume (pronounced *doom*) Malibu AA meeting has about fifty chairs. It is held in a converted grammar school classroom that once contained local ten–year-olds but now goes by the title Community Center Room 5.

The noon meetings almost always have several dozen attendees.

Most of the people who attend are locals—rich and jobless or rich and shaking one out. Some are addicts. There are also a good number of court-card alkies who, like me, were sentenced by the judge to come here for their DUIs. The swank recovery homes in Malibu bus in another dozen or so of their seventy-grand-a-month clients.

I'd met the secretary of the meeting several times before, a guy named Albert, a former alkie-dope fiend advertising guy who'd been in a few rehabs himself but now had five

years of recovery and apparently considered himself to be
some kind of AA guru hotshot. These days Albert is a coun-
selor at the Dume Treatment Center, a couple of miles away
in Ramirez Canyon. He wears a tie and jacket when he does
his meeting secretary act.

Albert is a pretentious asshole. His fifty-year-old face reveals a recent jowl-tuck and he smiles too much with perfect
capped teeth and always seems to pay particular attention
to the newcomer girls half his age and never misses an opportunity to introduce himself and pass along a few worn-
out snot-filled one-liners about recovery while he ogles their
tits and takes down their phone number to later make what
people in AA term a "support call." Somehow Albert is less
gregarious with the one or two transient, shit-in-your-pants
locals and guys like me: guys trying to get through the day
without drinking or blowing their brains out.

A PRETTY GIRL in her twenties, dressed in dangly earrings
and cutoff jeans and a short white top that exposes her
tummy, comes walking down the aisle toward my row in
the corner, holding a Styrofoam cup filled with the meeting's
free coffee. She was about to sit down in a seat in the row in
front of me when she paused to get my attention.

"Hi," she says, holding out a pretty, nail-polished hand
for me to shake, "my name's Meggie. I've seen you here a
few times. You're here a lot, right? Like almost every day. I
saw you take a one-year birthday cake a couple of weeks ago
at the Saturday night meeting."

"JD," I say back, shaking the hand with the red finger-
nails. "Yeah, I'm here a lot."

"Congratulations on your one-year cake, JD. I mean that's pretty amazing. It made me think that if you can do it, then I can do it too."

"One day at a time, right?" says I, parroting a recovery puke one-liner.

"I'll have forty-five days tomorrow, JD."

"Hey, good for you," my yap replies, wanting to sound positive, like I gave a rat's ass whether Meggie drinks again or smokes more crack or has Johnny Depp's baby, or not.

"Claude, my boyfriend, has ten days. He's French. He's a film composer. He's pretty squirrely right now and he sort of refuses to get a sponsor. Hey, would you do me a favor and talk to him, JD? Claude won't listen to me but he might listen to you."

"Sure. After the meeting. Whatever."

Then Meggie gives me her twenty-peso grin. "Thanks, JD," she says. "You're a real sweetie."

Then down the aisle comes Meggie's old man, Claude, a short, long-haired Frenchie, wearing an expensive sports jacket, jeans, and T-shirt. Malibu casual. He's carrying his coffee cup in one hand and two big, free chocolate doughnuts in the other.

Claude plants his dapper forty-five-year-old Froggy ass in the chair next to Meggie.

Next to Claude are three girls in their twenties, all wearing baseball caps and logo T-shirts. They're giggling and acting like morons, pointing at the nearby celebrity people and whispering. Apparently, the current gossip is that two young female Latino workers have gone missing without a trace. The girls somehow find this funny too.

After over a year off booze I am still disgusted by most people, especially the has-been actors and ex-rock stars who live nearby in their five-million-dollar châteaus above the cliff overlooking Point Dume.

I am forty-four years old, what in AA they call a retread because I have been in and out of sobriety twice over the last few years. When I meet people at an AA meeting I try to act like a concerned participant, but I'm not. It's just that—an act. I don't belong in Malibu and I don't like Malibu AA. My dead father, James (Jimmy) Fiorella, wrote movies for forty years in Los Angeles as a contract screenwriter. He was a transplant from the Little Italy section of New York City and moved west to Los Angeles, trying to become a newspaper columnist. A few years later, by mistake and by accident, he got into writing screenplays. Pop's street name as a kid in lower Manhattan was Jimmy Flowers. In Hollywood he became a script doctor, rewriting movies that had already been rewritten and further ruined. Jimmy Flowers almost never got a screen credit and didn't want it. He hated every minute of it. He moved us here to Point Dume thirty-five years ago when the place was a desolate, windblown plateau above the Pacific Ocean. Malibu was not pronounced *Maliboooo* in those days and dripping with glitz and two-hundred-thousand-dollar sports cars and big names. As a kid I could stand on our roof and not see another house for miles. Pop wanted to live as far away from the movie business as possible, so he picked Point Dume because no one lived there. Jimmy Fiorella had contempt for the film industry but he always cashed the large biweekly paychecks.

As it turned out, the joke was eventually on my dad because, somehow, with the passing of time, people like Barbra Streisand and Mel Gibson and Goldie Hawn and Bob Dylan and Cher and Nick Nolte and Anthony Hopkins and Louis Gosset and Robert Downey Jr. and Julia Roberts and a hundred other glitzy Hollywood transplants began to build their palazzos nearby. Jimmy had never wanted to be a trendsetter. In the years before his death, as he witnessed Malibu becoming *Maliboooo* and Point Dume becoming Point Glitz, his new dream was to cash out, sell everything, and evacuate his family to the Abruzzo mountains in central Italy. On his deathbed he held my hand and mumbled to me in Italian: "You're a good kid, JD. I love you. You'll figure things out someday."

NOTHING IMPORTANT IN my life has changed since I returned here to my mom's house three months ago, eight years after my old man's death. I arrived with all that I owned in three green plastic garbage bags, my mind still carving more of me up and killing more of me off every day.

My last and hopefully final shitstorm started eighteen months ago. Battling a perpetual headache, I'd gone on a three-week drunk, had a fight or two, and supposedly, underline supposedly, tried to off myself. During this time I had failed to show up at my Marina del Rey business, a high-end car rental agency that supplies the overrich population of Los Angeles with Hummers and Ferraris and Dodge Vipers by the hour and by the day. A good business too—until I blew it.

My serious drinking, and the headaches, began several years before that, after an incident in an apartment in the East Bronx when I was a detective. I killed people that day. That's when the headaches started. The booze, as it turns out, became the only thing that ever helped control the

headaches. But now I don't have the booze, just the headaches. They're less severe but they're not gone.

I don't remember much about the binge that caused me to
lose my rental car business, but it resulted in my having to pay
the tab—thanks to a clause in the partnership contract—by
signing over ownership of my company to my two acting
shit-for-brains minor partners. After I got arrested these guys
called our mutual attorney and, in a conference, decided it
was time to clean my clock, financially.

Knowing they had me by the short hairs, I rolled over and
played dead. In the end, I sold my fifty-one percent in LA
Dream Machine, the company I had started, for pennies on the
dollar and came away with thirty thousand dollars for a business that should have netted me at least three hundred grand.

I hadn't had thirty K in cash in my pocket, free and clear,
in quite some time, so I decided on a road trip and ended up
back in New York City, where I'd lived before coming to L.A.

Once back in Manhattan I made a few strategic and
spontaneous investments—mainly hookers and cocaine
and limo rides and then a suite at the Pierre Hotel—but
I did show up for a visit with the ex in the Hamptons to
settle up five back alimony payments.

A day or so later, when we talked again, I discovered that
Kassandra was having trouble with her newest live-in boyfriend. When I began to dig for answers in the conversation
she finally let me know that Cedric, after a few drinks in the
evening, enjoyed slapping her around a bit. So, one morning before breakfast, after an all-nighter at some downtown
clubs, I motored out to the Hamptons by limo to deal with
Cedric the asshole one-on-one.

That pre-oatmeal visit and the assault and B&E charge that came with it resulted in a permanent restraining order. The charges were eventually dropped, thanks to Kassandra, but I had to do a ninety-day recovery bit at the Croodmoor nuthouse.

JACK KEROUAC ONCE wrote that "the only people for me are the mad ones . . . who never yawn or say a commonplace thing, but burn burn burn like fabulous yellow roman candles exploding like spiders across the stars."

That's crap, but thanks, Jack. For the last few years in New York I'd tried to be one of Jack's people. In my spare time I wrote a book of poems and, before he died, I had even worked with my dad, Jimmy Fiorella, and coauthored a couple of screenplays, but eventually I discovered the truth about Kerouac, that crap, and those people: most of them wind up in the bughouse or with a mouthful of broken teeth and a jar of Xanax. Or worse. They wind up OD'd and dead.

In therapy at my nut ward, my shrink told me that I'd been suffering from a form of PTSD (with headaches) since I killed those people as a private detective. According to him that incident is when the wheels began coming off in my life.

NOW I LIVE with my mother and attend AA and make every effort not to punch people. The PTSD headaches are still there. The dreams too. It's almost always the same dream with two or three different versions: No. 1: I see the wounds but the bodies have no faces. No. 2: I'm buying cigarettes or at a market somewhere and I pull a bloody hand out of my pocket instead of my wallet. In the hand is my gun. No. 3: I'm holding my gun with blood all over me. There are two dead girls there but they are smiling and talking to each other.

Mom, who is now eighty-one, and her caretaker-companion, Coco, and their half-dozen cats occupy two of the six bedrooms in the house on Cliffside Drive in Malibu. Coco is a tall, strong woman. She's only seventy or so. She used to be Mom's neighbor until her husband died of colon cancer. The chemo treatments and other medical expenses lasted for two years and cost the couple every dime they had—their house on Point Dume, their restaurant, everything. After her husband's death, Coco was tits up—about to be homeless. Mom called her and made her the companion-caretaker offer and when Coco's house foreclosed she became Mom's full-time live-in companion.

Because Jimmy Fiorella had left a $1 million life insurance policy, Mom was now more than okay financially. She's been obsessed with astrology for years and never fails to let me know what new-shit planetary aspects are infecting my life.

My bedroom is the small one at the other end of the house.

MY NEW AA sponsor, Southbay Bill, says that I am what in AA they call a WILL NOT. A "will-not," as in, "will not completely give himself to this simple program." And in my last evaluation from my free biweekly state-supplied therapist in Santa Monica (who terminated our sessions, she said, because of my anger issues and my use of profanity), I was told that I should be back on medication, but I refuse to take any of that crap for the headaches or anything else because it doesn't help and it makes my brain stupid. And Southbay Bill has told me that he won't sponsor me unless I'm one hundred percent straight and off everything.

Two weeks ago I got my driver's license back after a long suspension for my last arrest and DUI in California. My license is restricted but I am now allowed to drive to and from my AA meetings and work—except, of course, that I have no job. Old Moms gives me fifty bucks a week for gas that I put in the tank of her oil-guzzling red Honda shitbox that fires on only three cylinders and emits a cloud of black smoke everywhere it goes.

A few days ago, when I began driving again, Mom and Coco were concerned that I might get drunk again and wreck the car, and on Mom's attorney's advice, she signed the title of her farting old Honda over to me.

CLAUDE AND MEGGIE are now holding hands in the row in front of me as the room continues filling up. The girls in the baseball caps are still giggling. Claude has finished gobbling down his chocolate doughnuts and is now scratching his goatee while scanning the room for the movie stars he knows. I can't help but notice that Meggie is wearing pink thonged panties that come two inches above the top of her jeans in back as she sits in front of me. Frilly panties. Very exceptional.

A couple of minutes later face-lift Albert stands at the podium to begin the meeting. "Hi," he says, "My name is Albert and I'm an alcoholic."

"Hi Albert," the room chimes back.

The former classroom is full now. There is only one open seat in my section—the seat next to me—and here comes a tall, fiftyish-looking woman in high heels and designer workout gear down the aisle. She stops at my row. Scary-looking bitch. All yoga muscle with perfect makeup. But the wrinkled skin on her hands and the liver spots are a dead giveaway that fifty is realistically sixty-five. Maybe older. The pulled face can't hide what she really is.

I have to stand to let the Glenn Close look-alike squeeze by me. But when I do, somehow the butt of my Charter Arms .44 snub-nose—a remnant of my New York City days—gets hooked on the backrest of my metal chair. The prick then tumbles out, clatters onto the seat, and falls to the floor.

I pick the gun up and tuck it back into the rear of my jeans, then sit down again.

Looking up I see that a dozen pairs of eyes are on me. The three girls in the baseball caps gawk but Claude's expression is one of alarm. He grabs Meggie (in the pink thong) by the arm. "Vee must mooff from ere," Claude hisses loudly, still glaring in my direction, "to anozer zeat."

Meggie snatches up her tote bag, then turns back to me. "That's pretty scary shit, JD," she hisses. "A fucking gun at an AA meeting."

"Yeah, well," I say, "shit happens. Have a nice day."

The two of them walk to the back of the full room and stand near the coffee table for the rest of the meeting.

THESE DAYS I attribute my black moods and my unpleasant evaluation of all humanity to my long absence from alcohol.

Sleeping at night has become impossible because of the off-
and-on headaches and the dreams of blood and massacres,
so I mostly busy myself by surfing porn sites, reading every
book I can get my hands on, and then nodding off when I
can. But I am usually awake until the sun comes up.

Since the age of twelve I have been into different forms
of martial arts. Lately I've continued to work out and have
walked the local beaches for hours. I have drunk coffee at
every Malibu café within fifteen miles and "talked" recovery
until I feel the onset of rectal cancer. I am unwillingly familiar with every snot-filled hard-luck story of every celebrity
tabloid knucklehead at every AA meeting.

I am not a "winner" in sobriety. I do not kid myself.
I now understand that booze is the great equalizer. I am
the same as everybody else at the Malibu meetings—in
the same fix. Beneath the cologne and Botox they are all
holding on to their ass for dear life, just like me. They sit
in these meetings in their sunglasses and Malibu Colony
tans and whine about their canceled TV series or getting
shafted in their divorce. Their kids hate them and are in
jail or have wound up in rehab themselves. These people
have what everyone in America thinks they want. If money
and fame could fix it, they'd all be fixed. But they're not.
Not by a long shot. They suck air and shit once a day like
everybody else. We're all the same. Nowhere.

AT MOM'S HOUSE that afternoon, with nothing to do, and no
interest in visiting the sex chat rooms, I sat down at Jimmy
Fiorella's old typewriter and began to type. The idea of
writing something on Pop's antique machine had suddenly

appealed to me and I decided to write like he had written. Before computers. So I began typing.

An hour later I looked at the clock. I had written two new poems.

Lighting a cigarette I leaned back and read what was in the machine and now on the desk in front of me. It wasn't very good but I decided not to throw out the page.

TWO

The car sales job interview I got came through an AA pal, Bob O'Rourke, who everyone calls Woody. Woody had been selling used iron at a Toyota dealership in Santa Monica and, after six months, was the top guy on the totals board, making six to seven grand a month. I'd met Woody and his annoying big-toothed smile at the Malibu AA meetings. What we had in common was that we were both sober and drove old red Hondas.

Woody was five years off booze. Older than me. Probably close to fifty. What in AA they call a winner. He didn't live anywhere near Point Dume but drove the twenty-two miles from Santa Monica two days a week to attend the meetings and network with movie people. He's written three Mafia-themed screenplays and is a starstruck screenwriter-wannabe after twenty years in the car business in Massachusetts. One bleak East Coast morning he dumped his condo, packed up his Honda, and rumbled west to chase his L.A. fame fantasy.

When we'd first met and he found out my last name, he was immediately up my ass because of my father's after-death literary fame. (Two of Jimmy Fiorella's forty-year-old novels had been republished and become successful.)

Woody liked to pump me with questions about writing screenplays with my dad. His idea was that we were both sober and had a lot in common because of our screenplay work, and should be friends.

At first I kept trying to blow off the association, and in the beginning I even tried avoiding him. The guy was way too friendly for my taste—way too slick and well-spoken and recovered for me. But in AA, dodging someone is tough to do if you attend the same meetings.

What finally made us closer was when I saw for myself that Woody was a for-real badass, an authentic tough guy. Behind his Turtle-Waxed salesman's grin and his Hollywood chitchat and perpetual cheeriness was the real deal. That, I liked.

And Woody was also a hope-to-die ladies' man, one of those guys who, just by walking into a room, attracts women. Whether it was by his looks or personal style, I could never figure out. The guy was just good with women. Real good. He was usually dating two at a time.

Our friendship began for real at the Point Dume meeting two months before. Some guy—some Hollywood stalker knucklehead with stainless-steel piercings up and down both ears, and tattooed arms—had tracked his skinny model ex-girlfriend to the noon meeting. Tanya was tall and humorless, a way-too-beautiful dazed-looking ex-crackhead and Victoria's Secret model who sipped one coffee after another through the hollowed stir-sticks off the tables.

When I first saw her, a couple of weeks before, she made a sort of half-assed move on Woody at the coffee counter, what in AA they call the Thirteenth Step. And, like I said, Woody's a charmer, so he blew her off in a nice way.

Now she was standing outside before the meeting, making chitchat with her girlfriend, when the ex, a guy who used to be in some famous rock band, comes up and starts a rant about her not returning his calls and how she'd ruined his life and fucked him over and how he was here to show her that she should be careful who she is dissing.

The yelling and the back-and-forth soon got intense. Woody and me and another guy named Manny, a pal of Woody's, who also sold cars, were drinking our coffees at our seats, just inside the AA room, waiting for the start of the meeting, when the ex grabs Miss Skinny and she begins pushing back and yelling.

The three of us step outside for a look-see. Captain Tattoo now has Skinny in a sort-of headlock and is screaming at her. She is attempting to fight him off by grabbing at his hair, with no success.

Enough becomes enough when we see the ex slide his hand into his jacket pocket, apparently for something sharp or with bullets in it. I did not see this part but Woody did, and for a change he wasn't smiling. The asshole turns on him, snarling that he should mind his own business, then gives Woody a shove. Mistake no. 1. A second later what was in the guy's pocket is now in his hand: a sharpened box-cutter shank. Mistake no. 2: Woody uses two or three nice moves, five seconds pass, and Tattoo is on the concrete, holding his nose.

From then on me and Woody were better pals. Later that day, we are drinking more coffee after the AA meeting with Manny at the Dume Café, and to my great annoyance,

Woody offers me a fifty-fifty split if I'll help him rewrite his latest Mafia screenplay so he can send it to his newest agent. I try to be cheerful. I even try to change the subject, but finally I have to tell him flatly that the idea is a loser and out of the question.

After that, thankfully, the conversation was dropped. To move on to something that does not piss me off, I ask Woody how he got the nickname Woody.

"Well," he says, "years ago I used to play semipro baseball in Florida. I was a decent outfielder and I could usually hit home plate on one bounce from dead center field. I had a pretty strong arm."

"Hey," Manny says, "you must've been a helluva hitter, too, to pick up a nickname like Woody."

"I batted .204 in my first season," says Woody.

"Okay," I say, looking at Manny, who's also confused and shaking his head, "we don't get it. Were they making fun of you because of your lousy hitting? Was calling you Woody some kind of a put-down?"

"It wasn't my batting average they were talking about. The first week I was with the team, after practice, one day I was getting out of the shower. One of the guys saw my johnson, and the name got tagged on me."

"So you're hung like a bull elephant," says Manny. "Is that it?"

Woody shakes his head. "Let's just say that some of us are more gifted than others."

"Great," I say. "And the fact that you've got women crawling all over you makes it even worse—a brutal curse, no kidding."

"Pal," Woody says, shaking his head, "it's a fifty–fifty deal. A poosh. I'll just say this: It never kept me sober. In fact I've been in more than one jackpot because of women. Like today, only worse. As they say around AA, I was born with a bad picker."

THREE

The job interview at the used-car lot was with Owen (Max) Maxwell, the used-car manager at Len Sherman Toyota. Max was Woody's current boss and Woody had put in a good word for me.

That morning, after waking up again with my head pounding and the sweats from another nightmare about blood and dead people, I'd showered and dressed in my only pair of slacks with a shirt and tie. It took me almost ninety minutes in rush-hour traffic to drive from Point Dume to the dealership in Santa Monica.

I arrived early for the interview and parked down the block. I own a fake, blue Handicapped placard, so I zipped into a fifteen-minute meter space, reached up behind my sun visor, and pulled it down, then hung the thing on the rearview mirror. A month before, I'd borrowed Mom's legal handicapped placard one day from where it hung from her Escalade's rearview mirror, then had it color photocopied. I'd then trimmed it down with a scissors and glued both sides of the thing back together. A perfect forgery. So now I enjoyed the privilege of parking for free at Santa Monica meters and outside businesses, or in the blue Handicapped zones.

While I waited to go into the job interview I performed my daily ritual of calling my sponsor, Southbay Bill, on my cell. Bill has a reputation for being strict about having his sponsees call him every day. Bill goes to at least six AA meetings a week and has for twenty-five years or more. He's a pretty chatty guy and dispenses a lot of AA snot advice. Conversely, I am not a loquacious person and had I known about Bill in advance I wouldn't have hooked up with him. I'd seen him at a few Santa Monica meetings and everyone apparently considered him a pretty seasoned, easygoing cat. But when he started sponsoring me I discovered a problem that wouldn't go away: Bill is a goose-stepping blabbermouth AA robot.

"Hey Bill," I say into my cell phone, "I'm getting ready to go for that car sales job interview."

"Good," says Bill, "remember, tell the truth. And take God in there with you, and no smartass comments."

"Good advice. Thanks."

"And try a little humility, JD. You just might have good results."

"Okay, I'll remember that."

"Call me when it's over," Bills barks. "I've got someone on the other line. I gotta go. Let me know how the interview went."

I'd gotten lucky. No lengthy AA sermon today. "Okay Bill," I say. "I'll call you."

THE USED-CAR SHOWROOM was a large, one-story glassed-in rectangle with three spiffy, freshly detailed cars on the floor and brochure stands everywhere. There were half a dozen partitioned cubicles for the salespeople. Each of these was just large enough to contain a desk with a computer and two opposing chairs. I asked where Max's office was and was told by one of the salesmen, who didn't look up, that it was in the corner. Its windows looked out on the showroom and the big car lot beyond.

Max was tall with wavy gray hair and looked more like a golf pro than a car man. He was in his midfifties and wore an expensive sports jacket and pressed slacks. He had a couple of rings on each hand and a fancy, thick gold watch with little dials on the sides.

"Hiya," he said, pumping my hand, a habit that appeared to be universal among used-car salesmen throughout Los Angeles. "Have a seat, James. It's James, right?"

"Right. James Fiorella Jr. But I go by JD."

Max tucked himself into a big brown leather office chair. His eyeglasses, which had been sunglasses when he came into the room, were now losing their tint. I hated glasses that did that. I handed Max my typed-out résumé.

"Woody says you're an ace at sales and that I should give you a job."

"Well," I said, "if you hire me I'll do my best. I'm serious about selling and I'll give you a hundred percent of a hundred percent."

Max eyed my résumé. "Ever sell iron? Used cars."

"No. For the last couple of years I owned part of a high-end car rental company. You know, Hummers and Ferraris, that kind of thing. Before that I did telemarketing. I was a phone guy. I also published a book of poetry and I was also a detective in New York City. It's all there on my résumé."

Max kept going. "Woody told me about the Hummer company stuff and the phone rooms. How'd that go? What did you sell on the phone?"

"Printer toner, mostly. The company had a business re-stuffing toner cartridges in China. I did pretty well at it for a few years, then I got sick of scamming people. I took the money I made from the phone room and started the upscale car rental deal."

Max smiled, then scratched his chin with a knuckle that held someone's Super Bowl ring. "You'd better explain that," he said. "Are you saying that when you worked at the tele-marketing job you had to exaggerate to make your sales? I mean, I'll be straight with you here, in the used-car business exaggerating is pretty much a part of the job description."

"Well, there's a difference," I said. "In car sales the cus-tomer gets what he paid for. What I did with my phone room clients was different. What I did was bribe people all day long. Half my time was spent sending out color TVs and lap-tops to IT managers' homes as incentives and buying Xboxes and football jerseys for their kids. They got all-expenses-paid vacations to Las Vegas and Hawaii and Disney World. We even sent them sets of golf clubs and tickets to the base-ball and basketball playoffs and the World Series. Stuff like that. See the difference?"

"Sounds like big business," Max said.

"Yeah, it was. I had two hundred corporate accounts. When I didn't sell them re-furbed toner cartridges I was pitching our other stuff: copiers and printers and memory products. Fifteen of my customers were Fortune 500 companies."

"Geez, sounds like you really hit the big bucks."

"My last two years there I averaged five sales a day and a thousand dollars a sale."

"And you got tired of that?"

"I wasn't selling anymore. I was bribing. I was doing what the medical companies and banks and insurance companies do in Washington with the geniuses who run this country, the congressmen and senators. I was in the kickback business. After a while it disgusted me. I had to pack it in."

"So how long were you in that business?"

"The dates are on my résumé. Too long."

Max was still smiling. "So what was this toner pitch like? Give me an example of your presentation."

For some reason I was now on my feet, gesturing. "Look at it this way," I said. "If you were the customer on the other end of the phone, between me and my thousand-dollar commission for that call, what do you think I'd say?"

"I don't know. What did you say?"

"Anything. Anything at all."

Then I sat down.

Max laughed. "You seem like a pretty intense guy, JD."

Then Max glanced down again at my résumé. "And you used to be a private detective?" he said with an amused smile. "In Manhattan?"

"Yeah," I said. "I did that too."

"A private dick? I've never met an actual private detective before. You know, you don't exactly look the part. I mean you're on the short side. You're thick but you're small."

"That's part of the reason I was good at it. People never look twice at me. I spent a lot of time in hard hats and polo shirts and overalls—blending in."

"Ever carry a gun?"

"Yes, I did. My boss was ex-FBI—and a bad drunk—but through him I got my carry permit."

"Ever use the gun?"

"Sorry, that's confidential. I don't discuss that."

Max rolled his eyes. "Well, then, any interesting cases?"

"I'll put it this way: I learned a few things."

"Such as?"

"On the whole, the human race is pretty much in the crapper."

Max lit a skinny cigar and returned to studying my résumé. "Okay," he said finally, blowing out smoke and looking up at me. "I'm reading here under Additional Training. You're also an MMA black belt?"

"I know self-defense. That's correct."

Another puff. Another cloud of smoke in my face. "And you went from L.A. to New York City and became a detective for five years. Is that how it went?"

"Right."

"After the detective business and the poetry you returned to Los Angeles and became a telemarketer. And then you took the money from phone sales and opened a car rental agency?"

"That's pretty much it."

More smoke in my face.

"So, look, Max," I said, fanning the shit away, "can I ask you something? Can we cut to the chase here? I need this job. I'm a motivated guy and I want to let you know that I've got the chops you're looking for. Bottom line, I can sell."

"I hear that, but I need you to be straight with me, JD. Woody mentioned that you guys go to AA together. Was

your drinking why you changed jobs and blew off a couple
of good careers? Was that it?"

"The answer is yes."

"So you've flamed out?"

"I'm in recovery. It isn't easy for me to talk about this
stuff. I'm a good salesman and I need a decent job to support
myself."

"And now you're drug-free? No booze? No bad habits?"

"For over a year."

"So you burned your life down and now you're looking
for a way up and out. You want a shot at the car business?"

The conversation had just become too personal. This guy
had climbed too far up my ass and I didn't like it. I was being
"honest" for the first time in my life in a job interview and
it was being used against me. I had a strong desire to lean
across his desk, knock the skinny cigar out of Max's mouth,
then grab him by his faggot paisley tie and punch him until
I could see blood—a lot of blood.

"Okay, look," I said, "Do you mind if we bottom-line
this conversation? I can sell. I can sell anything. I can sell
horseshit to quarter horses. You give me a shot at this deal
and I'll prove it to you. I'm a natural."

I got up from my chair again and held out my hand in my
best imitation of Woody O'Rourke. "So how about it, Max?
Do we have a deal?"

Max got to his feet, too, but he didn't shake. "Okay,
here's how I see it: you're a friend of Woody's. He's been our
top guy for months. Basically you have a good background
in selling and if Woody says you're okay, then that's good
enough for me. I'll give you a shot."

But Max still didn't shake my hand. Instead, his attention wandered to a notebook on his desk. He flipped it open and looked down at a list of what looked like upside-down license plate numbers. "Sherman Toyota supplies a demo car to all our salesmen. You'll get yours tomorrow. We pay straight commission every two weeks."

"Woody told me about the demo car and I know there's no guarantee," I said.

"How's your driving record and arrest record?" Max asked. "Sherman does a background check."

I'd been worried that the question would come up and my head began to pound. I had to lie. It was my first and only lie in the interview. My DUIs would surely disqualify me from the job, although one was old enough to have come off my driving record. The last one had been reduced from a felony DUI. There were other things too: I had a jacket with the NYPD, but that wouldn't come up in any California DMV search. My pal Woody had assured me that Sherman Toyota almost never does a background check for the first three months. By then, if I was selling well at the dealership, I might even be able to buy my own car and the problem would be moot. I wouldn't need their demo car.

"It's fine," I told Max.

Of course the demo car was the reason I wanted the job in the first place—otherwise I'd be stuck in Malibu forever with Mom and Coco and their goddamn cats, motoring the earth in my mother's worthless red Honda shitbox. Getting away from Point Dume was my only priority. The car job was my way out.

"Okay, JD," Max said, "be here tomorrow at seven forty-five A.M. The Saturday sales meeting starts at eight o'clock.

Rhett Butler is our new GM as of yesterday. You'll meet him tomorrow morning. Rhett has to okay you and then you're hired, but that's only a formality. All the sales people are usually hired by me."

"Rhett Butler?" I asked. "As in *Gone With the Wind* Rhett Butler?"

Max was grinning. "Not exactly. You'll see tomorrow."

WHAT I WOULD learn the following morning was that Len Sherman Toyota was in the middle of an upper-management housecleaning. This was something my AA pal Woody had neglected to tell me, probably because it had just happened the day before. The old co-manager of Sherman—Arthur Sherman, the nephew of the guy who started the company— and the finance guy and the former GM had been summarily dumped two days earlier.

Max had worked for Rhett Butler at another dealership, so he was not axed with the others. Apparently, abrupt purges of this kind were fairly common in the car business in Santa Monica. Heads rolled regularly up and down the boulevard and whole staffs were often replaced over a weekend. Rhett Butler and his ninja team of management hard-asses had gotten a reputation for traveling from dealership to dealership over the last several years, increasing sales by twenty-five to fifty percent wherever they went. To me, this stuff was right out of a Louis L'Amour cowboy novel: the new sheriff is brought to town to root out the deadbeats and restore order and big bucks to the dealership. Me and the rest of the used-car sales staff would find out about Rhett Butler the following morning—the hard way.

After filling out employment forms, I spent the next hour with Max. He showed me their eighty-car inventory of used vehicles and described the commission structure. There was no medical insurance and no paid vacations. This was the L.A. car business.

For me the odd, coincidental part about working a sales job at Sherman Toyota in Santa Monica turned out to be the car dealership's proximity to St. Monica Catholic High School, near Reed Park. My old high school was only a couple of blocks away. I was back where I'd left off twenty-five years before. At St. Mo's I had spent my high school life being disciplined and harassed by the diabolical and violent Brothers of Saint Patrick, the meanest sons of bitches to ever put on black robes and attain green-card status.

I knew the entire neighborhood like the back of my hand: the flooring shops and the bathroom wholesalers on Lincoln Boulevard, the massage parlors, the fast-food restaurants, even Reed Park itself, where as a ninth grader I had ditched wood shop at eleven A.M. every day with my pal Bobby Waco to smoke in the grandstand of the tennis courts. It was there that me and Bobby had received our first blow jobs for five bucks each from one of the drunken transient women who slept in the park every night.

Now, here I was, at forty-four years old, back exactly where I'd begun.

FOUR

As I was returning to Mom's place in Malibu after the interview, driving up the Coast Highway, the northbound traffic was thick but moving pretty well and my head-thumping was only moderate. I was sipping from my third Starbucks double latte of the day, holding the cardboard cup between my legs as I alternately sipped and smoked, congratulating myself on getting a new job and a fresh start. I was determined to do well.

On the cassette player in Mom's car I was listening to one of my favorite blues songs, an old Jimmy Reed number, "Me and My Baby in a '60 Ford."

If I did okay at the car sales job, if things worked out okay, in a few weeks I might be able to afford to rent my own apartment on the West Side of L.A. and attend normal, non-movie-star, non-Malibu-celebrity AA meetings.

In the Big Rock area, where the Coast Highway runs just above the ocean, a new yellow Porsche convertible with its top down cut in front of me so quickly that I was forced to hit my brakes and then swerve to avoid smacking the rear of the car the prick Porsche driver had just passed.

The act of slamming on my brakes caused my Starbucks latte's top to pop open and its contents to spill out on my only pair of dress pants, soaking the crotch, the bottom of my white dress shirt, and the cloth seat under me.

I was immediately pissed off. I honked several times, then punched my gas pedal to catch up with the Porsche prick, but Mom's three-cylinder turd reacted only by coughing and sputtering. The Porsche guy, wearing a black baseball cap and a black hoodie and sunglasses, was now a full car length ahead of me, still weaving in and out of traffic.

When I finally caught up and got his attention by honking, he sneered, then flashed me the one-finger salute, mouthing the words *Fuck you* as he cut off another car and changed lanes, moving ahead.

L.A. is notorious for road rage and I'd read somewhere that its citizens had been rated the most bad-tempered in America. People get aggressive in their cars all the time and wind up getting shot for their trouble. It wasn't in my mind to hurt the guy, at least not at first. I just wanted to catch up and tell him to take it easy.

The sun was out and the northbound two-lane beach traffic was thick enough for me to keep the convertible in view. A mile or two farther up the highway, I finally caught up to the Porsche.

I honked several times and then, through my passenger window, yelled, "Hey, you almost caused an accident back there! Take it easy, for chrissake!"

The next thing I knew, a heavy aluminum traveling coffee mug was heaved at me and bounced off the side of my passenger door, just below my open window. Again, the one-finger salute and the mouthed words, *Fuck you, motherfucker!*

I had to hit my brakes and slow down. This jerk was now over the line. Now he was intentionally trying to cause an accident!

Minutes later, when I passed Malibu Pier, the yellow Porsche was still in my sight, eight or ten cars ahead. It had just turned twelve o'clock on Mom's Honda's dash clock.

Half a mile later, at Cross Creek Road, I saw the convertible make a quick and dangerous right turn into a shopping mall, rolling through the red light. By the time I reached the intersection, the light had changed to red again. The Porsche was gone.

While I was waiting for the light to turn back to green I noticed that my hands were shaking from rage. Something inside me, some cog in my brain, had just snapped. It was like the old days in New York. It was him or me. I didn't care how long it took or what I had to do, me and this asshole were going to settle this—face-to-face.

Finally, the light was green again and I hung a right also, turning into the U–shaped Cross Creek shopping mall, hoping—suspecting—that the convertible's destination was a noon lunch appointment at one of the high-end eateries in the mall.

The Cross Creek Plaza isn't that big: a movie theater, a Starbucks, and several swank designer shops and restaurants. I knew the area pretty well because I often stopped at Diesel Books to check out the new arrivals.

I maneuvered the Honda through the L–shaped blacktop lot, looking up and down the rows of cars. The yellow Porsche was nowhere in sight. My brain was now hammering itself against the inside of my skull and I was still buzzed with adrenaline rage, but I could sense myself gradually becoming calmer. Reason was slowly replacing anger. It's just some spoiled L.A. asshole in a high-end ride, I told myself. You don't need to bust someone up over this nonsense, car dent or no car dent. Jesus, JD, cut the guy a break, for chrissake! Use the Twelve Steps. Live and let live.

I pulled into a parking space and stopped the car and began to take deep breaths. A couple of minutes later I was better.

I decided to pack it in and was about to back out and turn for home when, just for the hell of it, I told myself to take one more shot and try Guido's Restaurant on the other side of the plaza. The outside entrance to the restaurant is between the buildings but its parking lot is in back, behind the shopping center. Movie people and celebrities from the Malibu Colony come to Guido's for lunch.

Pulling behind the plaza and seeing Guido's in front of me, I spotted the yellow convertible again and congratulated myself for thinking that the Porsche guy must've been rushing to make a noon lunch appointment.

I watched as two busy kids in red jackets tucked spiffy cars into the valet park area.

The convertible's top was still down and it was parked ten slots away from the restaurant's front door.

I could feel anger returning. Screw it! This jerk has it coming. It was time to get even.

Since I knew where the Porsche prick was, I decided to give myself plenty of time to form a plan of attack. I pulled Mom's Honda into a spot several rows away from the restaurant entrance, in the public parking area. This punk was going to get a nice surprise for almost causing a wreck, ruining my only decent pair of work pants, and denting my mother's car with his metal coffee mug.

When I was sure no one was looking, I opened my trunk and removed one of the three quarts of 40-weight oil I kept in a cardboard box as backup. Mom's shitwagon regularly used a quart every two days. Then, from my toolbox, I grabbed the silver metal oil funnel that I kept wrapped in a rag and jammed it into a new quart. After that, from the box, I located a folding tool with a leather punch. Then I tore off a handful of paper towels from a roll I also kept in the trunk.

I carried the oil can wrapped in the paper towels behind my back, out of view, as I walked down the row of high-end rides toward Guido's entrance. The valet guys were busy working, parking a line of new arrivals, and didn't notice me.

I waited until neither of them was near the yellow convertible. Then, leaning in and across so I wouldn't trip the car alarm, I poured half of the oil on the seats and floor carpet. After that, ducking down, I circled the Porsche, my punch in my left hand, and jammed it into the side of each tire. I could have done more. A lot more. I could have slashed the seats and done electrical damage but I figured that a nice cleanup job and a tow-truck call for a couple of thousand dollars' worth of tires made us even.

WHEN I ENTERED the restaurant I noticed that my hands were shaking again. A pretty Asian hostess in heels approached me. She saw that I was carrying a quart can of oil wrapped in paper towels, then noticed my expression, and gave me a startled look. "No problem," I said. "I'm not here to eat. I'm just talking to a customer."

She stepped back, nodded, rolled her eyes, then turned to the couple in beach clothes who had come in behind me. "How many for lunch?" she chirped.

It took me a few seconds out in the main dining area to locate the Porsche motorist. His black hoodie was easy to pick out and he was sitting with two other people at a table. Both women.

Approaching the jerk, who was still wearing his heavy-framed sunglasses and cap, I noticed he and the women with him were eating salad. One of them had tattoos on both her arms and two or three lip piercings. Retro punk.

I waited until they stopped talking and looked up, thinking that maybe I was their waiter or something.

Without speaking, I first poured some of the oil on his salad, then trailed the dripping goo across the white table-cloth to his pants and sweatshirt. Then I pressed my oily hands against the guy's chest, rubbing the oil in.

To my surprise I discovered that there were breasts behind the baggy sweatshirt. Good-sized breasts.

She—now I knew it was a she—lurched backward in her chair. A nice blob of the oil was running down the front of her and soaking into the seat cushion of her chair. "That's for you, jerkoff," I said. "I never forget someone who tries to kill me on the highway. And I always get even."

Her face reddened but she didn't speak.

She opened the zipper on the sweatshirt and peeled it away. Beneath her hoodie was a tight-fitting, white T over round, large, braless breasts.

When I finally noticed her hands, I saw that there were

rings on at least three of the fingers. She had big hands for a woman.

"Go ahead, get up," I said. "I'll nail you right here! You think a yellow Porsche and bad attitude gives you the right to get crazy with people on the highway? Go ahead—get up, you psycho bitch!"

She didn't stand up. Instead, she adjusted her sunglasses. She didn't look scared either. "You grabbed me, mother-fucker! That's a serious mistake."

As her friends watched, I poured the rest of the oil from the can into my hands, knocked her cap off, then smeared it on her hair and face. She tried to duck but I was moving too fast. Finally, she lurched back in her chair and it tipped over.

Now she was on her feet. When she spoke again, it was in an even tone. "You're a dead man, bitch. That's a promise."

"Screw you, lady! You messed with the wrong guy today," I yelled. "Now the score's even!"

Heads were turning toward us from the tables nearby.

As I started to leave, two busboys and a beefy-looking guy in a cook's apron were blocking my path toward the exit. The beefy guy was holding a heavy metal soup ladle—ready for trouble.

"Back off," I snarled. "I'm leaving. If you don't want to get hurt, just back off!"

They backed off.

TWENTY MINUTES LATER, when I got back to Mom's house, I was okay again. Grateful I hadn't really hurt anyone.

Mom and Coco were outside on the patio in the sun and didn't hear me come in. Without saying hello I went to the bathroom and took a shower. After the shower, standing naked at the refrigerator, I downed a quart of milk. Then, wrapped in one of Jimmy Fiorella's old bathrobes, I went to my bedroom and called my sponsor, Southbay Bill, on my cell as I'd promised. I'd already decided not to share any of the details about what happened at the restaurant.

Bill was at work at his store. He owns a copy and printing business in Hollywood and when he talks about owning his own joint he always calls it "a gift of my sobriety."

"Hey, Bill," I said, "it's JD. Can you talk?"

"Yeah, of course we can talk. But I gotta go if a customer comes in. I'm working the counter. It's Friday and the girl's on a coffee break."

"So . . . guess what? I got the job."

"Hey, congrats, JD. Nice work. God is good. Small miracle. I was praying for you. When do you start?"

"Tomorrow morning. I feel okay about it too. I really need the job."

Then I added, "Look, Bill, I wanted to say thanks for your help. You were the one who suggested that I ask Woody about an opening at the dealership."

Bill chuckled. "First things first, my man. God's will and not my will. We take the action and leave the results up to the Big Shooter."

"Well," I said, "anyway, thanks again."

But Bill wasn't done. He had more spiritual input. "Speaking of miracles, I'll share one with you. Want to hear how a Higher Power works in another recovering alcoholic's life?"

"Sure. Okay," I said, knowing that I was in for another of Bill's spiritual AA harangues.

"My friend Stan. You know Stan. We always sit together at the Wednesday night meeting."

"Sure . . . Stan. He's got twenty-something years, like you. The bald guy."

"Well, Stan has a bad back. He's had laser surgery and he wears that metal brace 'n all. He's had a rough time for the last few years with that back. Naturally, because he's sober, he refuses to take any pain meds."

"Hey, that's a drag," I said. "I didn't know about Stan's back, Bill." And I didn't give a rat's dick if Stan had a bad back or not. I don't like Stan. In my book Stan is a shit-hole, a long-time-sober condescending prick. Stan makes it a habit of calling me "sonny boy" at meetings and makes every effort to infect me with the feeling that I don't know my ass from third base about sobriety and recovery.

"Well," said Bill, "here's the miracle: Stan is watching the evangelist guy, Joel Osteen, on the TV. He watches him every week. You listening here?"

"Front and center," I said. But now I was also wondering to myself why in the hell I had to hear about Stan's demented Jesus miracle.

"So Stan's watching this preacher, like he does every week. And the guy is talking about the healing power of God. How many have been cured by their faith in a loving God and all. So Stan gets this idea—an inspiration. His idea is to put his hands on the TV screen while the preacher is talking."

"Really?" I said. "No kidding. Stan actually put his hands on the TV screen?"

"Are you listening, JD?"

"Right. I'm listening."

"From that second on, Stan has had no more back pain. That's a miracle of faith! A product of the Twelve Steps of recovery."

"Well, wow, no kidding, I don't know what to say here."

"The point is, my newcomer friend with twelve months and two weeks of abstinence from booze, that through the steps of Alcoholics Anonymous and faith in a God of your own understanding, miracles are achieved. A great change is possible if you apply yourself to this work and make a commitment to grow into a new man. That's the reason I said what I just said."

"Well, I'll make it a point to catch that preacher's act on TV. I need better clothes and a new apartment."

Southbay Bill didn't reply. He had hung up.

AFTER I FINISHED my call with Bill, Mom and Coco entered my room, each holding a cat. Mom asked about my job interview. I told her that I got the gig. A faint smile crossed her lips until she saw my coffee-stained clothes, then she made a face. "What happened there?" she asked, pointing at my ruined shirt and pants lying on the bed.

"My coffee spilled in the car," I said. "A stupid accident."

"Mercury retrograde," she hissed. "I warned you, didn't I? At least twice."

Then Mom shook her head and she and Coco left the room. In a couple of minutes she was back, carrying her purse. She handed me her ATM card. "You can't start a new job and not look respectable," she said. "Go back to Santa Monica and buy some decent clothes. And bring me the receipt."

As she was turning to leave the room, she stopped. "Need I remind you that you now owe me over three thousand dollars in personal loans? I've written it all down, not including the outlay for that preposterous so-called treatment program. Another five thousand dollars down the waste pipe, as far as I'm concerned. As you know, James, I keep accurate accounts. Every penny. And now that you have a new job, I fully expect you'll be finding your own place again and making a beginning at a repayment plan."

"I'm doing my best here, Ma. I'm trying to turn things around."

"Really? Apparently you've forgotten that you lost a successful business and disgraced yourself and our family name. You call that doing your best?"

ON MY WAY back to Santa Monica to buy new clothes, on the Coast Highway, I had to stop for a red light at Cross Creek Road. It had been an hour and a half since my visit to Guido's Restaurant.

Looking over at the parking lot, thirty yards away, I caught sight of a white tow truck. Hooked to the back of the truck was a yellow Porsche convertible. The truck driver was writing something up on his clipboard while a woman still dressed in sunglasses and a black hoodie and jeans stood with her hands on her hips, looking on.

A moment later she turned her head and her attention wandered in the direction of the highway. Her eyes came to rest on Mom's tomato-colored Honda, then on me. There was no mistaking her expression.

FIVE

He loved the California coastline. Over the years he had made the spectacular drive from San Diego to San Francisco no less than a dozen times in his elegant Millennium motor home. Until last week those drives had always been recreational and rejuvenating. Then suddenly, one of the young female charges who worked on his estate had gone missing and, on a tip from her jilted boyfriend, he had driven to Ensenada to find the girl and reassert his authority. Sadly, when the child had resisted and refused to return with him, he had had no choice but to kill her.

It was early afternoon on day three of his Highway 1 tour when he reached Santa Barbara. The girl's body had been washed and dissected and was now stored in plastic bags in the cargo area of the motor home. The day's outside temperature was a perfect seventy-two degrees and above him the sky was blue and faultless. After a less than enjoyable luncheon with a former female TV star at the Four Seasons, he refueled the motor home, returned several phone calls, then continued his drive north to enjoy the exquisite coastline.

The sun was beginning to set as he approached the Buellton–Solvang exit on Highway 1. From behind his vehicle a California

Highway Patrol trooper's flashing lights caused him to pull over. The
tall woman who got out of the cruiser and approached his motor home
wore mirrored sunglasses beneath her wide-brimmed hat. He noted
that her tan uniform appeared tailored and fit her well.

As she rounded the front of his vehicle, he pressed his dash
button, heard the hiss, and watched as the automatic door popped
open.

He stood at the top of his carpeted steps as they began to speak.
From six feet away he was able to read the lettering on her gold
nametag. It spelled out the name, Trooper Spivak.

After handing the officer his driver's license, vehicle registration,
and insurance card, he was informed that he had failed to use his turn
signal when exiting the highway and that she would be issuing him a
summons for that offense.

He felt himself becoming annoyed and decided to speak bluntly to
the woman. This was patent nonsense, he said. There had been almost
no highway traffic behind him for several car lengths. Why then would
he need to use his directional signal?

Trooper Spivak's posture stiffened behind her sunglasses but she
said nothing.

Then, as she was looking over his vehicle documents, she paused.
"I smell something strange coming from inside your motor home, sir.
Something smells funny," she said.

Spontaneous killing had never been his métier. In fact he'd always
considered it unrewarding and risky. Yet, quite suddenly, his options
were limited.

Trooper Spivak set his license and registration documents on the
carpeted steps of the motor home and began boarding. "I am ordering
you to stay where you are, sir," she said. Then she unholstered her
service weapon.

His reaction was spontaneous but a bit sloppy. As she moved up the steps he kicked the woman in the stomach. She fell backward and her gun went off. The bullet entered her leg below the knee.

Ten minutes later, after gagging Trooper Spivak and restraining her on one of his motor home's two facing leather recliners, he used her uniform's thick belt around the injured leg to stop the blood flow. Following that he made his way to her vehicle, shut the motor off, then removed the car keys and a dash-mounted shotgun. In the cruiser's trunk was the woman's purse and a long-barreled stainless steel flashlight. He took these as well.

Heading north on Route 1, an hour passed before he reached the Bescara Resort Inn. It was dark now. He rounded the building's registration entrance and then pulled his motor home into the rear parking area. It was a weeknight and the lot was nearly empty.

Trooper Spivak was conscious and struggling though her leg wound continued to ooze. The bullet had entered and exited through her calf but was not serious. He used a sedative injection to calm her, then retightened the belt on her leg.

After registering in the lobby and getting his room key he returned to the motor home. Spivak was still alert but more docile.

Putting on his plastic gloves he cut away her clothing with a pair of thick shears and replaced the tourniquet on her leg. The last items he clipped from her body were her boots, police bra, and pair of white Kmart panties. The panties had small pink roses rimming the waistband.

He decided against removing the officer's mirrored sunglasses. To him the glasses symbolized the irony and absurdity of the situation she had put them both in.

After laying out his surgical tray he covered the motor home's carpeting and the facing of the recliner with plastic sheeting and cleaned up the bloodstains as best he could. He then selected an appropriate musical accompaniment: *Mel Tormé's Greatest Hits*.

Leaning close to the woman, jostling her to make sure that she was conscious, he untied each arm separately and, with deft motions, broke them both at the shoulder joint.

After resecuring her he picked up a scalpel and reclined her chair. The facts were these: This police person had jeopardized his freedom and was, he felt, annoying and inappropriately aggressive. The decision was simple; her death would be a slow and painful one.

He elected that his initial cut would be fairly wide, a six-inch opening just beneath her rib cage. While she looked on he would remove her intestines and place the coiled mass on her naked chest.

He was about to make the first cut when he saw that his hand was trembling. He realized that he had allowed himself to become genuinely upset. The incident had thrown him off center.

Setting his scalpel down he leaned back and took several deep breaths. He needed to reassess his relationship to this person. He chided himself. He should, at the very least, at a minimum, be objective.

A minute passed and then he leaned closer to Trooper Spivak's face, gently removing her mirrored sunglasses. He began stroking her cheek with the back of his hand. Spivak, whose eyes had been clamped closed, reacted to his touch by turning her head away.

Now he made a study of the woman before him. He observed that without the glasses, she was not displeasing. She was a big woman, certainly, wide-hipped, with acne scars on her face and jawline, but not unattractive—except for her nose.

He unfastened the clips that held her hair tightly in place against her head. In doing this the thickness of it fell to her shoulders.

Wanting to know more about her, he reached down and picked up her purse from the floor. From it he removed her lipstick, a makeup compact, her wallet, a postcard, a pack of Marlboro Lights, and a blue plastic lighter. He spread these across her naked chest and stomach and then dropped the purse back onto the carpet.

Trooper Spivak opened her eyes briefly, then clamped them closed again.

The postcard was the first thing he examined. It had a photo of the Atlantic City Boardwalk on the front. Turning the card over, he saw that it was signed by a person named Simone. According to what Simone had written, she and Willy were having a great time.

Setting the card down he opened Trooper Spivak's gold-toned lipstick. He tasted it by drawing an X on his tongue. After deciding that the flavor pleased him, he dropped the lipstick into his shirt pocket.

He then opened her compact. It was plastic and white. He smelled the powder, then closed the lid. He put the compact back on Trooper Spivak's chest, covering her right nipple.

Her California driver's license gave her full name. Marta Denise Spivak. Her birthday was August 4. She was six feet two inches tall. She weighed one hundred and sixty-three pounds.

There was an assortment of photographs in her wallet's plastic inserts, perhaps twenty in all. Most of them were of the same two women, both apparently Trooper Spivak's sisters—they all shared the same flat nose. There was a picture of a bulldog as well. The animal was huge, with a brown spot over one eye. Toward the back of the photos there were several of children: a boy of about seven and two preteen sisters who had brown hair. Absent, he noted, were any pictures of a man—a husband or boyfriend.

Marta Spivak had twelve dollars in the wallet—a five and seven singles—plus loose change. She had one credit card, a Visa.

As he was dropping the coins back into the purse's change slot she opened her eyes again and seemed to want to speak. The sock he had inserted into her mouth was her own filthy sock.

He removed the tape from her face and extracted the sock.

Spivak cleared her throat and spoke in a near whisper. "Take it all," she said. "Whatever you want. Take it."

As their glance met, he noticed that she had interesting eyes. Remarkable eyes, even. They radiated fear, of course, but in them there was also a dignity and a sense of what might be a quiet elegance. It made him recall the eyes and expression of the Egyptian statue of Nefertiti. He owned an original miniature from the Metropolitan Museum in New York and for years the tiny gold and black figure had been on view in a glass case on a shelf in the lower guest bathroom of his Malibu estate.

Mel Tormé was now crooning "Moon River."

He leaned closer to Spivak. "Your first name is Marta. That's a pretty name," he said.

"Please. Please let me go."

"Are your parents East European? Perhaps Ukrainian? The name Spivak means singer. Is Spivak your married name?"

"I'm not married. Look, take the money. Take the wallet. You can get more from the ATM too. I have about eight hundred dollars."

"You have remarkable eyes, Marta," he whispered. "In fact, you have the eyes of royalty."

"Please—just let me go, okay?"

It was only now that he came to understand the real purpose of their meeting. No question, it was her eyes.

For him the universe was one of symmetry and order. There were, of course, no accidents. True, Trooper Spivak had been the source of a possible summons that afternoon but he had nearly squandered their coming together by his haste and destructive emotions. He had nearly lost the opportunity for this . . . intimacy.

"You're quite tall," he said quietly.

"I know."

"Do you have a boyfriend?"

"Look—"

"Yes or no, Marta?"

"Yes. Okay. Sort of."

"You don't have his photograph in your wallet. Will you tell me why?"

"I threw it away."

"You threw his photo away? Why would you do that?"

"We had an argument."

" You strike me as a by-the-book type of person. Is that accurate?"

"I don't know. I just try to do my job."

"Is this boyfriend employed by the California Highway Patrol? Is he also a trooper?"

"He works construction."

"How long have you been dating?"

"Look, please listen to me. You can still let me go."

"Tell me, Marta, have you had an energetic romantic life with this . . . boyfriend?"

"Please—I won't tell anyone. I promise."

"What's the boyfriend's name? I'd like to know it, if you don't mind."

"Louis. His name's Louis."

"Does Louis look into your eyes . . . in romantic moments? Does Louis do that?"

"I don't know. Yes, I guess he does that."

"Has Louis ever told you that you have the eyes of royalty, Marta— the eyes of an Egyptian queen?"

"No. He's never said that."

"Well, you do. I assure you that you do."

"I don't want to die."

"Do you believe it possible that you and I are here today, let us say, for a purpose?"

"I just try to do my job. That's all it is—just a job."

"I believe that who we are is how we express ourselves in the world. If I may, I will quote Heraclitus, the ancient Greek philosopher, who said, *'Ethos anthropos daimon.'* Character is fate."

He looked down at Marta's brown boots and excised clothing. Then he picked up the contents of her purse from her chest and set them on the floor with her other things. He then brought his mouth to her ear. "I apologize for my rudeness this afternoon. I admit to have behaved poorly. In fact I now believe you to be a special person. I believe that you have been selected."

"You're going to kill me. Is that it?"

"I broke the law this afternoon by not using my turn signal. I am guilty as charged. I will send in the money. How much is the fine?"

"I don't know."

"I pride myself on keeping my word, Marta."

He picked up her mirrored sunglasses and put them back on her. Then, with his large hands, he forced her jaw open and shoved the sock back inside her mouth. Then he retaped her face.

Getting up, he crossed the carpet to a row of built-in supply cabinets made of natural mahogany. He had paid several thousand dollars extra during the construction of his motor home for natural wood instead of the standard laminate facing. Opening one of the cabinets, he removed a jar of petroleum jelly.

Returning to Marta he reached down and picked up the long-barreled stainless steel flashlight. As she looked on, he coated the tube with lubricant; then he leaned close to her ear. "It's time to begin now, Marta," he whispered.

It was after midnight when he punched in the number of his assistant Raoul at his Malibu estate. His call was answered on the second ring.

"Raoul," he said, "I'll need your help."

"Yes, sir."

"I'm at the Bescara Inn off Route 1 an hour or two north of Santa Barbara."

"Yes, sir."

"Bring two cars and two of the men."

"Yes, sir."

"Burn the motor home after you dispose of the remains inside. The motor home should look as if it were vandalized—torn seats, stolen electronics, broken fixtures. Do you understand?"

"Yes, sir."

"Burn it to the ground."

"Yes, sir, I understand."

"I'll be asleep. My suite number is 125. There are two tall potted cactuses on either side of my room's door. I believe they are *Adenia glauca*. Leave the keys to one of the cars on the floor behind the cactus. The one on the left as you face the room."

"Will you be returning to Malibu, sir?"

"Good night, Raoul."

"Good night, sir."

SIX

The next morning, after less than two hours' sleep, after another dream about reaching into my jacket pocket and finding the severed and bloody hand again, I reported for work. I parked Mom's red shitbox up the block from Sherman Toyota, on Ninth Street. A legal spot. No meter.

It was seven forty-five A.M. Saturday morning. I was wearing a new pair of pants and a stiff, new unwashed white shirt that was already scraping a red mark on my neck. I had a new tie, too, but I'd stuffed it into the glove compartment before I went in, in case I needed it later.

The conference room at Len Sherman Toyota had no windows and no pictures on the walls. In fact the room wasn't a conference room at all. It was a working replica of a high school classroom, complete with two dozen one-piece pine and metal student desks. There were pads and pens resting on the desktops and my friend Woody was the only other person in the room. I waved *hi*. Not only had Woody gotten me my job, but over the last several months he had come to be a good friend. On two occasions when I was freaked out and on the verge of getting drunk it was Woody

I'd called both times. He had driven all the way out from Santa Monica to Point Dume to talk me down and save my ass. "How's it going, big guy?" I asked.

"Just ducky, JD. Pull up a chair. The big show's about to get started."

Then he pointed to a large corkboard pinned to the wall to my right. "But first have a look at those mug shots and see who you're working for."

I turned and saw a gallery that contained all of Sherman Toyota's retail sales permit photo IDs. Stepping closer to the board I couldn't help but notice that Robin Baitz's ID was above all the others. Robin Butler Baitz, aka Rhett Butler, Sherman's new GM. Apparently Rhett Butler was a nice, spiffy, fake sales name.

I sat down in the back row next to Woody. He was sipping from his Pete's Coffee espresso cup. "Welcome to the shitstorm," he said.

"Thanks," I said. "Yesterday Max filled me in about the management shake-up. He also said they pay every other Friday. I gotta tell you, Woody, I'm a happy camper."

"You won't be, pal. I met with Butler yesterday afternoon and had a talk with him. Your new boss is a one hundred percent gold-plated ball-breaker. He bumped five of the old staff while I was out on the lot talking to a customer. Just walked in with his huge belly, holding that dumb-ass pink coffee mug he carries that's shaped like a pair of tits, and points at the staff: 'You, you, you, and you, and you, too. See me in my office.' Half an hour later their desks were cleaned out and they were gone. Ba-boom. All bumped on the spot."

"How come?" I asked.

"It's the car business, pal. Heads roll. Max let me know

that Rhett is changing the schedule too. I guess he's trimming the fat by cutting the staff. That's how a dealership can fire five people in one day. Charming shit, right?"

A FEW MINUTES later, as the wall clock got to eight, the room was populated by the rest of the sales staff: four more guys and one girl, the ones who had not been fired in the latest show-of-power car-business purge. Then, the great man himself entered with Max behind him, carrying a clipboard to make notes and Butler's coffee cup with the tits.

"I'm Rhett Butler," he snarled with a capped-tooth grin, "for those who don't know me yet. I'm here to increase sales. My goal and Max's goal is to up our gross by twenty-five percent in the next thirty days. That's what they pay me for. You'll soon find out that I'm hard on salespeople. But I have another side too—I'm also a greedy son of a bitch. I'm here to make you and me a shitload of money. If you produce, we'll get along and you'll make bigger bucks than you ever did before selling iron. If you don't, you're down the road. Understood?"

Most of us nodded.

"Next thing you should know: all days off are canceled as of today. Max has your new work schedule. Do it, Max."

Max handed Rhett his coffee mug with the tits, then pinned the new schedule to the corkboard by the door.

Rhett kept talking: "Bottom line, no more weekends off. No more banker's hours. No more split shifts. One shift a day for everybody. Bell to bell. And from now on, everybody works weekends. All salespeople will get one day off a week. A weekday."

Next to me, Woody groaned.

"You! You got a problem? Let's hear it!"

Woody rolled his eyes but didn't say anything, so Rhett snarled again: "Right, that's what I thought!"

Then he went on. "Also, now hear this: if you have to come in on your day off to deliver a car, then you'd better be here *at the store* to deliver it! If you are a no-show for a delivery and your customer arrives to pick up his vehicle, the salesman who delivers your car will get credit for the sale and also get your commission. Understood?"

Moans and grumbling from the asses seated in the classroom chairs.

"And here's the new dress code. This includes all managers: no more casual dress on weekends. From now on it's dress shirts and ties for the guys, skirts or dresses or slacks for the women, seven days a week. If you arrive out of uniform you will be sent home. Understood?"

Dead silence from the staff.

"Last thing, the demo car you are driving is not your car. That vehicle is for sale like everything else on this lot. It belongs to this dealership. Just because you drive it for your own use does not mean it belongs to you. It is a dealership spiff—a free gimme. And if the inside and outside of that car is not one hundred percent clean at all times, you will receive one ding on Max's attendance sheet. If you get two dings, you're a pedestrian for the next thirty days. That means everyone, sales managers included.

"Okay, now here's the deal with the ups: from now on everyone has their own sales area on the lot. No more number system. The number system is a joke. Max will assign each of you an area on the lot. Your personal patch. You are to be outside on the lot at all times on that patch unless you got a mooch in the box or you are at your desk, working a deal or making call-backs. Any mooch that stops in your area to check out a car, that mooch automatically becomes your up. And there will be no skating other salesmen. That shit will not be tolerated.

"Here it is again. Listen up: if the mooch stops in your area by a car, then he's your up. *If he stops.* If you are caught skating in someone else's area, and a sale is made, you will lose that sale.

"Okay, that's it. That's all I've got. Any questions?"

TRUDY, A TALL and skinny saleswoman in a short skirt and tight blue top, had a question and held her hand up.

"Excuse me, Rhett," she said, "I go to my second job twice a week at five o'clock. I have to be on time. Can I work something out?"

Rhett smiled. "No exceptions. Zero."

Trudy rolled her eyes.

"Now, all of you, check the board to see what your new day off is. Last thing: we have a new bonus policy at Sherman Toyota. Here it is. *This is the good news, so listen up, kiddies!* Beginning this weekend, the salesman who delivers the most cars will get a five-hundred-dollar cash bonus. And from now on, any salesman who delivers three cars in one day gets a five-hundred-dollar cash bonus. And any salesman who delivers ten cars in one week from now on will receive a five-hundred-dollar cash bonus in addition to his commission. And from now on, the first sale of the weekend gets a five-hundred-dollar bonus. In cash. All cash bonuses are off the books."

This information brought wide smiles from most of the sales force—all except Woody and Trudy.

Rhett went on. "This is the car business, my friends. You work for Rhett Butler now. If you give me my pound of flesh I'll make you a lot of money. If you don't, you're history. It's as simple as that. I know you think I'm an asshole. Everybody thinks I'm an asshole. I'm known all across L.A. as an asshole—a rich asshole. Play ball with me, I'll make you a fat paycheck every two weeks. Any more questions?"

There was only one. It came from Fernando, the dealership's only Spanish-speaking salesman. "Scuze me, Rhott. My dae hoff ez disa Sunday. Tomoro," he said. "I got me some planz to go out of tonn. I steel got my dae hoff?"

"Meeting's over," Rhett barked. "Let's go to work."

AFTER EVERYONE HAD left the room only me and Woody remained in the chairs. He made a face. "See what I said: This sucks," he said, "in plain fucking English. I got dinner with my sponsor twice a week. I go to two noon AA meetings. Now that's all down the shitter. I move an average of twenty cars a month for this joint. I've been the top guy here for months. My weekends and nights are now history—that means I start going to late-night AA meetings. Until ten minutes ago I had a sweet deal."

"I hear ya," I said. "Mercury retrograde."

"What? Mercury-fucking-what?"

"Forget it."

"Look, screw this shit, JD. I'm outta here. I'm done. I'm going home."

"What for?"

"To make some phone calls. I'll have another gig in a couple days. No big deal. Effective immediately. Rhett Butler and his plaid sports jacket can suck my ten-inch dick."

Woody unhooked his demo's car keys from his key ring and handed them to me. Then he pulled his cell phone out of his jacket pocket. "Do me a favor, pal, and give those to Max. I'm calling a cab to take me home."

"No so-long to Max and Rhett? No kiss-my-ass? Nothin'?"

"Don't you get it, JD? In the car business you're a turd—a photo mug shot on a bulletin board. Those boys don't give a rat's ass about us. Tell Max I'll be back to pick up my check."

Then Woody stood up and held out his hand. "Anyway, good luck, pal. You'll need it. I hope you make some money. See you around."

THE RAIN STARTED coming down half an hour after the meeting broke up. I had retrieved my tie from Mom's Honda, then I watched from the showroom as Woody got into his cab.

Rain came down for the rest of that day. Steady. It was Saturday—the best day of the week in the car business. The rain killed everything. The weather forecast was for two more days of it. I was the only male salesman that day technically in uniform. Skinny Trudy had gone into Max's office to plead her case about her second job. Five minutes later she, too, had cleaned out her desk.

By noon most of us were soaked and none of us had had one legitimate up. Three or four service department customers came into the showroom to wait but none of them wanted to buy cars and were just killing time. They picked up brochures or eyeballed the polished iron, got a free cup of coffee, opened and closed the doors and kicked the tires of the cars on the floor, but there was no action at all.

Max and Rhett both stayed in their offices watching sports on TV and the sales staff, me included, after getting drenched outside, spent the rest of our time reading or talking on our cell phones. An hour later Fernando and I played penny-and-nickel draw poker but that got boring quickly. At three o'clock Rhett marched out of his big office and passed out literature on the Avalon and the Prius. He told us to spend the rest of the afternoon testing each other on our hybrid product knowledge.

By six o'clock, with no business at all and the rain still coming down, Max told us all to go home, that the store was closing early.

SEVEN

By 9:30 A.M., two days later, after the rain finally quit, I had sold my first car and made the first sale in three days for the Sherman Toyota dealership. My mooch turned out to be a couple originally from Mexico City. They drove onto the lot in a twenty-year-old Toyota pickup that was a beater—no trade-in value. It was my area of the lot and the people stopped at a five-year-old 4Runner SUV, so I got the up.

This greatly pissed off Fernando, my poker-playing sales buddy, in our mutual area, because the couple were obviously Latinos and up until that day, he had been awarded all Spanish-speaking customers. But now, since Rhett had reshuffled the deck and I had greeted the customers, Fernando was SOL and he didn't like it—or me.

After I said hi to the couple, Fernando ran inside and bitched me out to Max, yelling that I was skating him and was stealing his customer. Max called to Rhett in the big office and Rhett yelled back, "Hey, if they speak any fuckin' English at all, then JD gets the up. It's his patch too. He greeted them first. Case closed."

· · · ·

AS IT TURNED out, Tomas Valenzuela was a landscape guy who had his own business manicuring the lawns and flower gardens of the rich and fabulous in Brentwood. Martina, his wife, was pretty much his interpreter and kept the checkbook in her purse.

I'd spent my own free time studying up on the 4Runner line so I knew a little bit about the SUV. But instead of talking about the excellence of the car, I did what Woody had suggested in one of our conversations after an AA meeting. Woody's advice was, "Just give the mooch the price and then start talking about them, what they like. Forget the bucket seats and the cruise control and the fucking GPS and all that crap. Ask the mooch how long he's been in L.A. Ask him where he lives. How many kids he's got. Does he like sports? That stuff. Remember, the car sells itself. People already know what they want when they come on the lot."

So I took Tomas and Martina on a demo ride up and down Santa Monica Boulevard, then across Lincoln Boulevard, with him behind the wheel. We talked about their kids (with Martina interpreting) and the landscaping business and then I asked her about her teacher's-assistant job, and how they liked living in Southern California. And then—you have to do this as part of qualifying the mooch—I asked if they'd ever bought a car before on payments and how much down they intended to pay. The only things I didn't discuss on the ride with Martina were world peace and her bra cup size.

The price I gave Tomas and pretty Martina from the typed flyer in my sports jacket pocket that listed all the prices for the used cars, was $11,995. This, I discovered later, was five grand over what the car was actually worth (what Sherman Toyota had paid for it). So the profit on the sale would be $5,000 at full price, less the dealership pack (the amount it costs to refurb the car and the cost of bank interest for retailing the car on the lot).

Tomas never blinked when I told Martina to tell him the retail ticket price. It was the first car they'd ever bought off a car lot and he and Martina were worried about their ability to get financing from our bank, so any price objection seemed to be settled right there.

When we got back to the car lot I took them inside to my desk and helped them fill out the credit application and got them each a cup of coffee. For a mother who said she had two boys, pretty Martina had a great figure beneath her snug black blouse and tight skirt.

They decided that the car would be in Martina's name. She was the one with the credit cards. So she took out her checkbook and wrote out a good-faith check for the four-thousand-dollar down payment.

With the paperwork and her check in my hand, I walked into the sales office and showed the deal to Max, who, before looking over the paperwork, reached into his desk drawer and pulled out a ridiculous-looking faded pink fly-fisherman's cap and put it on. Then he looked through his sales manager's window at my customers.

"Okay, now I'm ready," he said. "First deal of the day: we take no prisoners, right, JD?"

"Sure. Whatever."

"Pretty girl," he said. "Did you ask her if she sucks cock? We'll make my blow job part of the deal?"

"Look, I got lucky," I said. "I'm just glad I got the up."

Now Max looked down at my paperwork, saw the check for the 4K down payment, then made a face that registered glee.

Opening his finance sheet, he found the highest interest rate at the top of the page. Then he ran a computer credit check on Martina.

Five minutes later my boss had her printed-out credit report with her credit score. She was spotless on her two credit cards, a Mastercard and a Visa, and had never missed a payment on anything. Martina's credit score was a 721.

Max then wrote down a number on the front of the paperwork folder I'd handed to him: $469.00 (a total of over $22,000 for four years' worth of payments, plus the $4,000 down payment). The profit on the deal had just gone to over $17,000.

Max circled the payment and the number of months—$469 x 48—with his black magic marker. "Tell these delightful wetback foreigner cocksuckers they can drive the car home today. All Mrs. Valenzuela needs to do—after performing my BJ—is sign the contract. JD baby, you just buried your first mooch, big time. If she signs the contract you've got yourself one helluva big pop on your first sale in the car business."

"She'll sign," I said. "They want the car. I can smell it."

Max was beaming. "Like blood to a vampire," he sneered. "Four million spics in L.A. and ninety-nine percent of 'em are fucking grapes—perfect mooches."

I took the contract and paperwork back to my desk and pushed it across to Martina. "Four sixty-nine a month," I said with a straight face. "Can you afford that payment?"

"Jess, iz okay," says Martina. "We cah do it. *No problema.*"

I liked Martina a lot. She was the decision maker, the brains in the family. "My boss says you can take the car with you right now, today, if you sign right down there by the X," I said.

Martina and Tomas smiled at each other. They apparently had a nice relationship. Then pretty Martina wrote her signature across the contract, slowly, in bold script. Sherman Toyota had just sold a four-year-old 4Runner at more than the price of a new one.

Next, on Max's instructions, I marched Martina and Tomas into the finance manager's office, which was next door to Max's sales office. The finance guy was Mickey Goldman, one of the management henchmen Rhett had brought with him when he took over as general manager four days earlier. Mickey's name was in shiny gold letters on the fancy plaque stuck to his office door.

After I left the couple with Mickey, he further buried Martina and Tomas under the company's biggest, nearly worthless extended warranty contract, for another hundred twenty-five per month, for forty-eight months.

Caveat emptor, especially in the used-car business.

MY COMMISSION ON the sale was $2,550, plus the $500 cash bonus. Max called me into the office an hour later and handed me my commission voucher. He was still smiling. "Look, guy," he said, "they won't always be this easy. Those spics were a total laydown. They never knew what hit 'em. But you did a good job. Keep it up."

Then Max got up, adjusted his pink fishing cap, and

walked me down the hall to the big office overlooking the sales floor. Formerly Max's office, now Rhett's new office.

Rhett was eating one of three In-N-Out burgers and watching the Dodgers cream the Diamondbacks in the second game of a three-game series. Game one had been rained out.

Max tossed the sales folder on Rhett's big mahogany desk. When Rhett saw that Max was wearing his fisherman's cap, he grinned. "Okay, I see you guys got something for me? Make it good."

"Boss," Max yelled, "Fiorella here just put away the first kill of the day. Over seventeen K profit!"

Rhett checked over the paperwork, then smiled broadly. "Nice work," he said. "Nice deal. Now you boys go get me ten more and we'll have a decent fuckin' day."

"I intend to be the best salesman at Sherman Toyota," I said. "Top man. I'm here to make money."

Rhett looked at Max, then shook his head. When the commercials came on, the big boss muted the TV sound. He reached into his pocket and pulled out a roll of hundreds. A big roll. He counted out five bills and waved them at me. "These are yours, kid."

"I'm no kid," I said.

"Whatever. Don't be so touchy, Fiorella. Look, I can smell a good car man. You'll do okay here. Just calm down. Show up on time and keep your nose clean. And do whatever Captain Kangaroo in that goofy fishing hat tells you to do. I taught him everything he knows. Ha-ha!"

I scooped up the money and stuffed it into my new pants.

"Hey, Max," Rhett snarled, pointing at the TV screen,

"I'm about to dump two large on the fucking Diamond-backs! I hate Arizona."

Max smiled. "What'd I tell you? Never bet the Backs."

"Goddamn right."

OUT ON THE sales lot, with Max and Rhett out of sight inside the dealership, potbellied Fernando, fifteen feet away, began to hassle me. "Hey, esshoe," he hissed, "don't jou neber try tha chit again. Jou skated me."

"Kiss my ass, fat boy. Fair is fair. You heard the guy."

"We gonna zee ow tuff jou are. We gonna zee. Jou wait for later. We gonna zee."

THAT AFTERNOON MAX had hired a new saleswoman. Her name was Vikki Martin, a total L.A. cutie. Dark blonde with frilly curls and dressed to the nines in a tight-fitting skirt, and with red nail and toe polish. Midtwenties. Her low-cut black blouse advertised her two (what I was sure must be) aftermarket D cups.

EIGHT

At 9:20 P.M. I was done for the day. A thirteen-hour shift. The headache that had started five years ago in the East Bronx when I killed those people had never gone away, except when I was drunk. Today it was little more than a dull thump. Livable. I had five hundred dollars in cash in my pocket and had sold one more car, a two-year-old Camry, and made a total of three thousand five hundred for my first three days in the car business.

With mom's Honda parked and locked up safely around the corner, I was on my way across the darkened car lot to get in my demo Corolla, when Fernando stepped out of the shadows and into my path.

"Ho kaye, chithead," he snarled, "now we gonna zee whaz wha."

Fernando outweighed me by sixty or seventy pounds and was three inches taller. He gave me a two-handed push in the chest. I was knocked off balance, but regained myself. Before I could straighten up fully, he landed a nice flush right to my jaw and I fell back against the Corolla.

But, to Fernando's surprise, rather than go down or cover up, I straightened myself and stood there smiling. Then I lifted my hands and was ready to go. What fat boy didn't realize was that I like to fight and that long ago in New York City I discovered that I have the adrenal system for it. I'm like a boxer in the ring. When the juice begins to flow I can be hit, but the pain is minimal, not unlike a guy in a ten-round bout at the Olympic Auditorium. I simply ignore what hurts.

"C'mon, you potbellied cocksucker, try that again," I said, still smiling, waving him toward me.

Fernando made his next move, a wide right. I easily stepped back and it missed me by a couple of inches. After that I got in a series of three strong palm thrusts to the face followed by a nice kick. My foot found its mark and Fernando grabbed his crotch.

In some cases—in the past, in my private-detective days—I have taken pleasure in hurting people, but I didn't want to scuff up Fernando too much or break his nose or knock out any teeth, so I decided to take my time.

My best punch as a boxer is my left hook. I landed two of them, a few seconds apart, flush on his cheek. Fatboy reeled on his heels and went down. I could have kicked him nicely in the face but I decided instead to step back and wait to see if he had any spit left in him.

Ten yards away, Max, with a thick key ring in his hand, had walked outside and was just locking up the showroom. He could hear us scuffling.

"Guys," Max yelled, walking toward us, "that's it! Knock it the fuck off!"

Fernando got to his feet and straightened his shirt. I was pleased to see that I hadn't made him bleed. That would come later, if he still wanted more.

"We juss talkin, boss, iz all we beeng doin," fat boy said cheerily, still trying to catch his breath.

I pointed a finger at Fernando. "Your Latino salesman thinks I skated him, boss," I said. "He says that he wants to kick my ass. And, well, I'd sort of enjoy hurting him a little more, so if you don't mind, we can settle this after you leave."

"Shut up, Fiorella," Max snarled.

"Then tell fat fuck here to back off before I get angry and really do some damage."

"I said, shut up, Fiorella, if you want to keep your job!"

Then I turned back to Fernando. "Okay, moron," I said, pointing a finger, "how 'bout me scattering a few of your teeth in the driveway? You up for that?"

Max put his hand on my chest. I let him push me back. I had no interest in losing my job over a brawl.

"I said, that's it!" Max bellowed.

FIVE MINUTES LATER the deal was settled. Max ordered me to give Fernando two hundred and fifty bucks out of my salesman's cash spiff on the 4Runner. A settlement.

I refused. "No goddam way," I said. "I made that money fair and square. House rules. No goddam way!"

Then Max tried another angle. He decided that Fernando would get the first deal of the day the next morning if the up was in our area. I was okay with that.

. . . .

IT WAS MONDAY night, too late to go to an AA meeting. My
energy was flowing now. I'd had a short fight and I had five
hundred bucks in my pocket for the first time in a year, since
before I got sober.

I decided to buy myself dinner and drove my demo Corolla to the Broken Drum parking lot two blocks away on
Wilshire Boulevard. The Drum is a steak house with an attached bar. When I was in high school it had been our hang-
out after a day's classes or the Saturday night coed dances
and basketball games. In those days the bartender was a guy
named Sonny. He'd serve almost anyone provided there was
a twenty-dollar bill in front of them on the bar.

Inside, the place was the same as it had been more than
twenty years before—new paint, but that was all. It was
dark with a lighted fireplace at the center of the main dining
room. The bar area had pretty waitresses, fewer tables, and
another newer fireplace. I decided to sit there.

I ordered a steak with a potato and a salad. The waitress was named Betty. In her forties. Tall and attractive with
big, full lips. Red red lips. Very friendly. "Anything from the
bar?" she asked smiling. "Gin and tonics are three twenty-
five before ten o'clock."

"I just started a new job down the street at the car dealer,"
I said. "So I'm celebrating. I made my first sale today. I made
two sales today, in fact."

"Hey," Betty chirped, "good for you. Very cool."

"But just give me a tonic water—no gin," I said. "Put a
slice of lemon or lime in it too. Okay?"

"You know," Betty said, writing the order down on her

pad, a bit distracted, "I bought my car there. Last year. The guy's name was Woody. Do you know Woody?"

"Sure, he's a friend," I said. "He's the reason I'm selling cars. Woody got me the job."

"They come in here a lot. The heavyset guy from Argentina. Arnoldo. He comes in with that other guy from the service department. Buckie, I think."

"You mean Fernando," I said.

"Yeah, Fernando. He's nice. He's okay."

"Tell them to cook my steak medium rare, please? That's how I like it."

A couple of minutes later Betty set a salad down in front of me, along with my tonic water.

I started on the salad and was halfway through it when I took a sip of the tonic water. It tasted funny. A moment later I realized there was gin in it. It was my first sip of anything that contained booze since I'd quit drinking. My head immediately started pounding.

Just then Betty with the red lipstick was walking by, taking another order. "Everything okay?" she said, smiling. "How's your salad?"

"Jesus," I said. "There's fucking gin in my drink!"

"You ordered a gin and tonic, didn't you?"

"No! Tonic—no gin! I'm allergic to alcohol. Jesus!"

"Oh God, I'm soo-o sorry!" Betty said. "I'll take it back." Then she patted me on the arm, scooped up my glass, and walked off, shaking her head.

The taste of the stuff had made my brain crazy and it began chattering: *Hey, have the fucking drink. Just one. Fix your headache! Jesus, what's wrong with one drink? You already had a sip. Quit being a pussy. Enjoy yourself.*

I dropped a twenty on the table, then got up. I was terrified. One drink and I'd be back where I was before, where my madness had taken me—back to hell.

Once outside in my demo car, still freaked that I'd had a sip of gin and would now be back out of control—that the obsession to get drunk would come back—I punched in Southbay Bill's number on my cell phone.

No answer. I dialed again. When the call went to voice mail, I hung up.

Then I punched in Bob Anderson's number. The mean-ass old guy had fired me as his sponsee nine months before because I failed to show up for one of our appointments about discussing the AA Third Step.

I was desperate and I didn't care. I had to talk to someone who knew me and knew what to do. I was sure Bob could help and tell me how to handle the feelings.

When Bob answered I knew by his voice that I'd woken him up. "Hello, this is Bob," he wheezed.

"Bob, it's JD."

"Hey, buddy, how are ya? It's late. What's up?"

"I had a fucking drink! That's how I am. I'm crazy."

"Hey, my friend," he croaked, "that's what we alkies do. We drink. So, tell me what happened."

"I ordered dinner at this restaurant in Santa Monica, and a plain tonic water with lime. The waitress brought me a gin and tonic by mistake."

"And you drank it?"

"No. I took a sip and swallowed it but I didn't drink the rest."

"That ain't no slip, JD. You didn't order the G&T to get drunk, did you?"

"Hell no!"

"Just get to a meeting. You'll be fine."

"Are you sure?"

"Call me in the morning, JD. It'll all be okay."

Then Bob hung up.

THE HOOKERS NEAR Rose Avenue are mostly black because that area of Venice is near Ghost Town, where all the crack and meth dealers operate.

The girl I stopped to pick up was on the short side. She had beefy thighs with a close-cropped afro, big knockers, and fake gold hoop earrings. She looked to be an ethnic mix of black and something else. Asian—maybe Chinese.

I lowered the power window on the passenger side of the Corolla and she leaned in. "Hi babe, half and half is fifty," she whispered.

"Get in," I said. "You get a hundred more if you'll lick my asshole first."

"Uu-huh, you a spender. I likes spenders. Deal. My name's Dawn. What's yours, honey?"

"I'm JD. And I'm in love already."

ON MY WAY back through Santa Monica toward Malibu, an hour later, I swung off Lincoln onto Colorado Boulevard, then turned onto Ninth Street. I was feeling okay again after talking with Anderson, and the sex with chubby Dawn had been the tie-breaker.

As I was crossing Broadway, headed up Ninth, another car, what looked like a black four-door Beemer, almost sideswiped my Corolla demo. The other driver hadn't even paused for the stop sign and might have clipped me if I hadn't jerked my wheel the other way. L.A. has crazy drivers.

My plan, now that I had a nicer ride, was to leave Mom's Honda parked on Ninth Street until my day off on Wednesday, then drive her into town with me to pick up her beast and return it to her garage. The goddamn People's Republic of Santa Monica is well known for its brutal alternate-side street-cleaning tickets, so if you are parked on the wrong curb on street-cleaning day, you're screwed. The ticket is seventy-nine bucks. So I wanted to be sure the Honda was parked legally and okay.

As I drove down the block I saw flames thirty yards away. A car was on fire.

NINE

When I got closer to the flames, I could see that it was Mom's red Honda, my car. The hood and roof were ablaze.

I parked a safe distance away, got out, then approached the Honda. There was an acrid smell. Several solid streams of flame covered the hood and roof and the front bumper was burning too. Apparently, some jerk had squirted lighter fluid or something similar on the beast, then lit it up—some kind of idiot-style, high school prank.

The rear section of the Honda had only one strip of flame on it, so my first thought was to get my gun. I'm a guy who has been charged with felony drunk driving and I know that, in California, I will instantly go back to the slam if I'm caught with an unregistered piece.

I opened Mom's trunk, grabbed the gun, tucked it into the back of my pants, then pulled out a couple of grimy car towels I stored there to dry the Honda off after I'd washed it.

I threw the towels on the car's trunk and roof. Half a minute later some of the flames were extinguished.

Who the hell would want to torch my fucking car? Why?

Maybe it was that fat prick Fernando, carrying a grudge and still PO'd after I'd got that big sale. If it was Fernando, he'd find out very soon that he'd been screwing with the wrong guy. I'd really clean his clock this time. No one else came to mind except the crazy vengeful bitch in the Porsche in Malibu. Could it have been her? Was that possible? Then I remembered: She'd seen me at the stoplight on the Coast Highway but she'd been at least twenty-five yards away and too far from my car to have read my license plate. I dismissed the idea.

IT WASN'T YET midnight and one or two lights began to come on from the houses along the street. A door opened and a guy in a bathrobe walked out on his carport. He stood with his hands on his hips, watching the flames on my car. Then he called to me: "What's going on?"

"My car's on fire, for chrissakes," I yelled back. "Don't just stand there with your dick in your hand, get some water or something! Have you got a hose?"

"Right," he said, acting semi-dazed from TV, like my car on fire was a goddamn reality show. Then he cinched his bathrobe closed and walked to the corner of his house and began to unravel his garden hose.

The driver's-side window of Mom's car had been bashed in and the door was ajar. I flopped open one of my towels from the roof and, using it to protect my hand, pulled the door all the way open. Then I stood on the rocker panel and threw the other towel over the flames on the roof.

Half of the fire was smothered, but the grille section and the hood were still burning and there were intense flames coming from inside the engine compartment—smoke was beginning to billow out from under the hood.

The homeowner with the hose was behind me. "Hey, step back," he yelled. "I'll spray it down. Just get back!"

I stepped up onto the curb and stood next to him. He was blasting the hood and the grille with water just as we heard a loud popping sound and the engine compartment burst into flames.

"Hey, that's not good," Bathrobe yelled.

"You're right," I said. "C'mon, we'd better back off."

We were twenty feet away when Mom's car exploded. The blast and flames immediately ignited the car in front of the Honda—a Chrysler minivan. In seconds it was blazing, too, with its alarm howling.

HALF AN HOUR later, while the cops and firemen were mopping up, one of the blues who had already taken my driver's license and other ID was filling out a report. "Okay," he said, walking up to me with his cop notebook open, "tell me exactly what happened here?"

"I don't know," I shot back. "I was walking to my car and I saw it burning. I guess somebody torched it. Maybe it was a prank or something."

"A prank?" Blue barked. "Destroying private property and endangering the lives of the residents on this block is no prank, sir. It's arson. We're lucky someone wasn't killed."

"Whatever," I said, "call it what you want."

"Did you see anyone? Did you observe anyone leaving the area?"

"No. But I did see a car going around the corner at the

other end of the block. He didn't stop for the stop sign. It looked like he was in a hurry."

Blue looked at me. "He? You said, 'he.'"

"I'm not sure. I didn't see who was driving. I just assume it was a he. It was a dark four-door. Maybe blue. A Beemer, I think."

"Was the vehicle a newer car or was it older?"

"I don't know. Newer, I guess. It was shiny."

He held up my driver's license and Social Security card. "I already checked this out," he said. "Apparently, you're driving on a restricted operator's permit. You had a DUI."

"So what?" I said. "My car was torched. What's a restricted license got to do with a goddamn burning car?"

"Calm down, sir. I'm trying to determine the circumstances, what led up to the fire. Have you been drinking tonight, sir?"

"That's none of your business. I wasn't driving so that's got nothing to do with anything. But no, I wasn't drinking! I don't drink."

Blue sneered. "I think we have a problem here, Mr. Fiorella. In the trunk of your car we discovered a shopping bag containing five empty pint vodka bottles. Can you explain that?"

"They were in the trunk, officer," I snarled. "They're garbage. Undumped garbage."

Blue moved to the front seat of his cruiser, then returned with his plastic Breathalyzer unit.

He was stone-faced. "I suspect you of driving while intoxicated. I am now instructing you to blow into this unit."

I wanted to punch blue hard in the face. I wanted to

watch blood run down from his nose into his cop mustache.
I wanted to hurt blue badly. Instead, I stuffed the idea. "I
said I wasn't driving."

"Blow into the machine, Mr. Fiorella. I won't ask you
again."

When I was done blowing, Blue looked at the digital readout
on the gauge. "You are legally sober," he said in an even tone.

"No shit."

"Sir, it's Monday night. Not exactly a workday, as per
your vehicle license driving restrictions. You were on your
way to your car, I assume, to drive it, or were just getting
out after driving it, in possible noncompliance with those
restrictions. There are gaps in the account of what you're
telling me. I think you're leaving out information here—
omitting relevant facts. I recommend that you get your story
of the incident in order."

"I just told you what happened. Do your job, for chrissake! Find out who torched my car!"

Blue sneered. "I don't believe what you're telling me and
I find your attitude to be unnecessarily belligerent. I think
you somehow caused the fire yourself and are trying to shift
the blame."

"I don't give a shit what you believe, lawman. I told you
what happened."

"We seem to be having a communication problem. I can
have more backup here in five minutes. Do you want this
situation to deteriorate further?"

"No, I don't."

"Good. Now empty your pockets and place the items on
the hood of my vehicle."

"Do you think I'd break my own window when I'm holding the car keys in my hand? Wake up, for chrissake!"

"Last warning: Calm down! Let me investigate the circumstances of the incident or I'll cuff you right here."

"How about this: Go talk to the neighbors and see if someone saw what happened. That's your job, not hassling me!"

"I'm instructing you again: empty your pockets!"

"Jesus Christ," I said, pointing down the block, hoping like hell the asshole wouldn't frisk me and find the gun. "I work there at the Toyota dealer. On the corner. I was at my job."

Blue looked down the block and saw Sherman Toyota's big sign. "I see," he said. "So, for the third and final time, remove the items from your pockets and place them on the hood of my vehicle."

I reached into my pants and pulled out all my stuff, tossing it on to the cop car's hood: my wallet, my cigarettes, my lighter, a few Nicorets, a dozen generic Sherman Toyota business cards that Max had passed out to all the new salespeople on Saturday, and the wad of cash that was left over from my hundred-and-fifty-dollar hooker.

"Here ya go," I said, handing Blue one of the Toyota business cards, attempting to distract him and back up my story. "This is where I work."

"Is that everything?" he asked.

"You just saw me empty my pockets. That's it."

Fortunately Blue didn't toss me. Instead, he looked at the business card, then put it back on the hood of his patrol car.

"Okay," I said, hoping to Christ the frisking part was over, "now, how about finding out who did this?"

"Insurance card?" he said. "I need to see proof of automobile insurance."

"Look," I said, "my car was on fire. I can't get into it."

Blue smiled. "The interior of the vehicle was not burned, sir. The flames are out. Go get the insurance card, Mr. Fiorella."

"I don't have an insurance card," I said.

"Not good," Blue said. "That *is* a problem."

TEN

The morning after the car fire, when my mother and Coco came out to have their coffee and make their breakfast, I was sitting at the kitchen table. Dealing with the burning vehicle and the cop and the sobriety test, carrying a concealed weapon, and having no insurance card, was a cakewalk compared to facing my eighty-one-year-old D.A.R. (Daughters of the American Revolution) ex-librarian mother.

"Well," she said, pouring her and Coco's coffee with a still-steady hand, "you're employed again. A step in the right direction. I certainly hope you apply yourself and do well, James. And soon, very soon, we'll have a conversation about a repayment plan for the money you owe me."

"Something happened last night, Ma. I need to tell you about it."

"I'm listening."

"Can you excuse us, Coco?" I asked, looking up at Mom's companion. "I need to talk to Mom privately."

When Coco was gone, carrying her coffee cup, the newspaper, and a slice of toast down the hall, I turned to Mom. "Somebody torched the Honda last night."

"Speak English, James. Torched? Please explain what you mean by your use of that word."

"Some person—some asshole—poured gas or lighter fluid or something on the Honda last night and put a match to it."

"My car? Were the police contacted? The fire department?"

"Both. They were both there."

"You are telling me that my property was destroyed? Torched! My vehicle?"

"Technically, it's my vehicle. You put it in my name, remember?"

Mom was turning red. Redder. Her health issues were her clogged arteries and her high blood pressure—enough to allow her to drop dead after a strong sneeze some morning. I could see that she was beginning to shake.

"I hold you responsible, James. Your lifestyle—the way you conduct yourself—your addiction to alcohol and pornography. The smut I receive in my mailbox day after day is beyond horrific. You say you've now stopped drinking but your conduct has directly resulted in someone, some criminal type, destroying my private property."

"No, I wasn't hurt. Were you going to ask me?"

"You're a forty-four-year-old bum—probably a sex offender and God knows what else. You spent years as a detective—thug is the more appropriate term—hurting people, and you still own a gun! I've seen it with my own eyes. A gun, for God's sake!"

"Look, I have to know: did you ever cancel the insurance? The cop gave me a ticket for not being insured."

My mother considered the question while reaching across the table for her bottle of blood-pressure meds. Opening the vial, she dumped out two little bluies, popped them, then washed them down with a gulp of coffee. "No, is the answer," she said. "I never called the insurance company. I guess I forgot to do it."

"Did your lawyer do it? Do you know?"

"He reminded me to make the call. I must've forgotten. Are you going to jail again? Is that what you're telling me?"

"No, no jail. Looks like I'm okay. Just find the insurance card and give it to me. I'll go to court and straighten it out."

"I want you out of my home. Is that clear? By this weekend. Even Coco finds your behavior . . . unusual. She said so herself."

"Calm down, Ma."

"We'll call a locksmith today and I will have the locks changed. You are a danger to my welfare and my health. You're a recalcitrant fool with deep-seated psychological problems and I believe you actually take pleasure in hurting people."

Then Ma got up, tied her bathrobe in a stranglehold around her midsection, grabbed her coffee cup and the bottle of blood-pressure meds, and teetered off toward her bedroom.

AT WORK THAT morning, after the sales meeting, I stuck my head into Max's office. "Hey, boss," I said, "can we talk for a minute?"

"What's up, Fiorella? C'mon in. Got another deal for me—one like those wetbacks we hammered? I love it."

I closed his door behind me and sat down. "Look, Max,"

I said, "I'm in a spot. I have to find a place to live. I need to be out by Saturday."

Max rocked back in his chair. He loved playing the big shot. "Sorry to hear that. So . . . "

"So, can I get an advance? We both know I've got a good check coming. I just need about fifteen hundred for a deposit on a new place."

"Look, I hear you, Fiorella," he said, "but I've got to say something here. You won't like it, but it's part of my job and it's for your own good. The truth is you're sort of on thin ice around here. A couple of the staff have made comments about your attitude and rudeness and then there was that scuffle between you and Fernando. Do you see my point?"

"Max, I'm asking for a favor. I think I've proved myself."

"No can do, my friend. Rhett's GM now and he'd chew my ass from here until next week if I gave you an advance. He has a no-exceptions policy."

"I don't want to have to take time off. That's why I'm coming to you. My back's against the wall here, Max."

Maxwell hit the hands-free button on his phone's console. It started buzzing. Rhett pressed a button in his office and answered. "What's up, Max?"

"I've got Fiorella here in my office. He has an emergency. He says he has to move, to relocate. Can we make an exception and cut him an advance? Say two K?"

Rhett Butler, aka Robin Baitz, as always, came right to the point. "Tell Fiorella that payday is Friday after next." Click. Dead air.

Sitting back down at my cubicle desk in the showroom I

decided to try my pal Woody. He was fat city, money-wise, and I knew it. A couple of weeks back he'd mentioned that he'd stashed almost ten grand in the bank and was saving up for a late-model used Benz.

I called him on his cell phone and found out that in a few days he was starting at the Lexus dealer on Seventeenth Street in Santa Monica. "What's up with you?" he said after telling me his good news. "I've been looking for you at meetings. You weren't at the Sunday nighter at the Marina Center."

I didn't mention the torched car incident. I wanted to sound positive. "You know," I said, "work. That stuff. I don't get out of here until nine-thirty some nights."

"Right. A couple of people asked about you. Look, pal," Woody went on, "once I get squared away with Lexus, I'm putting in a word for you there with the used-car manager. Rhett's a fucking gorf. A jerkoff. And big Max is his gofer bitch. They've chewed through a thousand salespeople like us. They'll never change. Best thing for you is a gig at a decent, high-end store. From what I can see so far, the guys at Lexus are okay. The leasing manager, Manny—hey, you met Manny at the meeting where I popped that weird stalker guy—remember?"

"Right, Manny. I remember."

"He's a straight-up dude and sober three years. Look, when I'm on board I'll mention that you're looking for a new car gig."

"Hey, Woody," I said, "I've got something I need to ask you. Something I think you'd be interested in. Do you still want to write that screenplay with me?"

"Are you kidding? Hey, my man, anytime you say!"

"Okay, so here's the deal: My living situation just took a dump. I've got to get out of my mom's house by this weekend. That's the downside. The upside is that I made a decent hit on a 4Runner and some other cars and I've got over three K coming on payday. If you can front me fifteen hundred to find a new place, I'll get the money back to you immediately when I get paid, and I'll help you write the script. A fifty-fifty split on screen credit. How's that sound?"

I could hear Woody's breathing. Then, after a long pause: "And I get the money back a week from Friday, right?"

"A hundred percent. No problem," I said. "The day I get paid."

"When do we start the screenplay?"

"On my first day off after payday. Wednesday. We'll make the schedule work. I'm pretty good at screenplays. It's a promise. Okay?"

"Okay, deal," Woody said. "But hey, JD, you sound all wound up. Easy does it, my brother. You okay?"

"Yeah. Why?"

"You just sound edgy, is all. I mean, more edgy than usual."

"Hey, if you just found out you were out on the street in favor of a nursemaid and six overfed mongrel cats, you'd be edgy too."

"You're right, I would. One day at a time, pal."

"Right. I'll start to look for a place on my lunch break. How about coffee on Friday? We'll talk over the screenplay and I can pick up the money?"

"Sure, sounds okay. I'll meet you at that coffee place on Wilshire and Tenth. That's close to you. Okay?"

"Deal. Thanks Woody. I appreciate your help on this."

"No sweat, brother. I'm looking forward to getting into the screenplay."

AFTER MY CALL to Woody, I refilled my coffee cup for the fourth time that morning, then walked out to the lot to guard my sales area from Fernando.

There was no foot traffic and, after checking the showroom floor, I stepped up close to my lot partner, pushed my finger into his chest, and whispered, "Hey shithead, someone burned up my Honda. What do you know about it?"

"Jou tink I dee it? Jou acuzin' me?"

"If you were the guy, we can settle it right now. Right here."

"Majn, I done do thisa kinda chit. I neber seen jour car? I deen know jou had a fukkin' Honda."

I looked him in the eye. There was no tell in his expression—even with my finger in his chest. I decided to believe him.

THAT AFTERNOON ON my lunch break I drove east on the Santa Monica Freeway, got off at the Centinela exit, then turned south. In five minutes I was in West L.A. I copied down a few for-rent phone numbers, then returned to the Sherman lot.

Two hours later, on a break, I began a Google search on Sherman's main showroom's computer that had a search engine, typing in "West L.A. apartments for rent." There were two dozen on the list.

. . . .

ON MY DAY off, which had now changed to Thursday (Rhett got a bug up his ass and switched everybody's day-off schedule for the second time), I went to Santa Monica court, showed the clerk my proof of car insurance certificate, and had my No Proof of Insurance summons dismissed.

Then I stopped off at several apartments in West L.A. and finally settled on a smallish studio on Short Avenue off Centinela. The rent was $721. The place was clean, on the second floor, and bright, with a big window facing the street and two eucalyptus trees just outside. There was no A/C but good cross-ventilation from the main room and the bathroom. But the big bonus (for a low $721 rent) was the furniture it came with: a convertible couch, a coffee table, and a bookcase, along with the stove and refrigerator that were standard. The left-behind living room stuff saved me several hundred bucks in furniture expense. The place also had venetian blinds and even a shower curtain left by the last tenant, a woman. The building was on the old side but the apartment came with off-street parking for my demo Corolla.

I gave the manager, a baldheaded guy named Norm with melanoma scars on his blotchy noggin, a postdated check for the first and last month's rent: $1,442.

THREE DAYS LATER, still a week away from payday, I had sold three more cars. None of them were home runs like the 4Runner deal, but I'd made another five hundred dollars. Woody was right: pitching used iron had come easy to me. Even Max, who'd reminded me again that he didn't like my attitude, assured me that I was doing well as a car guy. The good news was that I'd stayed clean after the gin and tonic scare and even squeezed in a couple of AA meetings when the store closed early after more rain.

Eventually, dreading the deed, I telephoned my old sponsor, Southbay Bill, to check in. Before I could say anything, he fired me as a sponsee for not calling in for several days in a row. It was a relief. I hadn't had to cop to anything. I had come to loathe Southbay Bill and his Jesus racket anyway. Old Bob A. was my new guy, a total straight-shooter.

Later that morning an adjuster from Mom's insurance company came by Sherman's showroom to tell me that her Honda was a total. The value of the car was set at $660. I told the guy to mail the check to Mom at her address.

I met Woody three blocks away from Sherman at Pete's Coffee on Wilshire Boulevard. We'd changed our meeting because he was officially starting at the Lexus dealer the next day.

For the last couple of months we'd been talking on the phone at least a couple of times a week and e-mailing each other frequently. Woody was a good friend, and as much as I hated the idea, I told myself I would do my best to help him with his screenplay.

When he saw me at a table, Woody flashed me his eleven-dollar car salesman's grin, ordered his double espresso at the counter, then sat down. "Heya, JD. You look like shit," he said.

"You know, new schedule. Workin' my ass off."

"But hey, now you're an official car guy: sellin' cars to movie stars and tellin' jokes to all the folks. How's that feel?"

"It's a job, Woody. I'm glad I've got one."

Woody nodded and smiled. "Look, I'll tell you this; I'm

a hundred percent glad I did what I did with Rhett. It was the right move, no question. I even did a mini-inventory on Rhett and Max and talked to my sponsor. The AA program works, pal, that's no shit."

Woody pulled a white envelope out of his jacket pocket and pushed it across the tabletop.

Opening it, I saw a sheaf of hundreds. I folded the envelope, then stuffed it into my pocket. "Thanks, my friend. You're bailing me out here. Now I can cover the deposit check I gave to the manager at my new place."

"Glad to do it. No sweat."

"You'll get it all back next payday. That's a promise."

Then I saw that there was something different in his eyes. "Hey," I said, "you look more up than usual. What's going on? You just get laid or something?"

"Pal, if I was any better I'd be twins. I'm sober six years next week, and starting a new job. And ba-boom, I met someone. I mean I'm not talking about some ex-crackhead bubble-brain like most of the tail we bump into in the program. I mean, a real nice lady."

"So, you're actually dating again? I thought you only did one-nighters."

Woody's grin was ear to ear. "Last night was our first real night together. I kid you not, Laighne's a class act, in the program for over a year, dresses like a winner, and the girl has her own business. And, get this, she's in her early twenties."

"Gee-zus," I said, "a kid almost thirty years younger than you. Sounds like you hit the jackpot. So, what's her business?"

"Matchmaking of some kind. She runs a dating deal for

rich gay boys in Hollywood. And here's the good news: she's a real tiger in the sack. She's into yoga and all that stuff."

"Jesus, I'm jealous. Is she a switch-hitter or something? Is that how she got into the gay matchmaking thing?"

"Nah, she's straight, as far as I know. I really like the girl and she's a full-on nine plus. Her friend, some guy who is gay, and went into advertising, started the company. The way Laighne tells it, he got busy with his job and then made her the managing partner. She's in charge now. The girl's a whiz on the Internet too. She can do anything. You want some chump's background checked out, some producer or your ex-wife's new guy, she can have the dope for you in twenty minutes—with a webcam up their ass. The girl's for real—no joke. She used to be in security or something in Europe, but now that she's in the program, she says she won't go near ruining people's careers or taking any cheap shots."

"Nice," I said. "Sober, sexy, successful, and single. The four S's."

"She's got a pad in Santa Monica and a guest house on some big estate near Point Dume. I'm spending the weekend with her out there before I start the new job."

"Moving right along," I said. "Sweet."

"I'm havin' a ball. I also met one of her girlfriends, at a Brentwood meeting. She's okay, I guess. Kind of an L.A. bimbo, actually. Painted nails and aftermarket knockers."

"Okay, so what about me?" I cracked. "I'm single and sober and semi-sane. Maybe she can help me ring the bell too. This girlfriend might be dying to meet a broke, semi-homeless, fucked-up, ex-private detective with a nifty career in the auto industry."

Woody shook his head. "Nah," he said, "Laighne's cool—straight up—but her gal pal feels high-risk. About fifteen minutes sober from what I can tell, all about glitz and all that Beverly Hills celebrity clubbing jazz. My bet is that you'd be better off continuing to date your old standby: Mrs. Thumb and her four daughters."

I checked my watch. I would now be returning late from lunch and I still had to walk the two blocks back to work.

Woody followed me to the corner traffic light, then grinned his pearly grin again and shook my hand. "Okay, pal, stay in touch," he said. "Good luck with the new place. Call me tomorrow and maybe I'll e-mail you the script so you can read it."

"Deal," I said. "See you Thursday, your place, right?"

"Sure. That'll work. The two of us together can make that screenplay a total ass-kicker."

ELEVEN

When I reported for work several mornings later, the day before my new day off and move (Rhett had fired two salesmen and shuffled the cards again), Fernando and I had a decent conversation at the back of the car lot behind the company's detail van. He was smoking a joint and said he wanted us to be friends. He again denied that he had torched my mom's Honda.

As we talked I realized that I had misjudged my co-worker as an ignorant South American asshole thug. He was a step up from that. He launched into a five-minute tirade in Spanglish about Sherman Toyota—how he hated Max and Rhett and the management staff with a passion for bullying him and changing his day off three times.

Nando's style was to attempt to intimidate everyone he met. Even his bosses. When I had not backed down, and instead punched him out, I had earned his respect and affection. That day I found out that my lot partner was also an avid computer-dater and was consistently misrepresenting himself as a surgeon on several websites to the women he hooked up with, saying that because of his out-of-country medical license he'd had to settle for a career in investment banking, or some other whopper-snot. Fernando, on his first phone call to these women, would close the conversation with the all-important question, "Jou dell me somezing, my sweetz: are jou busty?"

LATER THAT AFTERNOON, to amuse me and himself, Nando, who was freshly annoyed at our boss Max for making him split a commission because he'd arrived at work late that morning, decided to square accounts. My lot partner reasoned that he now had nothing to lose: "Fuk disa cockzooker. I gonna fix hisa chit real goo. Jou zee."

Max kept his big brass key ring on his desk. It contained Sherman Toyota's business keys and his own car and house keys. While the tall oaf was in Rhett's office with the paperwork on a deal on a two-year-old Prius, Fernando walked in and snatched his keys.

Outside, my lot partner motioned for me to follow him around to the back of the building. He then heaved the key ring up onto the flat roof of the dealership.

An hour later, after discovering his keys were missing, Max spent two furious hours calling people. Even a locksmith. His annoyed wife, Margie, had to drive the fifty miles from their house near Magic Mountain to bring Max the extra sets of keys to the house and his Benz SUV.

Fernando, of course, was delighted. He took great pleasure in making his adversaries miserable.

THAT NIGHT, BEFORE quitting time, the showroom was empty. Nando had been instructing me on how to online date for free and I'd been chatting with a girl in Santa Barbara about us getting together for coffee.

The showroom PA blared. "FIORELLA! JD FIORELLA TO THE GM'S OFFICE. JD TO RHETT'S OFFICE."

On my way there, Vikki, who had just finished up with an Asian lookie-loo tire-kicking couple outside on the lot, walked in. Her customers were now leaving the dealership with a brochure.

She motioned me to her desk. This girl, for two obvious full D-cup reasons, had become the sales leader at the dealership over the last several days.

I walked over to where she was sitting. Her makeup was perfect, as usual, and standing above her, I was able to see down her low-cut blouse that accentuated her pink bra and hefty knockers. The only thing that might put a man off about this girl were her wide hips. Most men find hippy women unattractive. I, on the other hand, have always enjoyed a wide ride. Vikki was at least twenty pounds too beefy.

"Hey, JD," she cooed, "can we talk for a sec?"

"Sure," I said, "talk. But you heard, I've just been summoned by the company's brain trust."

"So you and Nando had an argument out back last week?"

"It wasn't a big deal," I said. "A territory misunderstanding, is all. As you know, Nando can be a knucklehead."

"I hear you're pretty good at taking care of yourself. I like that quality in a man."

"I do okay."

"And you also know I'm a single woman, right?"

"I know you've got an ex-husband. I've heard you on your cell with your lawyer at least twice."

Vikki smiled up at me, exposing expensive, pretty, perfectly capped teeth. "Divorces can be scary," she cooed. "My ex is also a lawyer. It's a nasty situation."

"I hear that."

"Well, okay. See, I was just wondering if you might like to have dinner with me sometime. Maybe after work tomorrow."

This was the first time in eighteen months that a woman who was not a hooker or a member of an online chat room had come on to me. I'd already pigeonholed Vikki as a West Side gold digger. I had enough recovery in me and enough ex-private detective horse sense to know she could be trouble. Plainly, the girl was out of my league. I had no intention of having anything other than a work relationship with her.

"Hey, that's nice," I said, "maybe another time. I'm pretty busy these days."

"Well, anyway—you just let me know, JD. The ball's in your court now."

Then Vikki pulled one of her business cards from the holder on the desk and wrote her private e-mail address on the back.

She handed me the card. While I was accepting it, she scratched the back of my hand with her half-inch-long red index fingernail. "It just might be fun," she whispered.

WHEN I GOT to Rhett's office I could tell that he and Max had been waiting for me—the room was silent and they were stone-faced.

Without saying anything, Max motioned for me to close the door and sit down.

When I didn't move, Max glared at me. "Over there, Fiorella," he ordered. "There's something we need to talk about."

I still didn't sit down. I could feel that something was about to hit the fan, and I already smelled the stink of it in the room. "Look guys, if this about those keys . . . " I said.

"Screw the keys," Rhett said. "Max'll find them or he won't. This isn't about the keys, okay? We've got a major problem."

"Involving me?"

Max stood up. "We got some very fucked news this morning, Fiorella."

Rhett lifted a hand to shut Max up. "I'll handle this," he said. "Look, amigo, we heard from our contracts guy at the bank. Turns out that your 4Runner deal went tits up."

"You're kidding!" I said. "What went wrong?"

"We got scammed, my friend. That beaner bitch used stolen ID and credit cards. The whole thing was a rip-off, from the get-go. I've been on the phone with the business office. The bank put a hold on their check days ago and then redeposited it. It bounced twice. Total flimflam. Pretty slick too. Christ knows where that 4Runner wound up. Probably some friggin' chop shop in East L.A."

Hearing this information was like a punch to the head. I took a deep breath. Now I was up shit creek—in hock to my best friend and out over two grand in commission. "Okay, so what happens next?" I said.

Max interrupted: "Look—I'll ask this point blank. I have information. Were you involved here in any way?"

I glared at Max. "Absolutely no way! *And fuck your information*!"

Rhett frowned. "Let it go, Max. He's clean. You can see it in his face. Back off!" he snarled.

"I don't like it. I don't like it at all," Max hissed.

I faced my manager again. "If you're accusing me of something, tell me now! Otherwise shove your information up your ass. Or maybe I'll shove it up there for you."

Rhett waved his arms for us to stop. "Look, JD, I checked over your commissions," he said.

"Okay. And . . . "

"If we deduct the money you earned from the sale, your check on Friday comes out to be $1,310, before taxes."

"Jesus," I said, my head now banging, "I'm screwed here."

"Then, there's the five-hundred-dollar spiff I paid you in cash. That has to come out too."

"C'mon, Rhett," I said, "that'd leave me with six or seven hundred bucks for two weeks' work!"

"Sorry, Fiorella, the store is getting short-sticked and so are you. I've gotta spend tomorrow morning at the bank to clean up this mess. It won't be fun."

"Okay, then how about this: spread the money out over a couple of paychecks. I'm really in a tight spot here. I borrowed fifteen hundred based on that sale. Now I owe the money back. You're my boss. Help me out here."

"I know," Rhett said, pulling out his handkerchief and blowing his nose, then picking more snot out with his fat index finger and wiping it on the handkerchief. "It's a tough break all around, but there's nothing we can do. Company policy is company policy."

. . . .

AFTER LEAVING RHETT'S office, I went back to my desk.
Vikki watched from two cubicles away as I tore my tie off
and picked up my sales tracking notebook. "What's up,
Tiger," she whispered. "You look like your dog just got run
over. What happened in there?"

I was angry. I couldn't talk. I felt like hurting Max—the
guy had developed a hard-on for me and my anger was starting to build, and that scared me. And tomorrow I would
have to face Woody with the news that I could not pay him.
I was royally screwed.

"Look, do you mind," I said to Vikki, "some other time.
I can't handle any chitchat at the moment."

My expression apparently startled her. "Hey," she shot
back, turning away in her swivel chair, "whatever you say."

OUT ON THE lot, on my way to my demo Corolla, I told Fernando about the situation. We were standing in our sales
patch, between cars, alone.

Nando sneered, then spit on the window of a Camry.
"Deeza preeks. Maz and Writ, dey fuk jou any way dey can.
Maybe becauz a da kees. I tink zo. Theysa make up some big
fukkin' lie to tell jou."

TWELVE

The following morning, out on Point Dume, with my head pounding after almost no sleep and another dream about dead-body parts, I woke up sweating.

While I was dressing I decided that I had no options. I'd make the move anyway, then worry about the consequences on the back end. Hopefully, I'd make a few sales and get even as quickly as possible. I'd tell Woody the truth and let the chips fall where they fell.

After packing up my clothes and computer I was ready to leave Mom's place. She and Coco were sunning themselves near the back patio table while Mom studied the astrology chart of one of her celebrity clients.

"Okay, Ma, that's it," I said. "I'm all done. I'm ready to hit the road."

She flipped her astrology book facedown, shuffled some papers, then looked up at me over the top of her glasses. "You and I need to have a serious and unemotional conversation, James."

Christ, I thought, *what the hell did I do now?* Then Ma

held up a chart. "I'm not pleased with your current aspects at all."

Happy to avoid another mother and son confrontation regarding my flaws and dogshit life, I glanced down at the diagrammed paper. "Thanks, Ma," I said, "but I'll be okay."

"I've already told you that Mercury's retrograde."

"Hey, that's no surprise—whatever it means. Talk to my boss."

"I've been sitting here pondering your chart. You must exercise extreme caution these next two weeks, especially in relationships. There's darkness here."

"I intend to, Ma. Thanks."

"Don't patronize me. Be careful. Very careful." Then she looked back down at my chart.

"Okay, it's a promise," I said.

Mom's expression got darker. "There's also your unpleasant Pluto. It may cause you mischief. It's a conjunction."

"Right, Ma," I said, kissing the top of her glasses by mistake instead of her head. "I'll keep this stuff in mind."

"Call me, James."

Coco was smiling. "Be well, James. You're a smart boy. This is a new beginning. I wish you great success."

"Remember, James: caution," Mom repeated. "Do you hear me?"

"Jesus, Ma, I hear you."

MOVING MY CLOTHES and computer into the apartment went easily enough. One trip in my demo Corolla did the trick.

At the door to my new place I met my next-door neighbor

as she was just leaving—a painted sixty-year-old L.A. floozie named Brenda who'd worked all her life, she said, as a barmaid. She was half-tanked as we spoke. It was one o'clock in the afternoon.

MY APPOINTMENT TO work on the script with Woody was at his apartment at Fifteenth and Arizona, in Santa Monica— two o'clock—only a fifteen-minute drive from my new place on Short Avenue.

Woody lived alone. I knew he'd be expecting me and I hated the idea of having to go back on my word to a pal, to put him off about the fifteen hundred I owed, but I had no choice. He'd be upset but it was time to work my program and face the music.

I'd already had too much coffee that day, plus a Red Bull, and I needed to pee badly when I got to the top of the stairs and knocked on his door.

There was no answer. I waited a few seconds, then tried again. The result was the same. I tried again, rapping more loudly. Still nothing. No footsteps either.

Pulling out my cell phone, I punched in Woody's number. After a pause I heard ringing from inside the door. He had to be home. Woody always carried his cell.

I decided to try the door. I was surprised to find that it wasn't locked.

Pressing the handle and pushing the door open, I stuck my head inside. It was the middle of the day and all the interior lights were on. I yelled, "Hey Woody, I'm here. Where in hell are you?"

Still no answer.

The living room was empty but neat, almost militarily clean. The TV was on and white dots were floating across its otherwise blank screen. In the upper corner green blinking letters printed out DVD. I saw the remote on the coffee table five feet away.

Walking down the hall I yelled again. "Woody, it's me, JD. You here?"

Passing the kitchen, I came to the bathroom. There was a smudge of something black on the door by the knob. I called again, "Hey, it's JD." Then I stuck my head inside the john.

The room was empty but immaculate too. All the towels by the shower were the same color and hung neatly on their racks. My friend was quite the housekeeper for a guy who lived alone. Impressive.

Then the smell hit me. It was nasty and unsettling. The stink of puke.

The other half of the bathroom was behind the door so I pushed it open all the way.

One almost-new toothbrush was tucked into its chrome holder and the soap dish contained a fresh bar. I could still see the letters on it. But the sink itself was filled with the contents from the medicine cabinet; toothpaste tubes and deodorant, itch creams and spare shampoos, several kinds of aspirin, a box of hair dye, and stuff for an upset stomach. The bottle of pink liquid had spilled and had soaked into some of the other items around it.

The toilet seat cover was down, so I lifted it up. There was a ring of puke inside—the source of the terrible stink. Leaning closer I stared down at what was in it—something floating in the water—a thick piece of flesh. A penis!

I leaned down to look more closely at the thing. Jesus!

. . . .

LEAVING THE BATHROOM I pulled my .44 out of the rear of my belt, my brain now slamming itself against the inside of my skull. Wham wham wham.

The bedroom door was closed but ajar.

I didn't want to go in. Something terrible was in there. Something I'd seen before and didn't want to see again.

After a pause, I crouched, readied my gun, then slammed the door open.

THE BODY ON the bed had been placed on a large piece of clear plastic sheeting that covered the light-brown, unwrinkled bed spread. Four blue pillows were above the corpse, at the head of the mattress. Arranged pillows.

The arms and legs of the body were splayed, pointing at the four corners of the bed. It was Woody.

I stood staring at the thing for a few seconds; this strange, white mannequin block of flesh with its tattooed upper arms and a thick chest and belly. Blood had pooled at the bottom of my friend's corpse. The color was purple-black.

I stepped closer with the gun still in my hand, aiming it at my friend Woody for some reason, still expecting something to move or jump out from somewhere.

My brain began sputtering—attempting to make sense of what my eyes were seeing. I was getting the same messages I had received five years before when I'd been at the East Bronx apartment building in New York City. The shock of violent death is something you never get used to. The unrealness of it scrambles the senses. It's scary shit.

Now, just inches from the body, the thing that was no longer Woody but a sort of purpled-stained porcelain mummy. I looked at it more closely.

My friend had been a big guy. He had hairy arms and a wide, hairy chest. The bruised slab before me appeared to have been shaved, head to toe. The body was on its back yet its arms, legs, and head were all facing down. There was massive bruising on all the limbs. The wound at the crotch had to have been delivered postmortem because there was no significant blood loss.

Prolonged pain had to have been the MO here. Hours and hours of torture before the relief of death.

I stepped back. To breathe. To take everything in.

Whoever had been here with this body was long gone.

I felt my head shifting into investigative mode. It had been a long time. My first boss as a detective in New York had been ex-FBI—Eddy Zakowski. Eddy had twenty-five years as a veteran field agent before he retired and went out on his own. He knew the job inside out. I had started with only one skill: I was good at martial arts. Then, over time, Eddy schooled me on photography, bugging, disabling security devices, effective bribery, surveillance, money laundering, basic kinesics, and so-so computer hacking skills. I had also learned the best way to visually dissect a crime scene in under five minutes without destroying trace evidence and DNA. We'd worked cases together time and again. But the most effective skill I had learned from Eddy was how to deal with death from the delivery end: I wasn't afraid to use my gun when I needed to. But my one weak spot had always been my shooting ability, hence the cannon I carried in my rear waistband.

. . . .

I MOVED QUICKLY back to the bathroom. In the sink was the box of hair dye. I opened the box and took out what I was looking for: the thin plastic gloves inside. I put them on.

Back in the bedroom, still being cautious, I moved to the closet with my gun in front of me. Keeping my hands free I opened the door with my elbow and cleared it. An overwhelming smell of vomit reeked from the enclosed space.

I flicked on the light and looked around at the walls in the narrow space. One of them had several drying stains.

Backing out of the room, I removed several tissues from a box on the dresser, then returned to the closet.

Holding the Kleenex between my fingers, I pinched enough of the puke away to have a sample. Then I wadded the tissue sheets into a ball and stuffed them into my inside jacket pocket.

After that, for another sample, I found one of my friend's dirty socks in a full laundry basket, then stuck it in my pocket too.

Everything inside the little room, all the clothes and shoes, had been pushed around. Half a dozen starched, long-sleeved car salesman's white shirts had been torn open and pulled off their hangers.

Woody had apparently owned three leather jackets. They were in a heap on the floor. Two black and one brown. Their arms had been sliced off and lay on top of a pair of boots in the corner.

I reclosed the door, hit the light switch, then tucked my .44 away.

The bedroom's shades were closed and everything electronic in the room appeared to be on. The stereo on the nightstand was softly replaying a CD and there was an open bottle of Hiram Walker's Ten High next to the machine.

Woody, of course, didn't drink. When I picked up the bottle by inserting my finger into the open top I noticed that it was one-third full. I felt my stomach wrench again involuntary.

Knowing better than to mickey any evidence and possibly get myself jacked up in the process, I began using more tissues to pick things up, just to be sure.

I turned up the sound on the CD player.

As I listened I realized I knew the album. It had been a favorite of my father, Jimmy Flowers, and it had played over and over again in his writing den when I was a boy: *Sinatra Sings Cole Porter*. The song was "At Long Last Love." Sinatra crooned, " . . . is it Granada I see, or only Asbury Park?"

SOMETHING WAS OFF about the music. This was not Woody's taste. My friend was a Fleetwood Mac and Eagles fan. I'd heard their songs often enough on his Honda's car stereo outside AA meetings, after the session, when we'd talk.

To double-check my memory I opened a drawer on the nightstand in search of Woody's music stash, again using more tissues in addition to the plastic gloves. Twenty CD albums lined the inside of the drawer. No Sinatra. Only seventies and eighties soft rock. The music playing on the stereo might have been brought in.

Is it Granada I see, or only Asbury Park?

Definitely, this was fucking Asbury Park.

. . . .

CLOSING THE DRAWER, still looking down, I saw that my friend's laptop case was open on the floor nearby. The computer was gone.

My eyes scanned the bed again and took in the other night table. On it I saw an absurd-looking seventies lava lamp with its green bubble floating slowly to the top. That was definitely Woody.

Then, on the floor, near the head of the bed, I spotted what I thought to be a stack of men's magazines. A *Penthouse* and half a dozen others. Near it on the carpet but not in the stack was a lone copy of *Cuffed*, with a seminaked girl on the cover, her wrists clamped to the headboard of a steel-framed bed, and her thonged ass extending toward the camera.

I flipped open *Cuffed* and saw page after page of mocked-up seminude torture scenes.

I'd had enough. I badly needed to take a piss.

RETURNING TO THE bathroom, I stared down at the penis in the toilet. Whatever blood there was in the water had drained to the bottom of the bowl, below the puke-stained rim.

I didn't want to piss in his shower and leave my DNA there, and his bathroom sink was full of junk that I should not move, and I couldn't bring myself to piss on my friend's cut-off cock in the toilet.

Back in the kitchen I opened drawers until I found the one with cooking utensils, the drawer next to the one with the regular knives and forks and spoons. Pulling out two wooden salad tongs, I returned to the bathroom. Then, leaning down, using the things like chopsticks in my gloved hand, I picked up the penis and carried it to the sink, then set it on the wide rim.

Screw the cops and the crime scene stuff. After I'd peed, I flushed the toilet. I let the bowl fill and flushed again.

Then I made a decision: I wasn't going to put Woody's dick back in the toilet water. That'd be an easy tell for the crime-scene guys. I'd leave the thing somewhere else, somewhere obvious, where they could find it.

Returning to the bedroom, still holding my friend's cock with the wooden tongs, I dropped it down on the bed.

That was wrong too. Would a killer slice off a guy's cock and then just leave it there next to him? No way. A severed penis had to be a trophy, otherwise why leave it floating alone in the toilet?

But this was getting too crazy. My brain went numb as it continued thumping in my skull, on overload. Screw it! I couldn't deal with it.

Crossing the carpet to the dresser, I pulled several tissues out of the Kleenex box, then laid the thing down on the dresser, on top of the tissues. The hell with it. Let the cops figure it out.

PULLING OUT MY cell phone I punched in 9-1-1.

The voice that answered sounded authoritative and metallic. A female voice. "Whaz your emergency?" it demanded.

"I've found a body," I said. "A tortured body. Cut up too."

"You're saying you have found a dead person?"

"Yeah, a tortured dead person. My friend is dead. Very dead. You need to send your people over here."

"Whaz the location, sir?"

The question stopped me. I couldn't remember the address. "I'm not sure," I said. "I mean I know I'm in Santa Monica. I'm at my friend's apartment on Arizona Avenue."

The voice was apparently writing the information down. "I needs an address. In full."

"Wait, okay," I said, forcing my still plastic-gloved hand into my shirt pocket, clawing to locate the slip of paper with Woody's address. "Hold on."

After pulling the crumpled paper open, I recited what I read. "Twelve-eleven Arizona Avenue. Apartment 201."

The aloof voice continued. "Okay, I've got that. Izzat where you're at now? You at that location now?"

"You mean, as opposed to Lego-Land!? Yeah, for chrissakes, I'm at the apartment."

"Okay, whaz the name of the deceased person?"

"O'Rourke. Woody O'Rourke. I'm pretty sure his legal name is Robert. Robert O'Rourke."

"Whaz your name?"

"Humpty Dumpty! You don't need my fucking name. Currently, I'm alive!"

"Stay on this line, sir. Don't be hangin' up. I'll contak a unit. We'll get you some officers there ASAP."

But I didn't stay on the line. I'd suddenly had a thought, an *oh shit!* thought. It made me click off my cell phone. I wasn't going to be talking to the bulls with my Charter Arms .44 tucked into the rear of my pants or, for that matter, with that puke sample and the sock in my pocket. I'd had my recent fill of dealing with the police after Mom's car fire. I decided to take my gun and the samples down to the demo Corolla and leave them there.

People do strange things—illogical things—in numbing emotional circumstances. Even trained people. They think through brain fog and overload, with their heads up their ass. At the moment, I was no exception. Later, I'd still be upset with myself for what I did next.

Returning to the kitchen, I opened drawers until I found a stash of plastic supermarket bags, used bags that Woody was apparently recycling for his garbage.

I went back into the bedroom, wrapped more tissues around Woody's dick, then stuffed it into a garbage bag. Then I returned to the bathroom and collected the hair dye box where I had found the plastic gloves. I didn't want to give away that I'd walked the crime scene.

I LEFT THE apartment door ajar and took the stairs to the front of the building.

I opened the trunk of my demo Corolla, looking for somewhere to hide the gun, Woody's cock, the hair dye box, the puke samples, and the sock.

I located a thick paper shopping bag that I'd forgotten to take inside my new apartment. It contained a pair of tennis shoes, paper towels, and a small box of laundry detergent. As I was unrolling a handful of the towels, my cell phone began buzzing. Knowing who it was—the law—I ignored it.

I wrapped my gun and my friend's penis and the dirty sock and tissues and the dye box and the plastic gloves in a wad of the towels, then opened the driver's door and popped the hood of the Corolla.

After looking to make sure no one was witnessing the event, I stuffed my bundle in the tight space between the battery and the fender's wheel well.

My cell buzzed again. I knew I'd better answer it. "Yeah?" I said.

The same 9-1-1 dispatcher's voice again. "We been tryin' to contak you. Are you Fiorella? James Fiorella? We waz disconnected."

Now they had my name, after tracing my cell's number. "What the hell's up with you guys!" I yelled. "Where are you? My friend's dead here in his apartment. You said you were on the way here ten minutes ago."

"The officers'll be there ASAP. We needs additional information—"

I clicked the off button on my cell again.

BACK IN THE apartment, sitting on Woody's living room couch, I lit a cigarette and tried some deep breathing as I sucked back half a dozen hits from my Marlboro Light.

This room was just as neat as the rest of the apartment. In front of me, beneath the wide, smoked-glass coffee table, was a stack of newspapers and martial-arts magazines. On the floor, too, next to the wastebasket, was Woody's computer printer. I concluded that my friend must've done most of his writing here at this table, not in the bedroom.

The screenplay he had wanted me to work on with him was also there. On top. He'd e-mailed it to me but I had not opened the file.

On the table was the TV remote, a Post-it pad, and a landline telephone. Woody's house and car key ring lay nearby. Next to the remote was a plastic container that held pencils and pens.

My friend had been a physical fitness guy and not a smoker and I could see no ashtrays anywhere, so I dumped the stuff out of the pencil jar and began using it for my ashes. My hands were shaking.

I didn't care what I contaminated in this room. I had a logical right to contaminate anything I wanted to contaminate. Screw the blues.

I picked up the Post-it pad. On it, in Woody's thick handwriting, was a phone number. An 877 number. I tore the top sheet off the stack and stuck it in my shirt pocket.

Taking more deep hits off my Marlboro, I took in the rest of the room, finally focusing on the TV set with the blinking green letters across the carpet in the center of a credenza.

Picking up the remote, I pressed PLAY. Nothing happened. I got up and crossed to the unit. There was no CD in the player, so I clicked off on the remote.

Then I scooped up Woody's screenplay. It was neatly stacked and on the floor, unbound.

I was waiting for the blues, trying to collect my thoughts, but the cock thing was haunting me. A very dumb mistake.

With nothing to do and my brain burning through my scalp, I decided to flip to the last five pages of the script to see if I could extract whatever punch would come from what I was sure was a very bad script. I've always been impatient when I read anything, much like my screenwriter father.

It was a death scene that would end the film. The wife of the Mafia don was in her room at the hospital, on life support—a girl in her twenties. She had taken a bullet for her son, a six-year-old kid named Michelangelo.

As I read the pages I felt myself beginning to tear up. The scene was run of the mill but the dialogue was good, very good, in fact, especially for a Hollywood screenplay.

FINALLY, OVER HALF an hour since my first call, I began hearing sirens outside. They were distant but becoming louder.

A couple of minutes later I was standing near the window when two patrol cars pulled up in front of the building.

Back at the couch, I sat down and I lit another cigarette.

The sirens from outside went silent and I began to hear voices and then radio transmissions—someone yelling something to someone else.

I picked up Woody's keys and shoved them into my pants pocket. Screw the blues.

NOW I COULD hear them coming up the cement stairs, taking them two at a time. They burst through the unlocked front door; both had their hands on their weapons that were still holstered.

The smaller one, a black guy, whose silver nameplate had "Ormond" printed on it, barked first. "Was it you that called 9-1-1?"

"Right, it was me," I said.

"Raise your hands, get up, and step backwards toward the center of the room," Ormond ordered.

I did what I was told.

"Do you have any weapons concealed on you?"

"No, I don't," I said, still moving backwards.

"Okay, now down on your knees—raise your arms over your head!"

I went along with Ormond's orders.

Then his partner, whose nametag read "Muskie," patted me down.

"You reported finding a body. Was that you?"

"Right. In the other room." I pointed. "That way."

Muskie turned to Ormond, who looked very young, probably twenty-one or twenty-two. "I'll check it out," he said.

Muskie left the room and then Ormond checked my wallet. After that, I was allowed to stand up again.

"How long have you been here?" Ormond wanted to know.

"I've been waiting for you representatives of law enforcement for over half an hour. Whoever did this murder could have mowed down half the old ladies in Santa Monica in the time it took you to get here. Nice work, guys."

Muskie had just reentered the room. "You shut the fuck up!" he barked.

"Look, my friend's dead in there and I didn't kill anyone. I'm just a little upset here."

"Shut the fuck up!"

"How about getting me a glass of water?"

"Shut the fuck up!"

HALF AN HOUR later I was still where I'd started, on the couch, smoking. Muskie and Ormond, having secured the scene and quizzed me with the standard stuff, were writing up field reports in their fat, wide notebooks.

Then the detectives arrived with what I assumed to be the ID techs, print guys, and a photographer—almost all at the same time.

The first detective I talked to was Archer. He announced his name when he saw me and came through the door. "I'm Detective Archer. What's your name?"

I decided not to answer. Screw being polite to these guys.

Archer stood there in his tan polyester sports jacket and cheap brown tie, and when I didn't answer, he began quizzing Muskie in a low voice.

Archer was tall and built like a tight end, with a skinhead haircut and a lean, mean, no-nonsense attitude. He was probably forty-five. I made him as an ex-Navy Seal or the equivalent. After talking to Muskie he glanced back at me, then went into the bedroom with the tech guys.

The second detective, who someone called Taboo, then came through the door. He was short—my height—and thick. He wore a dark suit that was probably Armani or something else upscale. His tie was red. He looked way more at ease than high-test, Special Forces Archer.

He walked over to me on the couch and shook my hand. "Hi, my name's Afrika," he said.

I decided I'd talk to Afrika. "JD," I said.

"Sit tight here, JD. We'll go over some things together if that's okay with you. I know this is a bad time."

"No problem," I said.

He then joined Archer in the bedroom.

While I was sitting on the couch doing nothing and smoking, it came to me that I recognized the second detective. We were about the same age. Maybe we'd been neighbors in Malibu a hundred years ago, although Afrika was

black, and in those days blacks were a scarce commodity in
California coastal towns where movie stars lived.

ANOTHER HALF HOUR passed. Finally Afrika appeared again
and pulled a chair up on the other side of the coffee table,
opening his notebook. He frowned, then pointed down the
hall. "Pretty sick stuff in there," he said.

"Woody was an AA pal," I said. "A good friend and a
damn decent guy. Whoever did him was a sick fuck and de-
serves all the payback they get."

Afrika rolled his eyes. Black, humorless eyes that spoiled
his friendly, nice detective act. "That's our end, sir. You can
be sure of that. . . . So, do you remember me?" he asked.

"Sorry," I said. "I don't. You looked familiar when you
walked in but I can't place you."

"We went to the same summer school in the tenth grade.
We were both in a science course. It was a make-up class for
you."

"St. Monica's? You went to St. Monica's? I don't remember you."

"I was just there for that summer. You and I sat in rows
next to each other, third from the back. The teacher was
named Jack Menotti. You were on the baseball team—
making up the F you got, so you wouldn't get kicked off the
squad."

"Geez, good memory," I said.

"I skipped tenth grade that year. I was a pretty quiet kid
in those days, but to get in the XL class, I needed the science
credit. You don't remember me because we almost never

talked to each other. But I let you copy my answers on all the tests."

"So you're some sort of a whiz-kid detective," I said.

"Nah," Afrika said. "I've got this kind-of memory skill—like playing the piano by ear or something. A doctor once told my mom it's a kind of autism. I had tutors and stuff and went to special schools. I guess you might say having a good memory is a blessing and a curse. It got me through college and law school."

"Hey, good for you," I said, not liking the chitchat or wanting to review old times anymore. "In my experience a good memory can be a shit deal."

Afrika removed two mini BabyRuth candy bars from his jacket, peeled the paper back on each, then popped them both into his mouth. "Yeah," he said, chewing. "I see a thing once and, you know, usually, that's it."

"I guess torture murders don't have much effect on your candy bar consumption."

"Hey, sorry," he said, "I skipped lunch. By the way, call me Taboo. That's how my co-workers refer to me."

"Look, Afrika, I'm just a little freaked here, okay? I could use a drink—several drinks—not a fucking candy bar."

Afrika ignored what I'd said. His black eyes were boring into my head. "So, let's get down to business, if that's okay. Officer Ormond gave me the time line. He says that you arrived twenty minutes before you called 9-1-1. What took you so long to make that call?"

"I was busy being upset," I said. "Then I watched my favorite game show, took a Jacuzzi, and waited for *Oprah* to come on. Gimme a fuckin' break here, okay?"

. . . .

AN HOUR LATER I was about to be released. The things I'd left out in my recital of the facts were the parts about me removing the samples from the closet and the Post-it with the 877 number, Woody's keys, the plastic gloves, and his dead, gray dick.

I had already made up my mind that I was going to square the books with whoever tortured my friend. Maybe I wasn't the mental equivalent of Taboo Afrika, my new good-buddy ex-classmate, but I'd been here before and I knew my way around. I was a guy who had been taught ways to get answers—something they didn't teach in Taboo's postgraduate criminology course or at detective school or law school. I, too, had a set of skills. Those skills had saved my life, then damaged it beyond repair. They had ruined a marriage and put me on suicide watch. In the time I had been away from New York City, I had hoped to have grown past those skills. But the truth is the truth: I am a man who will not quit or stop. I am a man who has pointed guns at other people's heads, then watched them explode. I am a man who knows how, no matter what, to get even.

AFRIKA STOOD UP from his chair. He handed me his business card. "If you can think of anything else, call me, JD."

Then he looked directly into my eyes. "Sooo, anything you may have left out by mistake?"

"I try to avoid mistakes, Afrika," I said.

"Uh-huh. So, are we square? You've told me everything?"

"Is that another question?"

"Just making sure. Doing my job." Then he smiled. There was a smudge of chocolate at the corner of his mouth. "Anyway, good to see you again after all this time, my man."

"Right," I said. "Just dandy."

DOWNSTAIRS IN MY demo Corolla, I lit up a Light. I watched as the rivers of smoke began to float above my head in the enclosed space. I thought of Woody's screenplay and how wrong I'd been about it, what a decent man my friend had been—my only real friend in Los Angeles. No matter how, I'd find the geek tortured him. It didn't matter how long it took or what the cost, or who it hurt, I'd find the killer. I'd square this.

THIRTEEN

Back at my new apartment, as the afternoon sun was streaming in over the tops of the eucalyptus trees outside my window, I sat down at my coffee table.

I opened the brown bag with the handles and pulled out Woody's penis, wrapped in a plastic garbage bag and the paper towels. My head was pounding relentlessly. What the fuck have you done here? You're completely crazy? You removed and concealed evidence in a murder! You've made yourself an accessory!

Enough was enough! "Fuck it!" I finally yelled out loud. There was no undoing what had been done. I lit another cigarette and looked around the apartment. My eyes stopped at the refrigerator.

Opening it, I looked inside. It was empty except for a quart of milk I'd bought, a jar of peanut butter, and a new loaf of bread.

In the freezer compartment were three bags of frozen broccoli that Coco had sent along as a care package. I returned to the couch, cut the end off one of the bags with a scissor, emptied most of the contents into the sink, then stuffed the plastic bag containing Woody's penis back inside.

That done, I put some of the broccoli back in, then placed the bags back in the freezer. That would have to do for now.

MY SINGLE THOUGHT now was to get very drunk, to stop the intensity of my headache and put the events of the day away. I told myself that after tonight I wouldn't make the same mistakes I'd made before in New York. I'd be less careless this time.

I picked up my demo's keys from the table. The nearest liquor store was Consumer's Liquor on the corner of Washington and Centinela, three minutes away.

Then something stopped me. It was almost as though someone had put his hand on my chest. Instead of leaving, I pulled my cell from my pocket and punched in Bob Anderson's number. I desperately needed to talk to another recovered drunk.

Anderson, as usual, answered on less than two rings.

"Hey Bob, it's JD, I need to talk."

"I'm here. I'm listening. Go ahead, my friend."

"My buddy was killed today. A damn decent guy with almost six years off the juice. I'm pretty crazy right now."

There was a long pause on the other end of the line. "Okay, here's what you do: Get to a meeting as soon as possible. Start telling people what's going on. Share about it. If you have to, grab somebody in the parking lot and just start talking. Don't go through this alone. You've got the tools,

JD, now it's time to use them. You're not in this by yourself, my friend. Take positive action now and leave the results up to God."

"Okay, good idea," I said, still not knowing or understanding what had stopped me from going to the liquor store or even what had made me pick up the phone. "There's a five-thirty meeting at the Marina Center every day," I said. "I've been there before."

"Call me afterward," Bob barked. "Let me know how you're doing. So—what happened? How'd he die?"

"He was tortured, then mutilated."

"Jesus Christ! Sorry, JD. That's the shits. Look, your job now is to control the thoughts. Short-circuit the crap your brain is telling you. Do you hear me? Getting to meetings and talking to other alkies will help. Do that and call me back."

"I don't want to drink, Bob. I know where that'll take me. And it won't be pretty. I was on my way to the liquor store but I called you instead."

"That's what we do. We pick up the phone. See, you're catching on. You're getting it, JD. A drink will only make it worse. There's nothing that a drink will make better. Just get into action and stay close."

I took a deep breath. "That's a deal. Thank you."

WITH NOTHING BETTER to do, I pulled out my laptop and turned it on. I went to my e-mail. There was only one that wasn't spam or a porn site solicitation. It was from Vikki-kat@yahoo.com. It read: Hiya JD. Hope you had a great day off. Just thought I'd check in.

The girl from work was hard-selling again. I immediately wondered how the hell she'd gotten my e-mail address. Then I remembered the notice on the wall of the sales office. It contained staff members' e-mail information. Somehow this girl—under thirty and still very pretty—had made up her mind to dip her cup in the Fiorella well. This puzzled me and made me think of something my state-sponsored shrink had once told me when we were discussing my chat-room dating prospects and my nonexistent love life: Women, she'd said, do the choosing. All a man really needs to do is to not say anything too stupid, open the car door, have a job, and tell the girl that she looks nice today.

I decided to ignore the e-mail. Taboo's black detective eyes and our conversation were still bugging me. His I'm-on-to-you expression had pissed me off. Taboo knew zip and would get zip out of me from here on out.

I ATTENDED A 5:30 P.M. AA meeting at the Marina Center in West L.A. The place was easy to get to from my new apartment.

The meeting turned out to be a one-hour speaker meeting. The guy's spiel was entirely useless to me. He'd been a crack addict. Nothing he said—not one word—resonated for me. I'd smoked coke twice in my life and didn't like the out-of-control rush. These days AA has become a catchall in recovery-speak. Everything's "anonymous." Fatties, gamblers, co-dependents, battered wives, and drug addicts were now allowed to participate in a program designed specifically for drunks. Where did that leave the alkies like me? We were SOL. What the guy said during his speech was useless pigshit to me. I didn't relate at all. Twenty minutes into his monologue, I got up and left.

Outside, I stopped to light up. A guy about my age in a leather jacket with a bandana around his head, a biker guy, was standing there, too, smoking.

He didn't smile. "Howya doin'?" he said.

"I've been better. My friend just got killed."

"That's it. That's right, brother. Life sucks and then you die."

I stepped closer to the guy. "Go fuck yourself," I said.

He looked me in the eyes, saw something that scared him, then looked away.

BY NINE THAT night, after a long walk, I was back at my place. Bob Anderson had been wrong about getting to a meeting. I'd come away empty-handed, with zip. I wasn't going to call him back. Not tonight anyway. But the good news was that I hadn't had a drink. Not one beer. I'd done the drill and gotten into action. I'd beat the odds for another day. That was something. Jesus, for a guy like me, that was a big deal.

Half an hour later, I'd watched an old *Girls Gone Wild* video and had something to eat and decided that getting laid might actually help shut my mind—and my headache— down. Digging into my pockets, I discovered that, after the pizza delivery, I was damn near broke. There would be no *LA Weekly* out-call massage for me tonight, or for that matter, any street hookers. My brain delivered an ironic piece of information: The fifteen hundred dollars I owed my friend Woody was now a wash. Dead men can't collect debts. The thought made me angry. Angry enough to hurt someone.

Then I remembered Vikki's e-mail. I had almost no interest in her. She was out of my league and for sure high maintenance, a girl in search of the L.A. brass ring and a man to give it to her. But she had come on to me, and by now she was home from the Toyota store. Maybe I'd get lucky. Right now the rest didn't matter.

I found her card after digging back in my pocket, and then dialed her number on my cell.

"JD," she answered in a chipper voice. "Surprise, surprise! So how was your day off?"

"Pretty shitty, to tell you the truth," I said. "But hey, I'm in your neighborhood. I thought I'd stop over and say hi."

"You don't know where I live. How could you be in my neighborhood?"

"That's why I called. I need the address."

"You think you're pretty cute, don't you, Fiorella?"

"No, but I am kinda bluesy at the moment. Like I said, it's been a pretty screwed day."

"You don't sound like yourself. Are you okay?"

"Compared to who? Rhett-fuckin'-Butler?"

A few seconds of dead air passed, then: "Okay, sure, I'm just fixing dinner and listening to some music. But just for a few minutes. I'm tired tonight."

"No problem," I said.

"So—got a pen, hotshot?"

"For you, blondie, always."

"I'm at eleven-oh-five Sixth Street. Apartment H, as in—"

"Hepatitis? Herpes?"

"Happy . . . stupid!"

I scribbled the address on the back of her card, then tucked it back into my pocket.

"Hey," she giggled, "I sold two today! One had a pretty nice gross. Over eight hundred in payable commission."

"You're the 'it' girl," I said. "No doubt about it. So, I'll be there in about ten minutes."

"See you then."

WHEN VIKKI ANSWERED her door I couldn't help but smile. My auto sales co-worker was wearing a light blue lounging outfit zipped down to her breast line, and her makeup and hair were, as usual, perfect. I'd read this girl as intense and complicated but nevertheless, she was very cute. And smart. A class act.

When I stepped inside she gave me a hug. I got the full D-cup treatment, chest to chest.

Leaning back, she eyed me cynically. "You okay, Fiorella?"

"Like I said on the phone, I've had a tough day."

Vikki stepped back. "Well, okay then—how about some coffee . . . or a glass of wine?"

"Thanks."

"The stuff I've got is red. It was a gift and it's been on a shelf for about six months. Is that okay?"

I thought the offer over for a very long second, then waved my hand no. "Just the coffee is fine."

She was smiling. "Whatever you say."

"So, you have other admirers? Not just me."

"Oh, now you're an admirer? When you left work yesterday I thought you were going to rip my head off. You have a delightful way of making people feel at ease."

"Yeah, I know. I'm sorry."

"I heard about your car deal going upside down," she said. "This morning Max sat everyone down and went over how to do the paperwork again—how to check and recheck IDs, drivers' licenses and credit cards."

There was music playing on her stereo. The volume was down. An old Bad Company album. Nice. This girl had good taste in classic rock.

Vikki's living room was composed of high-end sticks, maybe even decorated. Here was a girl who spent her money on nice things. Hopefully, without her clothes off, we'd actually get to know each other.

She brought the coffee over to the table by the couch and sat down. I began sipping mine.

"Look," Vikki said, smiling, "I heard what happened. And I know it wasn't just your deal going bad. Sherman Toyota is a weird place to work. For some reason Rhett and Max, especially Max, have a strange need to intimidate their sales employees."

"I believe it's called eating shit," I said.

"Soo-o, can I give you a compliment without you getting a fat head over it?"

"Sure," I said. "I could use one."

"You're the best salesman they have and they know it. In a strange way that might explain why Max is so tough on you."

"Thanks," I said.

"The testosterone level in that management office is neck deep. It can be pretty scary."

Looking across at Vicki I realized that I was beginning to like her. There was more there than I'd first thought, and I liked it. "Hey, look," I said, sliding across the cushion between us, "I think I'm getting, like, a thing for you. I've discussed it with myself, several of my alternate personalities, and we all agree."

Vikki smiled her *me, really,* smile. "That's nice," she whispered.

Then I went in for the kiss. As I did so, I eased my hand to the side of her left breast.

A second later she was on her feet, both hands on her hips. "Can I ask you something, Fiorella?" she fumed. "Did you think you were going to just pop in here and go for a quickie?! Is your head that far up your ass?"

"Hey," I said backpedaling, "I just wanted to show you I'm serious."

Vikki pointed a finger at the apartment door. "Well, how about this, Mister Suave: wiggle your goddamn serious back into your Jockeys and get the hell out of my house!"

AN HOUR LATER, back on my flip-out couch on Short Avenue, my TV on mute, I sat there watching an endless infomercial for a spiked energy drink and smoking my second-to-last Light. Again I resurveyed the ugliness of the day that had ended with my stupidity with Vikki. I'd blown it with a really nice girl.

But now there was no avoiding what I had to do. My life had changed unalterably in the last twelve hours. I knew I would see death again. I knew I would stop at nothing. This would only end one way. Some men are born to be scholars or preachers. Some guys will work at the post office all their lives, while others will fly at five times the speed of sound. Not me. I'm a hunter. I'm the darkness. I'm the one who gets even.

. . . .

I GOT UP, took a shower, then lay down on my bed. Maybe I could get in an hour or two of sleep. Maybe not. Tomorrow was the beginning. Tomorrow was Day One.

An hour later I was awake again. The headache wasn't too bad but I had just sweated through a newer and more vivid version of my blood-and-body-parts dream. Sitting up, I reached for my address book and my cell on the table next to my .44.

I'd known Carr in New York in my detective days. He'd been one of our go-to guys. It took five calls and about twenty minutes for me to hook up his new number. It wasn't easy.

It was after three A.M. in New York. We hadn't spoken in years but I was sure he'd remember me. We went way back, me and Carr. And he still owed me.

The call went to message and I talked into my phone. "It's me—JD," I said. "I've got a sock and a Kleenex that I need run. This is important. Get back to me."

Five minutes after I'd hung up my cell rang. The screen showed a 212 exchange. Carr was on the line.

"So, you're in town? You're back?"

"No, this's my old New York cell number. I still have it. I'm in L.A. Look, something's up, Carr. I need those samples run. As in yesterday. Okay?"

"Yeah, well, look JD, I can run your samples but it'll cost," he said. "It's double for a rush."

"No problem. I'll FedEx tomorrow morning before twelve, L.A. time."

I could hear Carr thinking—pausing—on the other end. "I always wondered what happened with you," he said finally. "You just dropped off the fuckin' map. . . . So, how's business out there? You still workin' alone?"

I was looking down at my Charter Arms .44. It was a decent piece at less than twelve feet but I needed something better, something repeating with fire power at a distance and one-shot kill capability. "I need Danny's number too," I said. "I need a clean Glock or a SIG and a box of hollow points. Should I call Danny myself or will you call him for me? I need to get hooked up."

"Clean SIGs and Glocks ain't cheap, JD."

"You owe me, Carr—that arms deal in Chelsea that time. You know you owe me."

"Hey, brother, that was years ago."

"Yes or no? Don't fuck with me on this. You know me and you know how I work. Do we deal or not?"

There was another several-seconds pause, then: "Yeah. Okay. You got it. I'll have the samples run. Then we're even. Deal?"

"Deal. What about the gun?"

"Forget Danny. He's out of the loop these days. But it so happens I know a guy. Wait, lemme get my book. Hold on."

Carr was back on the line in twenty seconds. "Ever hear of a place out there by you called Canyon Country?"

It brought a smile to my face. "Yeah—NRA Central. Yeah, I know Canyon Country."

"There's a guy lives there. Mendoza. We do favors for each other from time to time. Mendoza's your man. I'll make the call tomorrow."

"Make it now and get back to me. I need to move on what I've got going here. Give me an address to send the samples."

After I got the information I hung up.

FOURTEEN

At six-thirty A.M. my cell rang. I was sitting on my flip-out couch watching the TV news, drinking instant coffee. I'd slept off and on for two hours and smoked up all the half-smoked butts in my ashtray. In my dream I'd seen the faces again—they were covered with blood while they laughed and talked to each other.

I clicked the green button on the phone's face to On. It was a 310 number. "Who's this?" I said.

"Detective Afrika. Good morning."

"What's up, Afrika? I'm getting ready for work."

"We'll be in your neighborhood in about twenty minutes and we wanted to drop by to double-check a couple of things about your recollections. That okay with you?"

"Do I have a choice?"

Afrika chuckled. "Not really. We're just fact-checking is all. Just routine stuff. Or you can come down to the office."

"Okay, I'll be here," I said. Then I hung up.

. . . .

MY MIND WENT immediately to the freezer compartment
of my refrigerator and my friend's penis. Jesus! Afrika and
Archer in my apartment! My bet was that an apartment toss
would go with their fucking routine questions.

I went to the window and looked down. Outside, in the
tiny backyard of the building, were a line of half a dozen sad
rosebushes, a patch of lawn, and a flower bed of no more
than twenty square feet that contained geraniums of different colors.

It was a workday and only two cars were left parked in
the carport. I decided, fuck it! Now or never. I wasn't going
to get jacked up over my friend's detached cock. Not today,
anyway.

I OWNED ONE wooden salad spoon and I found it in an un-
opened moving box beneath the kitchen counter.

Downstairs in the small garden, between the geraniums,
the dirt was still moist from the last watering. After looking
around to make sure I wasn't being watched, I dug my hole,
then upended the plastic bag and let Woody's penis fall in.

Looking at the gray chunk of meat lying there in the shal-
low hole, I thought of my friend and his big salesman's grin.
Woody had been a good guy. A decent guy. But now the
clock was ticking.

Back upstairs, sitting on my couch after washing my
hands and my wooden dick-hiding spoon, I made another
cup of instant coffee.

. . . .

WHEN ARCHER AND Afrika walked in, Archer immediately began nosing around my kitchen, while Afrika sat down next to me on the couch.

"Got a cigarette?" I said.

Afrika removed a pack from his coat pocket and put it on the table with his lighter. "Sure, help yourself."

"I will," I said, lighting one up, then stuffing two more in my shirt pocket. "Thanks."

Special Forces Archer went into the bathroom first, looked inside, opened cabinets and drawers, then returned to the living room. He then searched the closet for a couple of minutes, opening and closing my cardboard boxes, seemed satisfied, put the stuff back, then closed the door. Then he opened the fridge, saw it was almost empty, and finally made his way to the freezer compartment. He looked at the frozen vegetables, took them out one at a time, and examined each bag closely, eyeing the one that had been torn open. That done, he put them back, then closed the fridge door.

"Just move in?" Archer wanted to know. "You've still got boxes."

"Yeah, I'm a new tenant. What's up, guys? I'm late for work."

"Want us to call them for you? We can do that," Afrika said. "A service of your local law enforcement professionals."

"C'mon, let's get to it."

Archer was staring at me. "Anybody ever discuss an attitude adjustment with you, Fiorella?"

Afrika chimed in before my mouth could start in on his

partner. "Your friend's house keys are missing, JD. Maybe one or two other things too. Can you help us out there?"

"Sorry, Detective. I don't know anything about any keys."

In one of the two side pockets of my jacket hanging on the back of my only chair were Woody's house and car keys—five feet away. In the other side pocket were my own keys. In my craziness about re-hiding my friend's cock, I'd forgotten to stash his keys. That cock and my absurd stupidity about it had caused me way too much trouble. I was beginning to hate that cock.

"Mind if we see your keys?" Afrika said. "Let's have a look. Where are they?"

I knew not to hesitate. "In my jacket pocket," I said. "Over there on the chair. I'll get them for you." Then I started to get up.

"Sit tight, no problem. Archer'll do that. Sit where you are."

I had no choice. I sat back down.

Archer walked to the chair, stuck his hand in the left-side jacket pocket and came up with *my* keys. He held them up. "These the ones?"

"Correct, Detective," I said, trying not to expel the air I'd been holding in my chest. "Outstanding police work."

"You're a smart-mouthed little prick, Fiorella. You're starting to piss me off. I'm beginning to dislike you."

"Look, guys, like I said, I'm late for work. I'd like to go now?"

Archer walked to my front door, located its key on my ring, stuck it in the lock, then flipped the tumbler. "Yeah, asshole," he said, "you can go to work now."

. . . .

AFTER THEY'D GONE I stood with my back to the closed door. I'd just dodged a bullet. Stupid. I'd been very stupid. And careless. Leaving Woody's keys in my jacket pocket had almost cost me my ass. And I hated that buried, dead cock. Enough was enough!

I went back down to the garden, dug up Woody's penis, brought it upstairs, then flushed the damned thing down my toilet.

I ARRIVED AT Sherman Toyota just as the big showroom wall clock clicked to 8:10. I was forty minutes late.

Fernando and Vikki and the other three new salespeople, Walter and Benny and Sheeba Perry, a tall, pretty black woman with a shaved head and hoop earrings, were collecting their paperwork at their cubicles and getting ready to head toward Max's office for the daily sales meeting. All carrying coffee cups. Three days earlier I had been the one to give Sheeba the tour of the car lot and then spent two hours showing her how to do the Sherman Toyota paperwork. We'd had lunch together at Jack in the Box and gotten along okay. She was a nice woman with a pretty smile and a spunky attitude. About thirty-five. I'd figured her for ex-civil service somewhere, but decided not to ask about anything personal.

As Sheeba passed by my desk she stuck out her hand. "Mornin', JD," she said with a sincere smile. "Hey, I sold one after you went home the other day. Third day on the job. You gave me some good tips. Not too bad for the token Negro at a Santa Monica car dealership, right?"

I had to smile back. "You're smart and you've got style. I'm a believer," I said.

In the coffee room, before going in to the meeting, I grabbed a quick cup, spilled some when my fingers wouldn't cooperate, then headed for Max's office, having forgotten to go back to my desk and pick up my call-back sales tracking notebook.

As I walked into the room the other salespeople nodded good morning. The air was still chilled outside and Vikki and Sheeba hadn't taken off their coats. Vikki didn't look up. Her eyes were fixed on her own fat sales folder.

Max set his cup down on his desk. "You folks go over your call-backs with each other for a few minutes," he said. "I need to meet with Mr. Fiorella, privately."

Outside Max's office he closed the door, then turned to me. "Sorry, Max," I said. "Sorry for being late, too. I had something I had to take care of. Jesus, and I forgot my tracking book again, too."

His expression was strained—nervous and tentative. "I assume that you heard about Woody," he said.

The bad news had traveled fast. I looked down at my shoes before I answered. "Yeah," I said, "I did."

"A terrible thing. A shit deal. A goddamn tragedy. O'Rourke was a good man. It was all over the news last night and this morning. They found his body. I know you guys were good friends."

"Yeah, we were. And yeah, it was a lousy deal."

Then Max's face darkened. "So, you lied to me," he said.

"What?" I said, not knowing what turn the conversation had taken. "Are you talking about Woody?"

"No, not Woody. Woody's gone. God bless the poor son of a bitch. I'm talking about your arrest record, Fiorella. Apparently, you were once charged with murder and assault. Tell me something, why was that information not on your job application?"

I hadn't been ready for the curve ball. "I don't understand," I said. "That was a long time ago. It was thrown out. Dismissed."

"Yes or no? Have you or have you not been arrested and charged with numerous felonies?"

"Yes, is the answer. I was. But being charged with lame bullshit is one thing—a lot of people who do what I used to do get charged with things. Call it the cost of doing business. Being charged and being convicted are two very different computer screens."

Max sneered. "Then, it's a no-brainer. You're fired, Mr. Fiorella. Effective immediately. You can pick up your paycheck tomorrow. I'll have someone drive you home."

"Did that arrest come out in my background check?"

"A lie is a lie, sir, especially on an official job application. Go clean out your demo and your desk. We're done."

"Answer my question, Max."

"You have twenty minutes to get off this property."

HALF AN HOUR later, my belongings from the trunk of my Corolla demo and from my desk were in a cardboard box. Vikki walked up to me wearing a tight gray sweater and matching skirt. She was flipping her key ring in her hand.

She wasn't smiling. "I guess I'm your designated chauffeur," she said. "Shall we go?"

"Swell," I said. "Exactly perfect."

WHEN MY STUFF was in her trunk, including the DNA samples from under my demo's hood that I'd transferred to a box in my backseat and we were on our way toward the freeway on Lincoln Boulevard, she turned to me. "Look, JD," she said, "I'm sorry, okay?"

"Because I got fired?"

"No, not that. I came off like a double-barreled bitch last night at my place. You didn't deserve to have me jump your case like that. Then, this morning, when I came in to work, I heard that Woody was . . . dead. Jesus! Did you know?"

"Yeah, I knew," I said. "It was a bad knock. I didn't take it very well and I didn't want to bring it up last night." I had no intention of telling this girl that I had been there and found the body.

"Woody and I were good friends," I said to end the subject. "But hey, about last night, I was probably over the line. So, forget it. You owe me zip. Drive the car."

Vikki wasn't smiling. "Listen to me, okay? After you left I realized that I was treating you like I talk to my ex. Call it a conditioned reflex or something. I mean, for sure, you were pushy, but I completely overreacted. So I'm really sorry. Okay?"

I smiled for the first time that day. "You mean you really will have my baby?"

Vikki rolled her eyes. "You've got balls, Fiorella. I'll give you that."

Now she looked away and said the next few words to

her windshield. "Can we try again?" She half whispered. "Maybe a real date or a reasonable facsimile?"

"Sounds like a plan to me. A very nice plan."

Then I realized I needed to make a stop. "Hey," I said, "can you do me a favor. I have to stop off at FedEx in the Marina. It's on the way. Just keep going on Lincoln."

"Sure, I know where it is. Behind the IHOP. FedEx, here we come. What's so important?"

"Just an errand."

"JD Fiorella, man of mystery."

"That's me, lady."

STOPPING AT THE next red light, she turned toward me again. "So, what happened back there with you and Max? It looked to be fairly quick and deadly."

"I was arrested in New York City years ago. But, trust me, I've never been convicted of anything important."

"You? What did you do?"

"I used to be a private detective. In that line of work, well, you know—things happen. You take your lumps. I was popped for something that didn't stick."

Now she was staring. "You were a detective? For real? I mean—who are you, Fiorella? Some kind of bad-boy tough guy?"

I shook my head as the light changed to green. "It all depends on your definition of the word "bad," as one former president might say. I've made my share of mistakes and stupid decisions. But that was before I met you, blondie."

Vikki gave me her hundred-dollar grin. "Gee-zus! What else have you done?"

"Me? A telemarketer; a high-end car rental agency owner in the Marina; a poet, and you know the rest; a newly shit-canned car salesman with a dead friend."

"A poet! Really? Geez, I'm a big reader—at least a couple of books a week. I hate TV. What kind of stuff do you write?"

"I don't write anymore. It was just a phase."

"C'mon, Fiorella!"

"Okay, I did write a book of poems."

"Tell me about them."

"Just a weak-ass collection of nonsense."

Vikki was smiling again—a strobe-light Hollywood-movie-premiere smile that filled her car. "Hey, look," she said, "I'd really like to read something of yours. Really."

"I guess that could be arranged. But what I'm interested in right now is that tight sweater you're wearing. Is it okay to say that, now that we're friends again?"

The pretty girl shook her head. "Jesus," she whispered. Then: "So, what's happening with FedEx?"

"Something's come up that I need to deal with."

"Something about Woody?"

"Why would it be something about Woody?"

"Just a guess. You guys were friends and now you're telling me you were a detective."

"You read too much Michael Connelly, kid."

WE HAD REACHED Washington Boulevard. Vikki caught the light and turned left, then made a quick right at the next block two hundred yards from FedEx.

She pulled up in front of the building.

"I'll be right out," I said.

"I'll be right here, boss, just as I said; at your service. Oh, FYI: I told Max I had a dentist appointment. I'm off for the next four hours."

INSIDE FEDEX I used my credit cards for the last time. After this my plan was to go completely off the radar.

Five minutes later, back beside Vikki in her demo, after telling the pretty girl, Thanks for waiting, I decided to go back to the subject of Max. "Hey," I said, "you know that conversation with Max is still bugging me."

Vikki rolled her eyes. "Really? Why?"

"No one at Sherman Toyota could have known about my arrest record. It was not public knowledge and it's only available on a restricted database."

"Did you ask Max how he knew?"

"Sure. But Max is a bitch. Too many years as a car business yes-man. He can't make up his mind if he's a goddamn vampire or a game-show host. His head's so far up Rhett's ass that he'll never see daylight again. Max was no help."

"Oh, so now it's Detective Fiorella again. Hey, you don't think somebody actually killed Woody? The TV just talked about finding his body."

We were on our way up Washington Boulevard toward Centinela. My place was a five-minute drive from FedEx.

"It's the blues' job now," I said. "I guess we'll just have to wait and see."

A knowing smile crossed her face. "So tell me, mister

jack-of-all-trades, out of curiosity, what does a man like you—a man with so many varied skills—do best?"

I had to smile again. "You may be on your way to finding out."

I TOLD THE blonde girl where to turn and we pulled into the driveway at my apartment house on Short. I knew that at this time of day there would be almost no cars in the parking area. I directed Vikki to slip her demo car in under the building's overhang garage. It was three-sided and private.

"Well, here we are," she said, smiling, popping the gear shift into park. "Door-to-door service."

Without saying anything I leaned over and kissed her. It quickly turned into a deep kiss—all tongue. She didn't pull away.

Half a minute later my hand was under her sweater, unhitching her bra. Then she pulled back. "Is that what you want?" she breathed.

"Yeah," I said, "that's a start."

"Okay, then, let's try doing what you want—but, shouldn't we go to my place? I have a king-size bed with pretty pillows."

"I like cars," I said. "I like doing things in cars."

Vikki smiled. "You sure?"

"I like it right here just fine."

"Sooo . . . what do you want us to do?" she breathed. "Tell me."

My tongue went from her mouth to her exposed tits. "Pull down your slacks. Then pull down your panties."

She leaned back from me then looked me in the eyes. "Here?"

"Right here," I said. "Right now."

Her dress slacks came down, revealing frilly pink bikini panties. She looked at me, breathing hard. "Do you like these? I like wearing sexy underwear," she whispered.

"Let me see what's behind 'em. Pull 'em down," I said.

I watched as Vikki removed her heels, then she slid her slacks off, then the panties. Her monkey was cleanly shaved.

I tossed the clothes into the back seat.

"Are you sure you don't want to go to my place? This would be more fun there," she breathed.

I smiled at her. "Here's just fine."

I picked up her hand then selected her two middle fingers. "Wet these in your mouth," I said.

"Why?" she whispered.

"You'll see."

She put her fingers to her lips.

"All the way in," I said.

After she'd finished wetting the fingers, I reached down and across and spread her legs. "Put them inside. All the way inside," I said.

I watched as she worked her fingers into her pussy. Deep inside. She began breathing hard. "What now?" she wanted to know.

"Take 'em out."

Vikki slowly removed her fingers.

"Now, stick them inside my mouth," I said.

I watched her eyes as I sucked the juice from her fingers.

"You like that, don't you?" she whispered. "Does that make you happy?"

"Yeah, I like it. I like it a lot."

"C'mon, let's go to my place. For real. I want to do this right."

"No. We're doing fine right here."

"Hey, you're smiling. You hardly ever smile. I'm making you smile, aren't I, Fiorella?"

I reached down between her legs and located the seat's adjustment lever, then pushed hers all the way back. "Turn around, with your ass toward me," I whispered.

"Whatever you say, Fiorella. Whatever you say."

AFTER VIKKI WAS gone, after cashing my final paycheck and buying a pack of Lights, a D-Coke, and three Pop-Tarts at the corner bodega, I picked up my cardboard salesman's box from Vikki's trunk that I'd hidden in my parking space and carried it inside the apartment.

Once I'd locked the door I opened all the widows to let in the cool air coming off the Pacific. It had all been too easy, me and Vikki. First the turn-down, then the submissive slut act. Something was off: the body language. Something wasn't right.

FIFTEEN

I downed the tarts with swigs from the Coke. Then I punched in Carr's number. One ring.

"Whaz up, JD?"

"Someone—I don't know who—has probably been running me through NCIC and the other state and fed databases. Somehow I was made on an old arrest. It so happens that arrest was squared long ago and only shows up in one place I know of. I need to find out who's been requesting information on me. I need ID, e-mail—the package, and I need to know how whoever it was managed to access an off-limits database."

"That'll take time. That's not what we do here. I'll have to shake the bushes, make some calls."

"My car was torched the other day and I've been tagged by someone—probably someone with computer smarts. There might be a connection to what I'm working here."

"Forty-eight hours. It's a deuce up front now, plastic only. And another deuce on the back end."

"I can't use my plastic. I'm hot. I'm off the grid. Help me out, Carr."

"This ain't charity, Slick!"

"Give me a day and I'll wire you the money."

"Done."

I gave Carr the e-mail address I never use. It could only be accessed through the New York Botanical Gardens website.

"Sit tight," he said. "I'm on it." Then he hung up.

AFTER I'D CLICKED off my cell phone it immediately rang again. I clicked it on. "Forget something?" I barked into the receiver.

"Fiorella?" a clip-toned voice asked.

"Who's this?"

"Detective Archer."

"Jesus, Archer, what now? You guys are way too far up my ass."

Archer began working me. Clearly, he didn't like me and I didn't like him. "More details, is all. Cop stuff," he said. "Just take a few minutes."

"The way you guys go over details ends up with me feeling more and more like your chump. For instance, you searched my apartment with no probable cause. A bullshit toss, Archer. So just leave me out of this from now on. You'll get dick when you dial this number."

"Calm down, hothead! Me and Taboo are just doing our job—trying to put the pieces together."

"Fine. If you've got a question for me, then ask it. I'm not your bitch and I don't deserve the heat. Quit dancing with me."

"That's the problem. You pretend like you're cooperating but you give us zip. Your answers to questions are always nonanswers."

"Hey, try some different questions."

"We were going over the inventory from your friend's apartment again. One of our victim's socks is missing. A dirty sock. How about that? Do you know anything about that?"

"That's the same kind of question, Detective. The answer is that I have my own dirty socks. I don't need anyone else's."

"Screw you, Fiorella."

"Is that all?"

"No it isn't," Archer hissed. "Here's something different. Something else came up—something else you left out."

"What would that be?"

"You are a former private investigator, apparently. You never mentioned that occupation."

"So what? You never asked. That was a long time ago. L.A. is a different planet."

"Let's talk straight here. Let's cut it right to the bone. That be okay with you?"

"You mean, as opposed to you working me like some kinda street rockhead slammed up against a black-and-white? I'm listening."

"There's something more than a little off about you—something kinky. I can smell it. I think you sort of fell into this thing and . . . "

"And what?"

"After Taboo found out that you did your detective work in New York, he ran a known-acquaintances search. That stuff set off quite a few bells. Bottom line, we all need to sit down again. Now. Today."

"Will I need an attorney, Archer? Because that's the direction we're heading in here. I'll make the call after we hang up."

"You know people—people in New York. You have, or used to have, interesting friends."

"I'm a car salesman, Archer. Period. My friend is dead. Period. You, Detective, are talking out your ass."

"*Were* a car salesman. As of today."

"Fuck you, Archer!" I said, then clicked the Off button on my cell.

TWENTY MINUTES LATER, now carless, I took the northbound bus across Centinela Avenue to Wilshire Boulevard, then transferred to the westbound Santa Monica bus. Both rides took over an hour.

I got off at Lincoln Boulevard and walked east to Woody's apartment building.

When I got to the corner I looked down the block and saw that a line of yellow cop tape was stretched around the entrance to his apartment house and there was still a patrol car parked in front.

Woody had lived in an older building and it didn't surprise me to find out there wasn't a garage at all. I just hadn't noticed. I needed to find his car. Apparently, my friend had been a street parker, a rough task in Santa Monica without a fake Handicapped sticker. In exchange for the lower apartment rent and no garage, street parking residents have the privilege of spending up to two hours a day looking for a legal spot in their neighborhood.

I began circling the block on foot from the opposite direction, searching for a red four-door Honda, hoping the blues hadn't yet gotten around to IDing the car and picking it up.

No soap.

So I widened my search until I located Woody's car, with a parking ticket on the windshield, tucked into a spot on Eleventh Street, two blocks north of Arizona. My luck was holding.

No pedestrians were nearby, so, after pulling the ticket off the windshield, I stuck my friend's car key into the door.

I fired up the motor, then made a U-turn in the direction of Ocean Avenue, putting as much distance between me and Woody's building as possible. Five minutes later, on Ocean Avenue, near the jogging path on the cliffs above the Pacific, I found a spot and pulled in.

My friend kept his car, like his apartment, very neat— there was nothing on the seats or the floor, no trash, no papers. Even the plastic black floor mats were scrubbed clean.

In the glove compartment were a few soft-rock CDs and a porn DVD. No Cole Porter.

I put the stuff back in the glove compartment, then began running my hand in the crack between the backrest and seat cushion of the passenger seat. I came up with two round, light-orange pills. They looked familiar. I remembered seeing something like them before, after the incident with my ex's boyfriend. The pills had been prescribed for me but I never took them.

My friend Woody did not take any meds—nothing stronger than Tylenol and antacids—so I stuffed the two tablets into my pants pocket.

The trunk of the car was like the rest of the stuff in Woody's life before he died: clean and neat. In it was a gym bag containing workout clothes and a razor, aftershave, and deodorant. That was it.

. . . .

HEADING SOUTH ON Lincoln Boulevard I drove toward the impound lot on Glencoe Avenue in Marina del Rey, the neighborhood where I'd been a few hours earlier with Vikki. Bruffy's Towing was where my mom's torched car had been towed.

I parked Woody's Honda down the block and walked back to the fenced-in impound entrance. It had been over ten days since my car fire and I was hoping like hell that Mom's shitbox would still be in the tow yard. If it was, I would soon have what I needed.

I showed ID to the guy at the booth, who was yakking on his cell phone, pinching the thing between his shoulder and his ear. He typed my name into his computer while he continued yakking. My last name was a match for the legal owner and the guy looked up and pointed. "Aisle three," he said. "About halfway down."

I'd caught another lucky break.

I made my way through the ocean of damaged and rotting metal until I found Mom's burned-up Honda backed into a slot in the middle of a long row.

There were surveillance cameras on both ends of the lane but by stooping down I was pretty sure I was out of camera view.

Using a Phillips screwdriver I'd kept in the glove box, I took off the license plates, which hadn't been damaged in the car fire.

I tucked them inside my jacket, stood up, then walked back to the exit gate. So far, so good.

. . . .

IT WAS TIME to do some grunt detective work with the pills in my pocket, but first I'd deal with Woody's car.

I drove his Honda back to Short Avenue, parked, and waited, three buildings away from my apartment house. Twenty minutes later, when I was reasonably sure there was no one on the building—no unmarked cars on the street and no activity—I went inside my apartment.

At the bottom of a half-empty cardboard box, in the closet that Archer had opened but had been a little too quick in searching, I found what I had hoped would still be there: a bogus New York City detective's badge I hadn't touched in five years. It was in the pocket of one of my wadded-up, out-of-date sports jackets.

Needing a safe place to swap out the license plates, I drove the Honda to the intersection of Culver Boulevard and the Marina Freeway to an unmanned self-storage lot.

Parking Woody's car in one of the many vacant spaces that faced Ballona Creek at the side of the building, I switched the plates: my mom's Honda for his. They were the same year. Barring a VIN number check, I had my own ride again. I was in business—at least until Archer and Afrika sorted out the details. That'd probably take a couple more days.

My hands were shaking. It wasn't my nerves or too much caffeine. It was something else. I needed a sugar fix. So I pulled a five from my pants and fed it into a soda-vending machine outside the storage units, got change in quarters, and bought myself two nice sugary Pepsis. My father had been a serious diabetic for many years before his death. I'd been told more than once that I was headed down that road. Without the booze, these days I often had an intense craving for sweets—whatever sugar I could get.

As I was standing beside the vending machine's alcove, drinking the first of my Pepsis, a man and a little girl came out of the storage building's double doors, pushing a wide, four-wheel dolly loaded down with half a dozen large cardboard boxes. The girl was seven or eight years old and on the thin side. The man, who I took for her dad, was midthirties, unshaved, and dotted with tattoos. He had a red drinker's face and was wearing a camouflage T-shirt and a blue Dodgers cap.

Their tan, beat-up SUV was parked three spaces from Woody's Honda. When they got to the car, pushing the dolly, I could hear the guy hissing at his kid under his breath: "Stupid! Stupid little bitch! Didn't I tell you just to leave the goddamn teddy bears? What's your fucking problem?! You're still a baby—a moron. You'll never grow up!"

"I'm sorry, Daddy."

"Screw it!" he yelled. "Just stand there and don't touch anything—you dumb twat!"

After he'd loaded the boxes inside his SUV he threw his arms in the air and turned back to the kid. "Where's the fucking microwave?"

"You left it, Daddy. It's back in the room."

"Why the hell didn't you tell me! That's one of the things we came for. What the matter with you?"

"I guess I forgot, Daddy."

"Shit! Okay okay, just stay here and watch the car. Do you think you can do that, stupid?"

"Okay, Daddy."

"I'll be right back."

AFTER HE'D DISAPPEARED into the building I crossed the
pavement to throw one of my Pepsi cans away in a large
metal bin that was near the little girl. She was sitting on a
metal bench against the side of the building, her hands in her
lap. We were five feet apart.

"Hi," I said, popping a new Pepsi.

"Hi."

"Was that your daddy who went inside?"

"Yeah, that's my dad."

"So—you must be moving. Is that why you're here today?"

"Uh-uh. We moved two weeks ago. Before school started.
We're picking up some stuff that didn't fit in the truck."

I sat down near her on the bench. This kid was very cute
and sweet. "Where did you guys move to? Close by?" I asked.

"We moved to Playa del Rey, near the beach. They just
painted our apartment. It's blue. I love blue. My mom and
dad are separated now and I'm going to a new school."

"Hey, that's nice. Do you like the new school?"

"Yeah, it's okay. My teacher is Ms. Alvarez. She's nice."

Then the little girl's eyes drifted to something on my shirt
and she smiled. "I like your cross," she said. "I like jewelry.
It's really pretty."

I fingered the silver crucifix hanging from my neck. It had
fallen outside my shirt. I'd owned the thing for twenty-five years
and never took it off. It had been a high school graduation present
from my mom. "Thanks," I said. "It's kind of my lucky charm."

"It's really pretty."

I smiled at the kid. "Hey, do you have a lucky charm?" I said.

"I have dolls on my bed at home but I don't have a real necklace."

"Do you want to see it?" I asked.

"Sure."

I worked the cross off over my head and collected it and the chain in the palm of my hand. "Open your hands," I said. "Put them together and make them into a cup."

She extended both cupped hands and I dropped the cross and chain into them.

"It's beautiful," she said.

"Yeah, I think so too. You know," I said, "you're a smart girl and you're really pretty too. You should have a lucky charm. My lucky charm has protected me for a long time. When is your next birthday?"

"I'll be nine in two months. Maybe I'll get one like that when I'm nine or ten—when I'm older."

"That's a long time to wait—two months. That's a long time to go without a lucky charm. A charm is a thing you can count on to make you feel better when you're sad—like when your daddy yells at you. You just hold it tight and then you feel better right away."

"My daddy gets upset. Mom says he gets upset too much."

"I know what we can do," I said. "You can have mine. Would you like to do that?"

"Sure. But it's yours. You won't have one if you give it to me."

"That's okay," I said, "I don't need it anymore and I've

been looking for someone to give it to. Someone who needs good luck. I want you to have it."

I took the chain and cross from her hands and slipped it over her head on to her neck. Her smile lit up the parking lot and could have stopped the traffic on Culver Boulevard.

"Thank you," she said. "Thanks a lot. It's really nice and beautiful too."

"So tell me your name," I said.

"Janie. I'm Janie. That's me."

"Well Janie, that lucky charm is for you but you can't tell anybody where you got it. Is that okay? I mean if somebody sees it and asks about it just say you found it here by this bench. Will you do that?"

"Sure. Okay."

"And any time you are sad or worried or unhappy, just hold it in your hand and remember everything will be okay. Will you do that?"

"Okay. I'll do that. What's your name, mister?"

"JD. My name is JD."

JANIE AND I sat on the bench and talked for a couple of more minutes and then her dad came through the double doors of the storage building, carrying the microwave oven. He saw us sitting together on the bench and made a face that reflected his mood. "Hi," I said, "I was talking to your daughter. Your little girl She's a great kid."

The guy eyed me up and down, then set the microwave at his feet on the concrete. His hands were on his hips. "Yeah, so . . . who are you?"

I tried to keep my expression even. "She's a great little girl. We were talking—making friends."

"Yeah, well, that's swell. So how 'bout minding your own fucking business, pal? How 'bout getting up from that bench and leaving my kid alone? I don't like her talking to strangers. That okay with you?"

"You know," I said, "I heard you yelling at her before. You might try to go a little easy on her. She's a sweet kid."

He glared at me, then took two steps closer. "So, okay, how 'bout this: Drink your pussy soda and get in your little red pussy car and leave me and my kid alone. Think you can handle that?"

"You need to be nicer to your little girl. That's my suggestion."

Now he was walking toward me. His face was red and he looked ready for trouble.

I stood up. My intention was not to bust the guy up. I didn't want to do that in front of his kid. So when he tried to push me, instead of delivering a blow that would break several facial bones and cause plenty of bleeding, I sidestepped the thrust, grabbed him by that arm, and used his momentum to trip him. When he was down, I slammed one knee into his crotch, then used them both to pin his shoulders. My hands were at pressure points at his throat.

"Have you got a cell phone, friend?" I whispered.

"What?" he croaked in pain.

"Have you got a cell phone?"

"Yeahhhh, I got a fucking cell phone."

"Pull it out."

I allowed him to reach down into his pants with a free hand and fish for the phone. He held it up.

"Punch in 9-1-1," I said, easing the pressure of my hand on his throat.

"Wha for?"

"You might need an ambulance, and if that happens your daughter Janie is going to need a ride home."

SIXTEEN

My next stop was at a Rite-Aid Pharmacy on Lincoln Boulevard in Venice. At the prescription counter I asked to see the pharmacist. The guy who came up to talk to me was a tall Latino wearing a white smock with a green nameplate on the front. It read "Roberto Galvan" in fancy calligraphy. He was young and hip and clearly gay, with two thick sterling silver ear piercings.

There was no one else with him in the department other than the girl twenty feet away at the drop-off counter.

I flipped open my New York City gold detective shield, then dropped the two pills from my pocket onto the thick glass counter in front of me. "Roberto," I said, "I need your help. I need some answers."

"Detectiff?" he lisped, rolling his eyes. "A New York City detectiff?"

"Correct, I said. "We're involved in an ongoing investigation. The person of interest we're looking for has been taking these pills. Someone from his school sold them to him. Can you tell me what they are and what effect they have?"

Now Galvan was all business. Unfazed. "Company policy, Detective. I'm not permitted to give out that information. You'll have to call corporate."

He began walking away.

I held up the badge again and spoke loudly. "This is an emergency situation, Galvan. There's a life on the line here. We need your help now!"

The young guy turned back and studied my face. Finally, he picked up one of the pills. "I'll be back in a minute," he said.

He stepped behind a tall partition. I could only see the top of his head. I wasn't sure whether he was making a call or examining the pill. All I could do was wait.

A couple of minutes later he was back, holding a hard plastic cutting board. The round, light-orange tablet I had given him had been crushed to a powder on the board's surface.

"Okay, look," he said. "You can't hold me to this and I can't be a hundred percent sure, just by sight."

I shook my head. "You're the pharmacist. Just give me your opinion of what it is."

"It's lithium. The pill is in a generic form. Lithium carbonate. Is the person taking this drug also on antipsychotic medication?"

"No idea," I said with an even face.

"There can be harsh side effects if this medication is stopped abruptly."

"That sounds right. I'm dealing with someone that's pretty unstable."

The pharmacist eyed me again. "That's all I can tell,"

he said. "By the way, what's a New York City cop doing in Marina del Rey?"

"Stalking an asshole, sir," I snarled.

I swept the remaining pill off the counter. "We appreciate your assistance in this matter, Roberto. Have a nice day."

I was making progress.

I HAD NO intention of going back to my apartment. It was hot there and I wouldn't go back at all if I could help it.

Back in Woody's car, I drove the two miles along Pacific to the ramp at Santa Monica Pier, then took it down the hill to the ocean. Once on the Coast Highway, I headed north.

Fifteen minutes later I was in the La Costa area of Malibu, where a steep hillside of three-million-dollar homes meets the coastline.

I pulled up in front of a tourist-type shop, just south of the old Malibu Sheriff's Station.

I got out and locked Woody's Honda.

Inside the shop, along with T-shirts and souvenir key chains, Malibu calendars, swim fins, and Styrofoam surf-boards, I found what I was looking for: a prepaid cell phone with a thousand minutes of talk time. I paid cash for the phone. I was now further off the radar.

HEADING NORTH AGAIN toward Point Dume, the traffic was moving easily. Twenty minutes later, when I got to the back gate of Mom's house, I parked fifty feet away on the street outside her wall, under a row of her tall fern trees.

This was not a social visit. I quietly unlatched her back gate, then walked quickly across the paved carport to her open garage.

Once inside I went directly to Jimmy Fiorella's old freestanding metal cabinet that had been kept in the garage for years. It contained personal junk. Athletic stuff mostly. His three sets of golf clubs, the baseball bats and gloves I had used as a kid, and an old cracked and worn leather jacket Pop had worn years before when he hiked the cliffs of Point Dume in the wintertime.

On the only shelf were two of his old, broken typewriters and a thick canvas bag tied shut with a long strip of rawhide. I was in luck. It was still there!

Pulling the bag down I untied the leather strapping, wiped off the dust, then opened the box. The gun inside was a wooden-cased .44 caliber 1851 Army Colt. A presentation piece. Pop had won it in a poker game many years before from a neighborhood bulldozer driver and had promised to pass it on to me when I was still a teenager. He had taken the gun in lieu of a three-hundred-dollar debt. His bulldozer gambling buddy had never come back for it.

I had come to have a decent knowledge of guns over the last several years and was sure the old Colt was worth considerably more in today's market—enough to maybe purchase the kind of gun I needed and maybe enough to spare to keep me going until I found out who had killed my friend, then evened the score.

I retied the rawhide around the canvas bag, then started walking to the back gate.

Halfway through the gate I stopped, realizing I wanted to check in on Mom. We'd been having a rough time these last few weeks.

I stowed the Colt in the canvas bag in Woody's trunk and headed back through the gate to Mom's kitchen door, then knocked.

Coco let me in, smiling. "James," she chimed, "always good to see you. Is everything okay?"

"Fine," I said, hugging her. "How's the old girl?"

"She's her usual self, James, working on a new chart; in good form, except of course concerning her blood pressure. Please come in and say hi."

When I reached the patio Mom looked up. I walked over and gave her a kiss. "Whatcha workin' on, Ma?"

She smiled up at me, then began flipping some pages. "Oh, I just started doing this man's chart today," she said. "He's one of the richest men in the film business in Los Angeles and, according to this, anyway, he's easily among the most strange."

I looked down at the printed and graphed white sheets in front of my mom. "Did you get him from your ad in *Malibu* magazine? Those clients usually pay you pretty well."

"I think so, but I'm actually not sure. His secretary telephoned, then put me on hold. It took my client five minutes to finally come on the line. He never told me how he'd found out about my work. But I am pleased to say I'm being compensated handsomely. By the way, James, did you hear about the two foreign girls who went missing at the beach near Paradise Cove? The paper said they were from Guatemala. They were nannies for a rich couple. It's quite odd."

"Yeah, I did. I heard about it at the noon AA meeting. Any news about what happened to them?"

No. They've apparently disappeared and no one seems to know why. We live in unusual times. Even a place like Point Dume isn't safe anymore."

"So fill me in on this strange new client, Ma."

"Well, he has one of the most unusual natal charts I've ever come across. It's a bit bizarre, actually."

"No kidding. Who is he? What's he like?"

"No names. Remember, he's a client. But I can tell you this: his natal Pluto is in the eighth house, squaring Venus. It's very odd. Violence and sexual obsession."

I rolled my eyes. "Geez, Mom, right here in Malibu? On stable, conservative Point Dume? First the Guatemalan nannies and now your weird new client."

"You have a tendency to trivialize what you don't understand, James. It's not your most endearing personality trait. In fact the earth—all of us—are undergoing a major transition cycle."

"More Mercury retrograde, right?"

"It's rather more complex than that. In fact many in my field see it as a day of reckoning, the possibility of impending transformation."

Mom took off her glasses and stared up at me as if expecting bad news. "So, to what do we owe the pleasure of your company today? Dare I inquire into your financial situation?"

"I wanted to say hi is all, Ma. I was out this way so I decided to drop by."

"Very thoughtful, James. Thank you. Please sit down with us and have a cup of tea. Would you like a sandwich? How about some pie? Coco made a nice mince. I know you like mince pie. I can put this chart aside. It's not pressing and not due for another week."

"Sure, Ma," I said. "Pie and coffee sounds good."

. . . .

ON MY DRIVE back toward Santa Monica I let my mind go back over what I knew—the swirl of disconnected crap that had invaded my life over the last half month.

1. Over two weeks ago I'd chased down a crazy woman (impersonating a man) in a yellow Porsche convertible on my way home from a job interview. Then, after that, I had caught up to her at Guido's Restaurant and evened things up. The woman had threatened me with death.
2. Three days later my mother's car had been torched down the street from Sherman Toyota. Perp still unknown.
3. My biggest sale at the car dealership had turned out to be a scam—identity theft. My commission was lost.
4. I'd found my friend's mangled and tortured body.
5. I was suddenly fired from my job for not divulging information the car dealer should not have had access to.
6. I'd met Vikki and begun an affair, for better or worse.

The swirl of sudden complications could not all have been coincidence. I didn't believe in coincidence. Somehow I'd made it to the top of someone's shit list. The question was who and how.

WHEN I REACHED the Cross Creek shopping center I turned left at the light. My job now was to find out if there was a potential link between the crazy girl in the Porsche and the other stuff. I needed to get as much information as I could about the incident on the Coast Highway and the confrontation with the woman at Guido's Restaurant.

After parking Woody's Honda, I approached the two red-jacketed valet-parking guys, who appeared to be ready to change shifts.

Fishing in my pocket I came up with a ten-dollar bill.

"Hey," I said to the good-looking blond surfer type, whose nametag read "Tim," "I could use your help."

Tim smiled. "Sooo . . . what's up? You a cop?"

"Cops don't hand out money, Timster," I said holding up the folded bill but making sure the number ten on it was covered by my thumb.

"Okay, so whose chimp do I have to screw while you film me? Ha ha."

"I'm doing backup work on an investigation. A couple of weeks ago a yellow Porsche got vandalized here on your lot. I need some details about the Porsche and the driver. Can you help me out?"

Tim looked at the folded bill in my hand. "Sure, I guess so. I remember filling out the insurance papers with the other guys who came out from town. I'm pretty sure I've still got my copy in my truck." He pointed. "Over there. You from the insurance too?"

"I'm following up," I said. "Double-checking the details."

We walked to Tim's yellow truck, which had a surfboard rack in the bed. He chirped the driver's door open. After fishing around in a plastic file box on the floorboard, he came up with a duplicate yellow form. He handed it to me. "There ya go," he said. "Now, I'll take my money."

"Thanks," I said, handing him the bill. "Do you need the form back?"

Tim unfolded the bill, then sneered. "Geez, pal, you're

quite the big spender. A guy can't take a leak in this town for ten bucks."

"Sorry. Next time I'll bring the gold watch."

"Yeah, whatever. Anyway, they said that the car insurance is gonna take care of the damage, so the restaurant skated and no one blamed us. So, you know, no biggie."

Opening the yellow insurance form I read down the checked boxes. The policy number was there but the Porsche owner's name was nowhere on it.

"What we have is a zero here, Tim. There's no plate number. I need to confirm the owner's information. How about the tow truck? The car was towed. Who did the owner call? Or did you call the truck yourself?"

"Auto Club, as far as I know," says Tim.

"Well," I said back, writing the information down, "that's a beginning. I can start there."

"Did you need the name of the driver?"

I scratched my head. "That's why I'm here, Timster. I did say 'owner's information,' didn't I? I sorta thought you'd put that together on your own."

"Hey, sorry. Ha ha. Well, okay, the car belongs to that producer guy, Karl Swan. His daughter Sydnye was driving it that day. They live on Point Dume. The big mansion with the gate on Grey Fox."

"That's what I'd call helpful, Tim."

"She never smiles. She's been here quite a few times. And she tips like for shit, too. Mikee helped her for an hour and a half that day. Made calls for her, got her two cold glasses of water—and guess what Mikee gets for his trouble?"

"What did Mikee get, Tim?"

"Zippo! Not even a friggin' thank you."

Back in Woody's Honda I now had what I needed. I started the engine. "Bingo!" I said out loud.

IN SANTA MONICA, at Ace Loans Pawn Shop on Lincoln Boulevard, I parked at a meter, then used my fake Handicapped placard to avoid dropping quarters into the meter. I stuffed my snub-nose under the front seat, then went inside with my dad's Colt in the canvas bag under my arm.

The store had strong overhead fluorescent lights fastened to the high ceiling by long chains. It was empty of customers but packed floor to ceiling with pawned junk.

The guy behind the counter was on the phone. I looked around for a few minutes at the watches and jewelry and knives in the showcases until he'd hung up, then I took the boxed Colt out of its canvas bag and set the box on the counter between me and the uncle who wore rimless glasses balanced on his forehead.

"I want to sell this gun," I said.

The middle-aged unsmiling guy reached under the counter and pulled out a rubber-tipped kind of screwdriver. He flipped his specs down onto his nose, then opened the case that held the gun, using this tool to prevent scratching the antique finish of the box.

Then he put on a pair of rubber gloves. Clearly, this uncle knew antique guns.

He carefully picked up the Colt with one finger on the barrel tip and the other on the heel of the wooden butt, making sure to not touch the steel finish of the single-action revolver.

Next, he tested the hammer and cylinder several times, making sure the action of the gun was in good working order. Then he rotated the cylinder and looked in each chamber. The whole procedure took a couple of minutes.

Finally, he unfolded the presentation document that came with the gun. He held it up to the light, read it, then examined the print and paper with a magnifying glass, then slid it back into the envelope.

"Nice gun," Captain Humorless finally grunted. "An original cased Colt in decent condition with a presentation letter. How much do you want for it?"

"Make me an offer."

"Where did you get this gun?"

"It's been in my family for years. On a shelf in our garage. Are you the Ace of Ace Loans? Are you the owner?"

"I am now," Stoneface replied without looking up.

"I used to come here with my dad when I was a kid," I said. "He bought sets of used golf clubs from you guys. We're longtime customers in this store. I'm hoping I'll get a fair shake from you, price-wise."

"We always make a fair price, sir."

"There used to be an older guy running the shop. He was . . . nice."

Uncle finally looked up and our eyes met. "My father started this business in 1955. We've been in the area since then."

The guy then pulled a stack of reference books out from under the counter and began cross-referencing the gun. "I'd like to see some ID, please."

I handed him my California driver's license.

He checked the license under a blue light, then looked on the back, saw the restriction, then glanced up at me.

"Everything okay?" I asked.

"Just checking," he said.

Finally, he handed the license back, then eyed me carefully again for a couple of seconds. "Look," he said, "this is a collector's piece—especially with the documentation. I won't loan you money on the item but I will buy it from you."

"How much?"

He opened another book then looked the gun up a second time.

"Cased Colt. In fair-to-good condition with a presentation letter. And you're a return customer. We value return business."

"How much, pal?"

"Sixty-three hundred dollars. It's worth more to a collector, maybe significantly more, but I'll have to list it in the magazines and take offers over the Internet. That all takes time."

I was shocked—and pleased as hell. The heavy old gun had been in Jimmy Fiorella's corroding metal cabinet for almost a generation. I hadn't had time to look up its value in the online collector's guide but I knew that with the letter it might be valuable. I just hadn't realized how valuable.

"Okay," I said, trying to keep a poker face, "make it seven grand and you've got a deal. Cash."

"Cash? Of course, cash."

"Seven thousand."

"Sixty-three hundred, sir."

"C'mon—make it sixty-five."

"Sixty-three hundred, sir. I'm allowing two hundred more in my offer because you are a return customer. We appreciate client loyalty in this store."

"Okay, I'll take it. And you've got a six-inch folding knife with carved ivory grips in that case over there. How about throwing that in too?"

He smiled for the first time. "Sure, I can do that. That's an excellent knife. It was custom made. Are you a hunter?"

"You could say that. I'm after a pig."

SEVENTEEN

On my way toward the 405 Freeway, with a roll of cash in my pants, I had the feeling I was now making progress. My ace in the hole had been Jimmy Fiorella's old Colt. Now I could afford what I needed: the samples research and the computer work. And the clean SIG or Glock I wanted to buy would be expensive, but was the right tool to get the job done. I'd hopefully have enough money left over to carry me for the next couple of weeks.

I'd tried Carr's number on my throwaway cell as I was getting off the 10 Freeway to the 405 leaving Santa Monica, hoping for some kind of update on my computer trace request and to confirm a meeting with Mendoza and get his exact address. My call went to voice mail. In my message I told Carr to use my new phone number.

Per usual, it took less than five minutes for Carr to call back. The Mendoza thing was on. According to Carr, the guy was a retired highway patrol cop and dealt guns as a high-priced sideline. Carr had never met Mendoza but had worked with him for the last few years on trade-offs and security and off-the-books private West Coast arms deals. I jotted down the address and directions as I drove.

FORTY MINUTES LATER I was in Canyon Country. Mendoza's house was in a recent desert development that, like many California housing tracts these days, was dotted with For Sale By Bank signs on the lawns. It was a mile from the freeway.

I'd been running Woody's A/C for the last half hour and was slammed by the outside temperature when I opened the car door. Easily a hundred degrees. Brutal.

Retired cops and city workers had colonized this haven for snakes and cactus and gila monsters over the last twenty-five years, seeking affordable new homes for their families. Their reward was a daily two-hour commute each way on the 405 Freeway back to L.A. at gas prices that had doubled over the last five years, while their home equity went into the tank. The bumper-to-bumper traffic to and from Los Angeles was only part of the price of relocated rural happiness. The big bonus for these rednecks was moving into the mostly white, working-class neighborhoods and a potential lifetime NRA membership. The folks in Canyon Country were armed and ready.

IN MENDOZA'S DRIVEWAY were two cars. One was a tricked-out off-road Jeep with roll bars, big tires, and a lift kit. Parked behind it was a late model black Lincoln Navigator SUV. Above the garage door, attached to the red brick facade, was a bleached white steer's skull complete with horns. It had a bullet hole between the eyes. There was a small row of windows on the garage door itself. They were blacked out by curtains or paint. My bet was that Mendoza did his gun business out of his garage. This ex-cop apparently was not a particularly careful man. But hey, this was retired cop country, and one shield protected the other.

When he opened the front door I saw that he was well over six feet and in his late fifties with a belly that might easily contain a fifty-pound sandbag. He wore the Southern California regional uniform: a Lakers T-shirt, a red baseball cap, and khaki shorts above his Nikes.

"Carr sent me," I said, after he eyed me up and down.

"Yeah. Who's Carr?"

I produced my cell phone with the printout of Carr's private phone number. It was the signal Carr had told me to use with Mendoza. "This is Carr."

"You Fiorella?"

"I'm here to do some business."

Mendoza smiled. "Follow me. Business is what I do."

INSIDE, THE FLOOR was bare wood and uncarpeted. His living room walls were picture-less except for a tall framed print of two-gun Bat Masterson over the fireplace. The old photo had a brass nametag below it. Old Bat was apparently not having a good day when this photo portrait was made.

The only furniture in the place was a widescreen TV and a large L-shaped velour brown couch.

On the coffee table were beer cans and two empty pizza boxes.

Mendoza glanced at me and sensed that I was checking

his place out. He sneered. "Wife packed up and took the kids six months ago. I'm a bachelor now. It's all good, friend."

"If you say so," I said.

But I didn't like the setup. I didn't like this fat, smiling, ex-cop fuck. I didn't like a nearly vacant house in a neighborhood full of foreclosed homes and the lack of concern for his sideline. I didn't trust what I was seeing. But I did trust Carr, who had never steered me wrong in the past. I decided it was best just to go along and then get my ass down the road.

Mendoza led me to the door to the garage and we stepped down and inside.

It was wall-to-wall guns. Easily 500K worth of weaponry. The room was spotlessly clean and everything was displayed and in neat order. The line of windows on the far wall were covered by thick black curtains, as were the garage door windows. The A/C kept the room temperature to under seventy degrees.

I began to feel better. Maybe this guy's slob act was for the folks at the supermarket, the Little League field, and the barbecue pit. Apparently Mendoza was a pro. For sure the place was vulnerable, but he knew his stuff. I had to assume that vulnerable worked okay in Canyon Country.

He motioned me to a large, wide stainless steel center table that contained handguns. It was covered by clear plastic sheeting. There were at least a hundred handguns, all in rows. Three Ruger LCPs, two S&W Airweight J-Frames, an S&W Bodyguard .380, a KelTec .380/.32, half a dozen Glocks, the 26/27s, and at least that many SIGs, and several 3-inch 1911s of various brands, a Beretta PX4, and a 93R with a 20-round magazine, a Springfield XD, and an array of Taurus small-frame revolvers, a Desert Eagle, and a Ruger MKIII, among others.

On the side table was a Tch 9, a Russian Stechkin APS, a Steyr TMP, an HK VP70, a 1908 Colt .25, a stainless S&W .357 (new in the box), a Taurus .25, a Hellcat .380, and some older-model Glocks.

I could feel myself reacting against the temperature difference from outside the garage. Mendoza smiled and picked up a SIG, then ejected the magazine. He handed the piece to me. "I like to keep it cool in here," he said.

I checked the action on the gun. It was a righteous piece.

"Clean," he said, repeating my thought. "One hundred percent. That one was originally sold in South America, then shipped to Mexico. Completely untraceable in the U.S. It belonged to a newspaper guy from the Netherlands. Over the last ten years, six hundred newspaper guys have been capped in Mexico by the cartel. My guy got it secondhand after the newsie guy got iced in a Mexico City hotel lobby. Broad daylight. The newsie guy never even fired the piece. He took two in the face. My guy picked it up later from the detective who worked the scene."

"How much?" I said.

"I'll make you a good deal. Carr pays wholesale and we do a decent amount of business together. He told me that you are definitely old-school and someone I should get to know."

As Mendoza was talking my eyes drifted to the other table. I stepped over and picked up the Beretta 93R hooked up with the twenty-round magazine. "Look, I'm thinking firepower," I said. "What's my price on this?"

Mendoza smiled. "That's my last one. I sold his brother a week ago. Nice gun. Originally obtained in a home-invasion situation in the Carson City, Nevada, area. Totally clean, of course. Just touch the trigger and you get three-, four-, or five-round bursts."

"I know the gun," I said. "I'm not much of a shot and I don't like to miss. I'll take the 93R. And I want two boxes of hollow points too."

"For the man who doesn't want any mistakes."

"That's me," I said, fingering the action, "no mistakes."

"Whatever you hit with this will go down and not get up."

"That's the idea. So, how much?"

"Thirty-five hundred. No haggling. That's Carr's price. He asked me to take good care of you so that's what I'm doing. Final price. Cash, of course. Take it or leave it."

"Deal," I said, "I'll take it." I dug in my pocket and counted out the money, then handed it across to him.

Mendoza spread the bills out in stacks on a metal workroom table behind him, then made a big deal out of recounting the bills, then picking them up and restacking them, reminding me of a slow-witted bank teller.

"Signed, sealed, and delivered," he said finally.

He deftly disassembled the Beretta, then placed the sections in a thick brown chamois bag with leather thong tie ends. He then slid the bag and the ammo boxes into a neatly folded and doubled supermarket shopping bag. "You've got my number," he said. "If you need anything else, I'm here."

"I'll remember that," I said.

I began heading toward the door to the house with my shopping bag in my hand, pausing to wait for Mendoza.

"Look," he said from behind me, "Carr tells me you're good. He says you're very good, but that you work alone."

"He's right. I do work alone."

"Well, here's something to remember: If you need anything else—anything else at all—keep my number. And bear in mind that I've got a roster of trained guys who all qualify, mostly ex-lawmen, with one or two retired feds. All solid guys. All ready to move with one phone call from me. You can have one man or a team."

"Thanks," I said. "I'll keep it in mind."

Now Mendoza was smiling. His big body filled the door frame. "You know, you don't look like such a hard guy. I've met 'em all over the years. You're not what Carr described. You don't seem like such a—a badass. You seem pretty low key, but you're edgy too. I can feel your edge."

I smiled back at the gun dealer. "I've been told that more than once," I said.

"So how do you keep that edge?"

"You don't want to know, Mendoza. Just leave it there, okay?"

"Whatever you say."

EIGHTEEN

Later that afternoon, back in Santa Monica, I stopped at the Goodwill thrift store on Santa Monica Boulevard and bought two used pairs of pants and four shirts, underwear, and a rainproof black hooded jacket. The total cost was thirty-eight dollars.

At the Walgreens on Wilshire and Fourteenth Street, I picked up some disposable razors and a toothbrush. My new residence, from today on, was Woody's car.

THE NEXT MORNING, after parking the Honda nearby in the big parking lot adjacent to the boat slips in Marina del Rey, with three one-dollar bills in my hand I joined the line of guys outside the shower facilities at the Marina Yacht Club. These guys, half of them in bathrobes and carrying shaving kits, all owned or lived on boats moored in rented slips at the marina—boats without bathing facilities on board. An AA guy I knew who'd lived on his boat illegally for several years had put me on to the idea months before.

After I'd showered and dressed, I stopped at Starbucks

for coffee and a sugar fix, then drove the Honda to Sherman
Toyota on Santa Monica Boulevard. I parked a block away,
using my Handicapped placard at the one-hour meter, then
walked back to the dealership's showroom.

Fernando saw me come in and walked up to me. *"¿Que
paso, hombre?"* he whispered out of earshot of the other
salespeople.

"I'm here to get paid."

"Majn, tso sorree to hejr abou Woodee. He was a goo
guy. I deen know hijm real goo but I liked hijm."

"Thanks. Yeah, tough break," I said.

Fernando handed me his Sherman Toyota business card
that had his cell number written on the back. "Jou call me,
meester badass. We go to ga drunk, ho-kay?"

"I'll call you," I said.

Vikki was next, sitting in her cubicle wearing heels, a
tight maroon sweater and skirt. The perfect L.A. used-car
sales associate. Sheeba Perry, in her civil-service-looking
dark suit, was sitting on the corner of Vikki's desk, a coffee
cup in her hand.

I walked over and said hi to them both.

Sheeba took the hint, got up, rolled her eyes at us, then
walked away with her coffee cup.

Looking down at Vikki, I whispered, "Sooo, did you miss
me? I've been thinking a lot about our little auto adventure."

"Keep it up, mister poet-detective. You'll get yours."

"Again? Sooner than later, I hope."

"I'd like that. I'd like that very much."

I wrote my new cell number without my name on the
back of one of her business cards from the holder on her
desk, then pushed it to her across the desktop. It was a test.

A way to find out who Vikki really might be. The risk was worth it. "That's a new number," I said. "Make sure no one sees it or uses it but you. Okay?"

"Your privacy is safe with me, Fiorella," Vikki cooed.

I was on my way to Max's office when Sheeba Perry stepped in front of me, holding a Sienna brochure. She was smiling slyly. She nodded in the direction of Vikki's cubicle. "So, Fiorella, you been tappin' that ass, right? Vikki's a class act, right?"

I winked at Sheeba. "Are you moonlighting in the Sherman Toyota gossip booth, lady?"

"Nah, just making observations—separating the players from the chumps."

From twenty feet away, the door to Max's office swung opened and he stuck his head out. "Step in here, please, Mr. Fiorella."

I nodded good-bye to Sheeba and walked to Max's office. Inside, with the door closed, Max reached into his desk drawer, then handed me an envelope. I tore it open and looked first at the amount of the check, then at the sales summary paper clipped to it.

"Four hundred and sixteen bucks!" I hissed. "What's the deal here, Max? This check should be at least several hundred more, and you know it."

"Two of your deals are pending finance. We had to go to an outside lender. You'll get yours when we get ours," he sneered. "So long, Fiorella."

I turned to go, then changed my mind. I walked back to the side of his desk and faced Max, two feet away in his swivel chair. "Do you have something on your mind that you'd like to let me in on, Max? If you do, I'm standing right here."

Max got up and folded his arms. He was a head taller than me and his Super Bowl ring and gold watchband glistened under the fluorescent lights. "I don't like you," he said. "You're a loose cannon and a shit magnet. You brought stink into this dealership. Hiring you was my mistake. The Santa Monica detectives have been here twice asking about you."

Then he rolled his eyes. "Know what, on second thought, I don't want to see you back here again. I'll have your next check, when it's ready, mailed to you."

I looked at Max for a long moment, the way I like to look at people I'm about to hurt. "I'm standing in front of you. I'm right here, Skippy," I said. "If you'd like to try me, go right ahead. Do it now. But here's a promise: if you do, you'll be picking up your next check in the ICU. I'd actually enjoy busting you up. I enjoy hurting assholes."

"Now you're making threats! Get out, Fiorella, before I call the cops!"

"Hey, Max," I said without moving, "maybe we'll meet up sometime away from the dealership. Just sort of bump into each other somewhere. A surprise when you least expect it. I'm looking forward to that. I'll keep that in mind."

OUTSIDE, LEAVING THE dealership, walking to Woody's Honda, I knew immediately that I was being watched. Picking up my paycheck and seeing Vikki again had been a calculated risk—a dumb-shit move. I should have enlisted Fernando to do it for me.

I walked quickly past the car and continued down the block, turning right when I got to Broadway. Out of the corner of my eye I spotted the beige Crown Vic behind me.

Just as I made the turn, a few feet away—off the corner—
was a new building under construction. The lot was surrounded by a six-foot-high chain-link fence.

I scrambled up and over the fence quickly, then crossed to
a stack of covered lumber and ducked behind it.

A second or two later, from behind the plastic tarp, I saw
the beige Crown Vic roll through the intersection and turn
right. Archer was behind the wheel and Taboo was sitting
shotgun. They were looking in the direction of Bay Cities
Deli across the street, not in my direction.

Instead of turning left at Lincoln, Archer hit his light,
gave a brief blast from his honking siren, then cut off traffic
and made a right.

I had to act fast. They'd be back soon enough.

I decided to take the chance on going back to get Woody's
car, hoping Taboo and Archer didn't have a second unmarked as backup.

I was over the fence again and around the corner in less
than ten seconds, with Woody's car keys out and in my hand.

Getting into the Honda and turning my head ninety degrees, I saw nothing to worry about.

I fired the engine, then tapped the gas pedal, rolling
slowly the half block toward Broadway.

In my rearview mirror I again saw the Crown Vic making
the turn off Santa Monica Boulevard by the dealership.

I turned left on Broadway, then turned left again on Santa
Monica, hoping that circling the block was the best way to
evade them.

I got lucky. It worked. Seeing Vikki again and picking up
my check had been clumsy. I wouldn't make that mistake
again.

NINETEEN

When the phone call came in from Carr, I was on the 405 Freeway headed toward Malibu, going the long way—on two freeways instead of the Coast Highway. It was a circuitous route but less obvious.

Carr's news was a dead end. "I got the results back from your sock and the sample," he said flatly. Prelim, of course."

"Yeah, and . . . "

"Male. Same person. No second party. I'll have my guy hit the database next."

I knew it had to have been Woody. "No," I said. "Tell 'em to stop there."

"Whatever. It's your nickel, pal."

"What about the other thing?" I asked. "The computer trace. I need to know who's on me."

"Not much to report. Whoever did the work was up on their shit. Dummy IPs and a spiderweb of dead ends. Whoever the dude is, my guy says it did not originate at any federal or local law-enforcement source. So it's definitely a hacker. My guy feels like he was outsmarted and he doesn't like it. He says he's not giving up. He thinks he's a better hacker than whoever's on you. He told me he won't quit until he has something solid."

"Good," I said. "I'm thinking there may be a direct connection between what I'm working on and that hacker. Tell your guy I said thanks, and to keep at it."

"Will do," Carr said. Then he barked, "Hey *you* owe *me* now! I did you a solid with Mendoza. I need five hundred more today."

"I'll wire you the money," I said. "You're covered."

Then I hung up.

IT WAS FIFTEEN minutes before the start of the Point Dume AA meeting when I made it through the nine miles of Malibu Canyon to the Coast Highway. As a teenager two of my friends, under the influence of booze or drugs or both, had met their end on this road. Halfway through the canyon the turns become treacherous and it is almost three hundred feet to the bottom and a rocky grave.

Turning right at the Coast Highway I punched the Honda's gas pedal.

I arrived a few minutes late to the meeting because the parking lot, that had spaces for about seventy-five cars, was uncharacteristically full. Driving up and down the rows of cars took additional time. Finally, at the very end of the lot—at the entrance/exit—I found a spot.

As I was getting out of the Honda, my cell buzzed. I didn't recognize the number so I clicked the red Off button. Only two people had this number and the number on my phone's printout was neither of those.

I was about to enter the room when I saw a guy everyone

called Boxcar, a regular at the meeting. Boxcar was a big dude with long, dirty hair and dirty clothes that he changed once a month whether they needed washing or not. He'd grown up in Malibu as a surfer kid and now lived in a trailer at the rear of his parents' property somewhere near Trancas Beach. Boxcar had done two tours in Vietnam at eighteen and had been trained as some kind of killing machine/explosives expert, but had lost his mind in the process behind heroin and alcohol and what he'd experienced in Southeast Asia. He'd been unemployable for years and was now a casualty of an uncaring VA system, collecting a grand a month for sacrificing his life and sanity for his country. The guy had been in and out of recovery homes and nut wards for over twenty-five years.

Boxcar never attended the actual meeting. He always stood outside and, for his own reasons, listened at the doorway. He also had a serious profanity problem and he tended to fart loudly in public whenever the urge came to him.

"Hey," Boxcar whispered, "howz it hangin', shitwad?"

I nodded hello.

"Yo, JD, look inside, brother, these cocksuckers have taken over our meeting."

"Who?" I asked. "What cocksuckers are we talking about?"

"Look for yourself."

I stuck my head inside the door and saw that the room was packed. Near the front I recognized several new celebrities—TV and movie people.

"What's it all about?" I asked the big guy.

"Some asshole's AA birthday. Look in the corners near the podium. See them two pimpshit fuckin' bodyguards?"

"Bodyguards?" I said, playing it dumb.

"What do you take 'em for, ballerinas? Wake the fuck up!"

When Boxcar began scratching his head and beard crazily, I left him at the door and made my way inside.

THE SECRETARY OF the meeting for that day was an AA Malibu fixture, a woman named Dotti Patrick, once a sixties and seventies daytime TV queen and now an eighty-five-year-old recovery zealot with over forty years of sober time.

Dotti stepped off the podium and some scattered-looking newbie guy began reading Chapter Five from *The Big Book*. A room that held several dozen people was now at twice its capacity.

Hearing the new guy read made me smile. He announced himself as Chad and he was very nervous and stumbling over the unfamiliar words. You can always pinpoint a newcomer to AA when they read Chapter Five because it is a long chapter and the new people always jumble Bill Wilson's unfamiliar syntax and blow it the first few times. Their lack of time in recovery is a dead giveaway.

I made my way down an aisle toward the left side of the podium where I normally sit. There were no seats but just as I leaned back against the wall, listening to Chad continue to fumble through Chapter Five, a child began screaming in the chairs near me. The mom looked around, saw twenty pairs of accusing eyes on her, then got up to remove her unhappy kid and allow the distraction to continue from the parking lot.

Me and another guy took the empty seats.

I recognized a lot of the regulars but Boxcar had been

right, this was a true L.A.–Malibu AA lovefest. Many more big names than usual.

Looking down my row I also saw Meggie and her Frenchie boyfriend, Claude.

When I caught Meggie's eye, she looked away. Then Claude's expression bored into me. My reaction, after Claude had turned away, was to reach behind me and adjust my new Beretta under my jacket. I didn't need another public embarrassment with a gun.

The only person taking an anniversary cake that day was called to the podium by Dotti. Walking toward the front of the room, he looked like a Ted Turner stand-in. In his late seventies or early eighties, over six feet tall, tanned, and workout fit. He was wearing a starched, light-blue thigh-length long-sleeved shirt, turned up at the cuffs. It hung loosely down over his expensive tan slacks. High-end loafers with no socks completed the ensemble. His thick, wavy gray hair had to have been professionally cut and he had two gold hoop earrings that fit snugly over his right earlobe.

I was less than six feet from him as he stood next to the podium with his arms folded. From there I could make out what looked like a faded tattoo behind the sleeve of his shirt, on his left forearm. This man's presentation spelled fame and money: Hollywood money. Bo-coo bucks.

Dotti was now holding a cake with eight lighted candles on top, while a girl in her twenties, probably the guy's granddaughter, stood up and came forward to join him near the podium.

Next to come up front, waved forward by Dotti, was a famous male movie star whose name I couldn't remember. The little group held hands and began a chorus of "Happy

Birthday." They were immediately joined by everyone else in the room. Dotti's theater-trained voice was the loudest.

After blowing out his candles, Iron Pops stepped to the podium and straightened the mic before speaking. "My Name is Karrrl Swaaaan," he drawled, "and I am an al-co-holic."

I picked up that the accent was British by way of some German-speaking country. Now the ink I'd seen on his arm began to make sense.

The dapper old guy in front of the room was one of the most successful men in Los Angeles—a famous film producer of space movies, *the* Karl Swan. Everyone in the room had their full attention on him.

"I would like to thank and acknowledge my daughter Sydnye for giving me my birthday cake today. I am proud to say that she will have eighteen months of recovery shortly. And of course I must also gratefully acknowledge the support and love I have received from my good and old friend. The handsome fellow you see standing next to Sydnye. We've made four films together and his sponsorship, forbearance, and unwavering dedication to my recovery have allowed me to change my life."

I looked at Sydnye again. My brain quickly took away the high-end clothes and earrings and makeup, then replaced them with a hoodie and sunglasses. It made me smile to myself. Bingo!

Old Karl was four times his daughter's age. That was weird, but this was Hollywood, where the rule book doesn't apply. Seventy- or eighty-year-old movie stars and directors married teenagers all the time.

I listened as Swan went on in his honeyed voice. "And Chad, thank you for that stirring rendering of Chapter Five."

I thought, *What goddamn rendering did this guy hear?* Chad had almost passed out while stuttering over what he was reading.

Swan continued. "Sadly, I regret that I don't get to as many meetings as I would like to these days. My production schedule often does not allow for the time and opportunity. That notwithstanding, may I simply say that I owe everything I am today to Alcoholics Anonymous. Thank you, AA. Thank you for showing me a new way to live."

Well done, Karl. You parroted the party line perfectly. I was sure that, outside, my pal Boxcar was snarling to himself and grunting curses.

THAT DAY'S MAIN speaker was, no doubt, chosen by Dotti to complement the presence of the great Swan. She identified herself as Natasha. She was fiftyish and still beautiful—thanks to the skills of her surgeon—and also a former TV star with a long-running female crime-show series, who kept smiling down at Swan as if to say, I'd be willing to put your shriveled old pecker in my mouth right here, in front of everybody, for a gig in your next blockbuster.

By the end of the meeting I wanted to puke on Natasha and her pandering star-fucker pitch, filled with insider movie-industry tidbits and having almost nothing to do with the Twelve Steps and recovery. I was beginning to hate the secretary of the meeting, Dotti, for selling out AA that day and making my recovery program a Hollywood/Malibu circle jerk. I felt alone in the room except for Chad who, like me, was holding on to his ass for dear life. I understood Chad. We were brothers.

THE MEETING HAD been a waste of time, recovery-wise, but not a loss by any means. Fate had allowed Sydnye and me to see each other again, up close and personal, less than ten feet apart. Though she hadn't let on, I was pretty sure she'd made me.

IN THE PARKING lot the Swan daisy-chain and swooning and kissy-kissy continued while I talked with Boxcar about Woody. "Goddamn shame about that dude," Boxcar hissed. "The good motherfuckers are the ones who always go down first."

Swan, with Sydnye by his side, stood next to his silver Bentley convertible as the group of movie and TV people continued with the hugs and handshakes. Nearby, observing the action, were the two well-muscled Latin-looking dudes in sport clothes that Boxcar had accurately made as Swan's bodyguards.

When I'd finished talking to Boxcar, before walking away, I took a last look over at Sydnye, hoping to make eye contact again. Her smile was painted on and her eyes were set on her famous father. No soap.

A couple of minutes later I reached my car at the far end of the lot. Looking back I saw Swan and his daughter getting into the Bentley convertible. The car's top was down. A few seconds later the Bentley began slowly pulling down the long driveway toward the exit. A black BMW, close in looks to the one that had left the scene of Mom's burning car two weeks before, was right behind the Bentley.

Half a minute later Swan, with Sydnye sitting shotgun, paused at the stop sign next to the lot's exit and Woody's Honda. There were two dogs in the backseat. Rottweilers.

Then something odd happened: The old guy seemed to be looking at me, watching me as I unlocked my car door. He was smiling, but the expression in his eyes wasn't joy; it was strange—like a cheetah eyeing a lone chicken from behind a wire fence.

Then Sydnye looked my way too. She wasn't smiling. Not smiling at all.

I could hear music floating in my direction from the convertible's expensive sound system. It was a Cole Porter tune from the thirties, sung, it sounded like, by Tony Bennett or Vic Damone, or someone like that: "You're the top, you're the Coliseum . . . You're the top, you're the Louvre Museum. You're a melody, a symphony by Strauss . . . you're a Bengal bonnet, a Shakespeare sonnet—you're Mickey Mouse!"

"Have a wonnn-der-ful day," Swan chimed over the music.

My mind immediately went to the songs I'd heard playing on Woody's speakers in his apartment the day I found him and his tortured body. *Sinatra sings Cole Porter.* Bingo!

"Yeah, you too!" I called back, not looking at Swan but putting all my attention on the daughter, Sydnye.

As I got into Woody's car and closed the door, Swan's Bentley turned left, and was heading toward Grayfox Drive and his estate.

Inside the car, with my windows rolled up, I yelled out, "Gotcha, Sydnye! I gotcha now!"

TWENTY

I started the Honda, dropped the tranny into R and began to back up, but as I did, glancing into my rearview mirror, I saw the bottom half of a man's torso just behind my car, blocking my way.

I popped the transmission back into P.

Two seconds later, Santa Monica detective Jim Archer was at my door. I pressed the power window button once and lowered the glass an inch or two.

"Time to talk," Archer said in his flat, Special Ops voice.

"About what, Detective?" I said.

"You're lucky, Fiorella."

"You call this luck?"

"Open the window now, before I kick it in," Archer snarled. "Do not fuck with me! Open it, or I'll take you down right here! You know I'll do it too."

I lowered the window. "Okay, now what?" I said.

Archer scanned the parking lot, then turned back to me. "We need to talk. Let me in. Open the passenger door."

A few seconds later he was beside me in the front seat.

Sneering. "So, you snagged your friend Woody's car. What'd you do, swap out the plates?"

"No idea what you're talking about, Detective. This car once belonged to my mother, Nancy Fiorella. It's my car now."

"Well, if it is then you got nothin' to worry about. But if it's the one we have the BOLO on, you might be parked here in deep poop, sonny-boy. Know wh'am sayin'? Anyway, FYI: we know all about the car and your friend's keys and the other shit you took. It's old news."

"And . . . "

"But today does happen to be your lucky day, nutball. I'm not here about that stuff and I'm not here to jack you up. I'm serious."

Archer pivoted in the passenger seat and was taking me in, studying my expression. "You're on to it, aren't you? I know you're on to it!"

"On to what, Detective?"

"Listen up. Let's pretend just for half a minute that I'm on my day off and I'm doing some backup case work on my own, okay? Let's also pretend I'm not here and I didn't see you. How's that?"

"Better. I like playing pretend."

"You're on Swan! Somehow you added it up. He made you just now—and you made him. I saw it for myself. You're not as dumb as I thought."

"Keep talking."

Detective Archer rolled his eyes. "Pay attention. Okay? I come out to Point Dume once or twice a year—I even take a sick day when I have to—for one purpose. Call it a mission; I've done it for the last eight years. Any idea what that mission might be?"

"You like looking at dried-up movie stars whose kids hate them? You're a daytime-TV fan?"

"I come here to let Swan see me. To rattle his fucking cage. That's why I come. I come on his AA birthday. Today, as you somehow found out, is his AA birthday."

"And . . . "

"Stop dancing, Fiorella! You're pissing me off. For your information, the MO of your friend O'Rourke's homicide fits the profile of eleven unsolved murders going back almost twenty-five years."

"Now that is interesting," I said. "I'm listening now."

"I worked those cases."

"You?"

"Yeah, me! That was before I was kicked sideways, then forced to resign at the sheriff's department. Before I stepped on my own dick over Swan."

"You just said twenty-five years' worth of murders."

"Eleven homicides. So, you might say I have a special interest in Citizen Swan. Okay, so I am here now, pullin' your coat. I'm saying you're on the right track. However you made the guy on your own, your moves so far are above the line."

"Thanks for the heads-up. I appreciate it."

"Apparently you do know your ass from Catalina Island. I had you down as some kind of loose cannon, a New York City burnout. I also know you did time in the bughouse. By the way, what were the real names of the Russians you killed? It took me a while to dig all that up."

I decided to avoid the question. "Look," I said, "just tell me what happened with you and the cases. Eleven homicides? Seriously, that does interest me."

"Maybe, just maybe, we can help each other."

"Okay, so fill me in?"

"There were no arrests. One suspect only."

I shook my head. "That's not much of a batting average, Detective."

"In the immortal words of Johnny Cochran—out of the side of a mouth that occasionally did tell the truth—Cochran once said, 'The color of justice in Los Angeles is green, as in dig-deep expensive.'"

"I hear that."

"Keep listening. Those eleven unsolved homicides featured dead illegals from Mexico and south of the border, illegals that meet the MO of your pal Woody's murder. Torture mutilation killings. All buried on Point Dume. Some— the more recent ones—also with multiple amputations. And just last week, as I'm sure you are aware, two Latinas also went missing near Paradise Cove. But we haven't found those bodies yet."

"You matched Woody with the MO to the Point Dume bodies?"

"Up until now all those bodies were buried, less than a mile from Señor Swan's mansion, up on Grey Fox hill. You may or may not know that Point Dume is an ancient Indian burial ground."

"That I knew, Archer. I was brought up here, remember? So you're looking at Karl Swan and his daughter?"

"Not the daughter. Just Swan. He was ninety percent good for one murder. One murder was all I wanted. Just one murder. Then, he and his ten attorneys and his eight hundred million dollars and his political pull had me locked out of the case and eventually transferred."

"But you had one solid homicide?"

"It was close. I had a decade-old DNA match and one witness who could corroborate Swan's involvement. Unfortunately, that witness disappeared and is, I assume, presently dead. I was less close on the other murders but I was still working them. I had all eights and some nines but no witnesses. It turned out that my DNA match guy had been Swan's driver, so there was poop in the duck pond on that one, but I was on my way. I was close."

"And no one stepped up? No arrests were made?"

"Like I said."

"Police work is crap. Pointless bullshit."

"My book was good. My work was solid. If it had been anyone else but Swan we'd've gone to the grand jury. Now, just a few days ago, when I saw your friend's body, I pretty much knew that Swan was back in business. The sick fuck. I want him down for this one. The only variable is that your friend's killing was in Santa Monica. That's the only thing that queers the profile."

"Jesus, Detective, if you think Swan could be good for Woody, then make your move. You've certainly got enough to make a pinch. Go for it."

"I tried. I took it up the ladder a few days ago. Me and Afrika. We ran Swan and the old MO and half a dozen cases passed the brass. There were too many matches for them to shitcan our pitch. We gave it a nine."

"And?"

"This morning we were called into the big guy's office— the big guy is a woman these days—and told, point-blank, to stay off Karl Swan."

"C'mon," I said.

"Our orders are to steer clear of anything to do with Mr. Swan. Supposedly, the way they're spinning it, I've overreacted again, trying to nail the asshole to my old Malibu files, and in the process, I've roped Afrika into it."

"Long live police politics," I said.

Archer kept talking. "Then, two hours after the meeting, after I got my dick handed to me like a Pink's hot dog, I'm sitting at my desk considering a new career in the nightwatchman industry, and I received an e-mail from my *L.A. Times* contact. That e-mail informed me that the instructions for me to back off came down from up north in Sacramento, at the highest level. The whole thing gets a pass."

I decided to trust Archer. He'd leveled with me and now I was going to give him what I had—at least some of what I had. "Look," I said, "you may be wrong about Swan—at least on this one."

Archer's face twisted. "C'mon, Fiorella, what are we both doing here?"

"For your information, I'm not on Swan. I'm on the daughter, Sydnye."

Archer rolled his eyes. "What? You're kiddin'? You're on Sydnye for your friend Woody's death? Why?"

"A few weeks ago she cut me off in her car. I didn't know the girl from Madonna. I chased her down after she got crazy and threw a metal coffee mug at my car on the Coast Highway and almost caused an accident. Then, a few minutes later, after I caught up with her, we butted heads inside Guido's Restaurant at Cross Creek Road."

"I know the place. What happened?"

"I smeared oil on her hair and her tits and knocked her off

her chair. She stood up and threatened me. Then, a couple of days later, the car I was driving got torched. Then my friend Woody wound up dead."

Archer was sneering. "Jesus! Sydnye Swan? Now that *is* a curve ball."

"Karl Swan was not on my radar until you mentioned him a minute ago."

Archer leered at me, then began shaking his head. "Jesus, you know, it so happens she could have done that before, Fiorella. I mean the road-rage act. She has no jacket with any law enforcement agency—Daddy and his lawyers saw to that—but I know from the digging I've done that she once supposedly held some guy hostage for several hours on Kanan Road, soaked him with gasoline, and almost sliced him up over the same kind of thing. There is another incident too. Also hearsay. Naturally, nothing stuck."

I stared at Archer. "So, is it possible?" I asked. "Could they both be psycho killers? Like daddy, like daughter?"

"Look, like I said, our Santa Monica murder profile isn't a one-hundred-percent fit because all the killings we know about happened on Point Dume. You pal Woody was the only exception."

"Can you give me what you have on Sydnye?" I said. "I'll do the rest."

Archer looked around the now empty parking lot, then faced me. "You're not trustworthy, Ace. You're a material witness in your friend's murder."

"If you say so."

Archer sneered. "I just haven't found you yet. By the way, where's his cock? Did you take it?"

"Get real! Why would I take my friend's cock?"

"His DNA was on the kitchen counter in your apartment on a napkin I took, along with a pubic hair. A single pubic hair."

"Can you just keep me out of this?" I asked. "I don't need the heat. I think we can help each other."

"We know you didn't kill the guy but the moves you made so far have pissed off a roomful of people. I can't do much but I'll do what I can. Anyway, we've been reassigned —me and Afrika. Now they won't let me anywhere near the murder book."

"Just give me Sydnye. Point me in that direction."

Archer adjusted his belt holster and leaned back in the seat. "Look, the girl's a ghost. She's managed to stay almost completely off the grid. But fifteen months ago I interviewed an ex-maid of her dad's in Ensenada. I speak enough Spanish to get my point across so I made the drive down there trying to dig up more on my one murder."

"You're a stubborn guy, Archer," I said. "I admire that in a cop. And I promise you, I don't admire cops."

"Turns out that my boy Karl does what that Scientologist actor, Tom Cruise, does with everyone who goes to work for him. He's done it for years. All employees sign a binding contract with a code-of-silence clause in it in front of a tableful of attorneys. Anyway, when I finally got to Leticia, the maid, who's sitting there scared shitless after quitting him eighteen months before, I eventually got her talking about Sydnye and her relationship with Swan. Just bear in mind that all this basically comes from one source, okay? According to Leticia, the kid's a whack job. She's been on heavy meds for years. Hey, maybe you two were roommates in some nuthouse in another life. I know that you still get the headaches, right?"

"Keep going, Detective, unless you'd like me to start drooling and speaking in tongues."

"You're not really crazy at all, are you?"

"No, I'm not. I'm an ex-drunk with a short fuse. That's about it."

"Sydnye was educated in Europe—Switzerland, Leticia says—and she's been in and out of institutions over there since she was ten or eleven. Diagnosed, Leticia remembered, as crazy by a roundtable full of shrinks at the UCLA nut ward."

"That's my girl," I said. "Rich and spoiled and batshit nuts."

"From what Leticia told me, when Sydnye goes off her meds, her personality runs to extremes. Swan's been bailing her out and covering for her most of the kid's life. So Pops teaching her all he knows sort of fits, in a rather extreme and very sick way."

"I'm betting she's the one who did my friend Woody, Archer! Without Pops. All I did was pour some motor oil on the girl's tits and she starts killing."

"One more detail," Archer said. "Supposedly, she's also some kind of high-level computer hacker. She might have worked for the government. Not here—not our government—in Switzerland. She's fluent in German, or so the maid told me."

"That could be a fit," I said. "I think she torched my mother's car and dug up my old arrest jacket and got me fired and probably was behind an identity theft on a car I sold for the Toyota people—and Christ knows what else."

"Can any of that stuff stick?"

"Only this: Woody got killed. Two days before I found him, he told me he was dating a new girl who he called Laighne—a computer whiz, he said. Sydnye and Laighne sound like they just might be the same girl."

Archer nodded. "Look, here's the deal: I can't make any moves. But I think we can help each other."

I met Archer's eyes. "I'm the outside man."

"I was wrong, okay," Archer snarled. "The pieces might add up to something."

"Look, Detective, I've got nothing to lose here. I've got nothing on the table. I'm not like you. I'm no cop. I'm in this for the payback. Just tell me, can I have what you have on Sydnye. I need your notes. E-mail names, websites, known associates, previous jobs and relationships and addresses. Whatever you've got."

Archer pulled out a personal business card—not his detective card—and circled a number on it with his pen. "Call me tomorrow at this number. Like I said, it's a pretty thin file, mostly computer trace stuff and what I got from the maid, Leticia. But I do have a list of known acquaintances and a European website that I tracked down."

"That's a start," I said. "And I'll give you as much as I can on Swan's involvement as it comes down. That's a promise."

Archer grinned. "They've got me and Afrika sweeping the floor and sorting through cold cases at our desks these days, but I'll do what I can."

"You'd better know this about me, Detective Archer: I'm not concerned with indictments and court trials. I'm not interested in bringing anyone in. Those things are your department. You and Afrika. You didn't dig far enough into my jacket. Here's the bottom line on me: I don't quit. I don't give up and the only way I'll be stopped is when I'm dead. That's how I roll. I'll get Sydnye. And if Swan's involved, I'll get him too."

"Wake up, tough guy! You're chopped chum for Swan's attorneys and the people over at his fortress. There's too much money on the table and too much power involved. If Swan finds out you're on his kid, he's got an army on his side."

"Like I said, I don't care who gets hurt. I don't interview witnesses and I don't collect evidence. I don't give a rat's ass about the justice system and I can't be stopped. I won't quit until Sydnye's dead or I'm dead. Just look at it like this: You've got someone on your side willing to do a little community service for the city of Santa Monica."

Archer shook his head. "That's the wrong road. Just help me and let us do our job."

"How about this: I'll do what I do and you do what you do."

Archer opened the car door. "You're nuts. You've got no idea what you're up against. You'd better call my number before Swan's kid or Swan himself calls yours. And like I said, ditch this car. It's hot now."

"Thanks for the advice. I'll deal with it."

Pulling out of the parking lot, I could feel my head begin to pound. I was in for a long night.

TWENTY-ONE

I'd been on Gusarov for three days. My boss at Priority Investigations LLC, was Ray Alvarez, who everybody called Two-Tone. Ray got his nickname because of the large burn mark that covered the right side of his face and the thick, pink scar it had caused.

Two-Tone had authorized only a couple of days on the surveillance and had flatly told me that morning, "It's a dead end, JD. You got nothin'. Get off the Russian and go with the girl's aunt on Staten Island. Work that. Stay with that."

I didn't agree and decided to keep going on my own. Two-Tone was always worried about overruns on client costs and that shit. I liked Gusarov on this and I wanted to stay with him until it burned out or I had my bingo.

The night before, I'd changed rental cars again in Midtown. Then, the next morning, Gusarov had began altering his established pattern. From the plumbing store on Eleventh Avenue at 7:54 A.M., instead of his normal route of stops, he'd driven to an apartment building in Queens and then to a private house in Sheepshead Bay. Two hours on the road.

Unlike in the previous two days, Gusarov had done no business at either of the first two locations and had never opened the back of his van. Each stop had lasted less than half an hour. I could feel my guy beginning to make moves.

At Sheepshead Bay I called Two-Tone again. "Something's up, goddamnit! This guy is rolling," I said. "He's not plumbing today, for chrissake. Plumbing repair contractors plumb. This guy hasn't plumbed anything. He's doing another kind of plumbing. I'd bet on it. I can feel it."

Two-Tone had known for some time that I was a serious drinker but he didn't know yet that it had deteriorated into a 24/7 jones. He wasn't aware that I was getting up at least twice every night to fill a water glass with whiskey, down it, then go back to sleep. But my boss did know that my judgment had recently been confused by my moods and over-amped emotions. I knew that he'd stopped trusting me.

My boss was immediately pissed. "I told you to dump the Ruskie, goddamnit! The client won't authorize any more time on this. Last warning: Get back here. You're off the clock as of now!" Then he'd hung up.

I was parked around the corner on the street; the second car in a line of five, next to a row of houses. I only had a partial view of the old beach house, two houses in, down the block at a right angle.

I checked my watch. I'd been here twelve minutes.

Killing time, I changed hats again on the front seat, added several ounces to my cardboard coffee cup from the bottle in my inside coat pocket, then got out to put on my tan raincoat.

I was about to get back into the car when, fifty yards away, Gusarov came out the front door and stopped. He took his time looking up and down the street.

I moved behind my car and pretended I was walking a dog on the narrow grass patch between the street and the curb. I clapped my hands and yelled, "Goo boy! That's my boy! Here ya go, boy!"

Gusarov bought the act and began walking the other way down the street toward his truck.

A minute later, I was behind the wheel and ready for him to make a move.

Instead of pulling away, the Russian was now backing his van down the block to the house's driveway. He made a wide turn, then reversed up the driveway toward the side entrance of the house.

I waited.

Five minutes went by.

I had no direct line of vision but when I heard what sounded like the van's rear doors slamming closed and then a motor starting, I knew we were back on. My guy was moving.

Twenty-five minutes later the Russian had driven to the Grand Central Parkway, then taken the turn toward Manhattan.

Half an hour after that, instead of using the Fifty-Ninth Street Bridge via Stewart Street, which is the cheaper and faster route to midtown, the van continued heading for the Triborough Bridge, then crossed into the Bronx exit lane.

I called Two-Tone again. He answered on the first ring. "I told you," I said. "He picked up something in Sheepshead Bay. Maybe people. Maybe kids. He's on his way to the Bronx. He hasn't been to the Bronx before. I'm thinkin' he's hot now!"

"Okay, fuck it," Two-Tone hissed. "In for a penny, in for a pound. Stay on him. But call me, goddamnit."

Ten minutes later the van turned off the Grand Councourse at 149th Street, then headed east.

At Third Avenue Gusarov turned left, then pulled to the side under the El.

I slowed as I drove past the van and made the next right turn. I'd seen Gusarov talking on his cell.

Five minutes later the van had moved to a parking space near the front of one of the tenement buildings.

I could feel it. This was a drop—or a pick-up!

Standing outside my tan Dodge sedan, after changing hats again and tossing my coat into the backseat, I looked down the street to the front of the building, fifty yards away. I saw something. Gusarov had a passenger or passengers.

The sidewalk was narrow and the distance between the open van door and the side of the building wasn't more than a few feet, but I could make out colors—at least two different colors—of people being hustled inside. And someone else, a second man I'd only caught a glimpse of, was holding the building's door open.

Then I saw the van's rear doors slammed shut and Gusarov walked to his driver's door, then clicked his remote to lock it.

I hit my cell and called Two-Tone. "Okay, we're hot," I whispered. "I think Gusarov has two pieces, maybe three. I'm north of One-Forty-ninth on Third Avenue. Three buildings in from the corner on the east side. I couldn't make out if he's got boys or girls but they just went inside the entrance to the building. There's a second man too. He was at the door, holding it open. I saw him for half a second. Better get me some backup. I'm thinking we can make our move here."

"I got no one, JD," Two-Tone snarled. "Iggy's on Fifty-seventh Street watching the gallery and the kid's at the dentist until after two o'clock. Look, I'll come myself! I'll take a cab and be there in forty-five minutes—if I'm lucky."

"Okay. I'll go in and sniff it out. Like before. But I won't make any moves until you get here. Just get here!"

"Hold back!" Two-Tone barked. "Do the drill. Just wait for me. Do not go in there alone, Fiorella."

"He's got kids in there. I know it. The son of a bitch has kids."

"I said hold tight! I'm on my way."

"Just get here," I said. Then I hung up.

The building was a four-floor walk-up, easily a hundred and fifty years old. I pulled the Dodge into the red zone a hundred feet off on the corner, a safe distance down the block from the main entrance—but closer.

Shielded behind my car's open driver's door, I pulled my Charter Arms .44 from the rear of my belt and slid it into my right front pants pocket. Then I dipped my head inside and took a long pull from the pint of Ten High in my coat pocket.

After that I went to the trunk of the Dodge and pulled out one of the two decoy outfits I had with me—a white jumpsuit with a matching hard hat. The arced red lettering across the back of the jumpsuit read, INSTANT EXTERMINATIONS. The phone number below it was a dummy and went directly to a dead line.

I slipped the jumpsuit on, put on the hard hat, then picked up the clipboard that came with the getup. A fake work order form was anchored beneath the spring clip.

Back by the driver's side of the Dodge, reaching in, I clicked the car's hazard lights on, then locked the door and walked toward the building.

There was an aging sign taped above a panel of the building's entrance buzzers that read, OUT-ODER.

It took me less than a minute to pick the front-door lock with my picks and my two-ounce spray bottle of WD-40.

Once inside, I left the door ajar, making sure the lock's latch did not engage.

Then I began checking the first floor for sounds. There was a TV playing in the front apartment. A corkboard and dangling pen were attached to the door for messages. It had to be the super's place. I kept going.

Working my way down the hall slowly, I went from one door to the next. There were no sounds or red flags in the second, third, or fourth units.

Then I climbed the stairs to the second landing. As I reached two, the smell of piss was overwhelming, as if this was someone's personal spot to take a leak twice a day. I kept going, telling myself that I'd just find the right door, then back off and wait for Two-Tone to catch up.

I took even more time on two, listening for almost half a minute at each door.

There was only one fixtureless bulb at the other end of the dark hall. The hallway floor itself was composed of ancient half-inch tile squares laid in swirling patterns, and my thick rubber cop shoes were soundless against them.

Halfway up the hallway I heard voices as I neared no. 209—the first live voices I'd heard in the building.

I listened for a full minute. Two men were speaking in raised voices. It sounded like Russian. But I could hear no children's voices.

Satisfied that 209 might be the right apartment, I padded to the end of the hall, slid the casement window open, and leaned to my right, looking for the fire escape. I'd failed to notice it was on the street side of the building. The front window of 209 would face it.

I looked at my watch. I'd hung up from Two-Tone fourteen minutes before. He was still at least twenty minutes away.

I climbed the interior stairs to the roof, then exited on the wide, tar-coated surface.

I crossed to where I saw the top of the fire escape and began to descend on the heavy metal stairs. As I did this, the frame clanged against the building's brick surface. Too much noise. Way too much.

I soon found that by pushing myself against the exterior wall while holding the metal handrail with the other hand, I was able to prevent the steel-framed railing and stairs from making contact with the brick.

I took my time. I wasn't worried about the pedestrian traffic below and someone seeing me. New Yorkers seldom look up and if they did they'd see a guy in a white workman's uniform, then ignore it.

When I got to three, I stopped for a full two minutes, sat down on a metal stair step, and studied my surroundings while waiting for any signs that I'd been discovered.

Now I slowed my descent rate even more, heading toward two, taking a long time between each metal step.

When I was half a dozen steps from the bottom metal platform, I removed my .44 from the pocket beneath my top layer of clothing and tucked it into the wide, chest-high front folding flap pocket of my overalls. I then set my white hard hat on the stair above.

I decided to play it safe and descend the steps upside down, reversing my body, hooking my feet on a step rung several above me and stretching my torso in a downward angle against the metal stairs so that the top of my head would be even with the top of 209's front window.

There were ancient venetian blinds on the window. They were cracked slightly and I was able to see in.

The room I was looking into was the living room. I could see three one-person cots against one wall. The setup was like a barracks and not like a home.

On the last cot's sheetless mattress, farthest from the window I was looking through, was a girl. She was naked from the waist down and wearing a sort of pink nightshirt that ended at her midsection; a quiet, unsmiling little girl, no more than ten or eleven years old. She sat without talking, nodding her head while someone, probably Gusarov or his buddy, out of my line of vision, was apparently talking to her.

A couple of minutes later another man came into view. He stood beside the bed, obstructing my view of the girl.

Then another girl entered my line of vision. She was wearing a long, faded blue T-shirt and appeared to be about the same age as the first girl. She was blonde. Both of the kids were blondes.

The second girl sat down on one of the two remaining cots, then drew the blanket up and around her, to above her chest.

Having seen enough, I pulled my body back up the metal stairs, put my hard hat back on, then made my way up the fire escape stairs to three.

I needed a plan. Two-Tone was on his way and his presence would even the odds. But we'd still have to have a plan—a way in. A distraction.

Looking across Third Avenue, past the El, I surveyed the storefronts and spotted one that advertised takeout: FUEGO'S PIZZA. WE DELIVER. The 718 phone number was larger than the painted-on name on the orange banner. The store's faded fabric sign covered the original store sign and stretched the width of the facade.

I had used food delivery before as a way in. I didn't like it. One time it had worked and one time it had backfired, and Iggy, my sometimes partner, had narrowly missed being hit by a blast from a sawed-off 12-gauge. The takedown had been set for an absurd drug deal where the buyer and the supplier had both gone to the meet to rip each other off. No one was shot or fatally hurt but the would-be buyer had had his feet crushed when the seller and his boys made their point by dropping a fifty-pound vise on each of the guy's shoe tops as he sat strapped to a chair. The food-delivery ruse had come too late and only a swing of the metal door Iggy was closing had saved him from a sure trip to the boneyard.

I quietly made my way back up the fire escape to the roof. Once on the flat surface I pulled out my cell and punched in the pizza store's phone number. I ordered a cheese and pepperoni, gave the address, and asked how long. "Twenty minutes," the kid on the other end said.

"Make it twenty-five minutes. No sooner," I said. "I gotta pick up cigarettes at the candy store. Oh, and look, the downstairs buzzers don't work. Just push the door. It's open."

"I know your building. Who's this? You're not Vladdy? Two-oh-nine, right?"

"Right, he told me to call," I said, vamping now but hoping to be read as convincing. "How much?"

"Seventeen-oh-seven, with tax. Vladdy always gives me a twenty."

"You'll get your twenty. Just bring the goddam pizza in twenty-five minutes," I said. "No sooner. Okay?"

"Sure. Okay." Then there was a pause. "And what about extra napkins for the kids? Vladdy always wants extra napkins."

"Right," I said. "I forgot. Extra napkins too."

Then the kid hung up. So far, so good.

I continued to check my watch, waiting for Two-Tone to pull up in a cab. Below, on the street, I could see a cop walk up to my Dodge rental. He wrote out my second red-zone ticket in three days.

Twenty minutes after I'd placed my pizza order I clicked my cell phone on and pressed redial to get Two-Tone back.

He answered right away.

"Where are you?" I said. "I've got a pizza on the way to the apartment. Gusarov's in there with at least two kids, both girls."

"I told you to hang back. Step down, JD! Screw the pizza thing. We'll put something together when I get there."

"Where are you now?"

"I'm on First Avenue heading toward the bridge. The FDR had construction so we got off at Ninety-sixth Street. My ETA is at least ten to fifteen minutes."

"I'm going in, Two-Tone! When the pizza gets here, I'm doin' it! Gusarov has kids in there. He's our guy and he's got little girls in there! They're screwing and pimping out little girls. Fuck it! When you get here, go to apartment two-oh-nine. Second floor. Go heavy."

Then I clicked off.

Five minutes later, still on the roof, looking through the El's tracks I saw a kid in street clothes and a leather jacket holding a cardboard pizza box exit the take-out store. He waited for the car traffic to slow, then began crossing the street toward my building.

I moved down the fire-escape stairs as quickly and quietly as possible.

When I got to three, I set my hard hat back down on one of the metal steps, then pulled my .44. I padded quietly the rest of the way down the stairs, then stood to the side of the window, waiting, hoping to time my move to a few seconds after the knock when it came. I'd checked the window before. It had upper and lower panes divided by a wooden cross-member. The thing looked to be as old as the building itself and was thick with layers of decaying paint. I hoped it would cave in on my first kick.

I waited.

Several seconds passed and I didn't hear the knock, but I did see Gusarov through the crack in the blinds as he became startled, then stood up and headed toward the apartment door. As best as I could see, he wasn't armed.

With my gun in my hand, I backed myself up on the fire escape platform. I aimed a foot thrust at the cross-member of the window and put all my weight behind it. The glass and frame shattered in all directions.

Gusarov turned from the door. The pizza kid was startled and stepped back into the hallway.

I jumped down to the floor, feeling crushed glass under my feet.

One of the girls was between us on a cot, but The Russian was still unarmed.

Then, to my left, in the bedroom, I heard a sound I knew: someone jacking a round into an automatic.

I turned instinctively and heard the roar of my .44 as it spit two hollow points in the direction of the sound I'd just heard.

Now I saw Russian number two move to his right, out of view, and I assumed I'd missed both times.

A second later, stepping to the bedroom's doorframe, I cocked the .44. Gusarov was making a move toward the girl on the cot until I waved him back with the barrel of my gun. Crouching low in the doorway near the floor, I stuck my gun hand in the opening and fired blind twice more in the direction of Russian number two.

A second later I heard a groan, and then a body hitting the floor. Number two was down.

Standing quickly, I moved inside the bedroom. The first thing I saw was girl number two. She was on the bed, naked, holding her arms and palms up to shield herself. Terrified.

Russian two was grabbing at the right side of his chest with both hands. He'd taken a second bullet in the upper leg, near his crotch. His automatic, a Glock .40, lay a foot away.

I knew Gusarov was behind me and to my right. I only had one round left in my .44 so I scrambled into the room and snatched up the Glock.

Glancing at the girl on the bed I could see her expression had changed suddenly. I spun right, into the living room, and pointed the Glock.

Gusarov had a knife in his hand. The blade was six inches and thick. A hunting knife. He was ten feet away.

Using the first girl as a shield, he was moving toward me. "Put fucking gon down! I kill girl. She dieee right here."

He held her in front of his face and head. I decided not to risk the shot and stepped back.

Now Gusarov yelled something in Russian to the girl in the bedroom. Frantic, she came out and started moving toward him. I tried waving her back with my free hand. "No, kid," I called, "get back inside."

Now Gusarov had them both. He was grinning. "You like dis game?" he snarled.

Before I could make a move or say anything, his knife had cut the first girl's throat. He slashed deeply into her neck. The arterial spray sent a three-foot arc on to the wall and the linoleum floor. As the child convulsively turned her body, a gush of her blood covered Gusarov's face and shirt.

After she'd gone down, still flailing her arms and legs, he moved his grip to the other girl. The fucker looked like some sort of blood-soaked ghoul—the child's blood was impairing his vision. He wiped it away with his shirtsleeve.

I fired twice, quickly, intentionally wide, not wanting to hit the other kid.

Gusarov didn't even blink. He was grinning as he forced the second girl down and, with his free hand, slashed her across the belly and chest. Long, diagonal wounds.

He looked at me, leering. "Cut like pig," he yelled. "Cut like pig!"

Terrified, the second girl grabbed at her body and began screaming and thrashing, rolling from side to side on the cot.

"Now girl die," he hissed. "You watch! Watch pig die!"

I fired twice more as he plunged the knife into the child's stomach.

One of my shots was a center mass hit and the force of its impact threw him against the wall.

Gusarov was a big guy and he was strong. He began trying to right himself and even grabbed for the knife.

I was close enough now to deliver a solid left elbow to his face. That spun him away. Then I hit him again.

I stepped back and quickly squeezed off another shot. This one caught him in the shoulder.

His hand was at his chest wound but somehow the crazy smile was back. He pointed a bloody finger at the dead girl beside him on the cot. "You see? You did this. You are a fool."

I fired again, into Gusarov's stomach. He grabbed at his wounds, then rolled on his side.

Then, from the bedroom, I heard a noise. Something moving.

I walked the few paces to the doorway, then looked inside.

The second Russian was still alive. He was struggling to get to his feet, his shoes slipping in a wide, dark pool of his own blood.

Moving to him I pointed the Glock, then executed the Kossack prick with one bullet above his ear. His head came apart in the explosion.

When I reentered the living room, Gusarov was barely conscious, clutching his hands to his shirt as deep crimson flowed up between his fingers.

"You ready, asshole?" I said, raising the gun.

He spit blood at me as he spoke. "Fukk you," was his answer.

I held the Glock between the Russian's eyes. He looked straight at me as I squeezed the trigger.

Nine days later I was released from jail and the murder and numerous felony charges were all dismissed, thanks to Two-Tone's client, the Russian Immigrant Coalition. But I was done and I knew it—done with the detective business, done with New York. Done with death. My headaches started that day in the Bronx. The only way to deal with them was to stay drunk enough to kill the pain. So I stayed drunk for a month at the Oasis Motel in Queens, then bought a one-way ticket back to Los Angeles.

TWENTY-TWO

For the next eighteen hours I sat on Swan's house, hoping to pick up Sydnye's trail. The place truly was a fortress in every sense of the word. The stone walls were ten feet high and a foot thick, like a prison. They surrounded his fourteen-acre estate. The security system was state of the art and encompassed the property and its perimeter, along with four one-hundred-pound Doberman pinschers. I'd once known a guy in New York who'd been an installer of what looked to be the same kind of security setup. I was pretty sure, with a little time, I could disable it. The problem, of course, would be locating the master unit itself.

The main front brass gates had a guard house with a man inside. Rotating cameras were mounted every thirty feet on the walls, and Swan's two beefy bodyguard/security men—Mutt and Jeff or Sonny and Cher or whatever grunt they answered to—could alternately be spotted coming and going from six P.M. until three A.M. They each had one assistant.

THAT NIGHT, BANKS of motion-tripped spotlights came on if so much as a stray cat mistakenly climbed a wall.

The one time Swan did go out, he was followed by the black BMW sedan carrying the two bodyguards. There was no trace of Sydnye.

The next morning three groundskeepers in green uniforms and sombreros came and went. Their apparent assignment had been to clear the brush on the outside of the wall, at the periphery of the estate. To do this they used a small tractor. It pulled a corkscrew tiller that turned the dirt into even rows and plowed under all the growth in a twenty-foot border beyond the wall. One guy drove the tractor while the other two walked behind, using rakes and hoes to decapitate the stubborn shrubbery that the tiller missed.

I knew where there was a war surplus store on Venice Boulevard in West L.A. that sold green khakis similar to the ones the groundskeepers wore. I'd shopped there a few times. I made a note to pick up a uniform and some wasp spray in case I had to deal with the guard dogs inside the wall.

For the next hour I watched the clearing guys work from Woody's Honda on Grasswood Drive, drinking coffee and eating the last of a packaged sandwich from the market on Dume Drive. The night before I'd had to relocate three times when a yellow private neighborhood security 4x4 rolled by. With a BOLO out on Woody's car, I couldn't take a chance on being reported to the local sheriffs.

By ten A.M. it was time to pack it in. I'd had no sleep and there'd been no sign of Sydnye.

I decided to drop by my mom's to take a shower. It had been a foggy and cool morning on Point Dume and when I walked in I found Mom and Coco at the dining-room table drinking breakfast tea and eating toast and jam, instead of sitting outside on their patio. A long-corded phone was resting between them, and the Malibu phone book was on the table. Nearby was Mom's computer. It was on.

When I kissed her on the cheek I knew something was off. "What's up, Ma," I asked.

"Two of our cats are missing. I'm contemplating making a police report."

I shook my head. "The blues can't help you," I said. "Better call someone private. Maybe a neighbor or a local kid. Pay 'em by the hour."

"I am a taxpayer. Are you implying that the Malibu police—the blues—are ineffective?"

"They don't hunt stray cats, Ma. They have other things to do."

"You have a point, James. I'll telephone Chuckie Melber, down the block. He's a nice boy. He'll help me."

"Hey, Ma," I said, biting into a slice of toast, "mind if I take a shower and get cleaned up? I worked late last night."

"Of course, dear. Use the spare bathroom. You're not in any trouble, are you?"

"What trouble would I be in, Ma?"

The new information about Karl Swan and Sydnye that Archer had given me had been churning in my mind for the last twelve hours. I looked down at Mom's laptop, then realized I could save myself a little grunt work.

"Hey, Ma," I said, "mind if I do a quick search on your machine? It'll just take a few minutes."

"Of course, dear," she said.

I sat down and Mom asked Coco to make me some real coffee. Then Mom minimized the astrological web page she had on the screen and turned the computer toward me. "Help yourself, James. Just don't lose the page I'm on."

I clicked to the search engine, then typed in a name: Karl Swan.

What came up wasn't a surprise. A color photo of a younger, grinning Swan, then several more photographs of the guy with movie stars and other film-studio bosses at gala events. Then the bio:

Karl Swan, (born Kella Swirsky in Stuttgart, Germany, June 1930) is one of the most successful film producers in Hollywood history. Nine of his twenty-four films have grossed over 100 million dollars. As a boy, young Swirsky survived an Austrian concentration camp in Flossenbürg, during World War ll, where both his parents and his sister perished, to eventually immigrate to England in 1944, where he attended Eaton College and Cambridge. Having developed an interest in photography as a teenager, he began a hobby as a still photographer, and soon gravitated to filming documentaries of bombed-out European towns, interviewing dozens of civilian survivors of WW ll. At nineteen he was awarded the Kandinsky Prize for what later became his 1954 film, *The Aftermath*. International attention followed and Swirsky immigrated to America, where he began his Hollywood career. Good fortune awaited the young man. His first assignment was as an assistant cameraman working for famed producer Harry Goldman in the box-office success *The Texan*, starring Paul Morrow and Sandra Turner. Goldman saw talent in the young man and Swirsky became his protégé. It was on the screen credits to *The Texan* that Kella Swirsky's newly adopted name, Karl Swan, first appeared. What followed was a series of successful assignments where Swan went from cameraman to associate producer and, ultimately, to producer. In 1963 his first box-office triumph (financed by Goldman) came with the film *The Great Escapade*, about soldiers in a WW ll concentration camp.

I COULD FEEL Mom standing above me, looking over my shoulder, being nosy. "What's your interest in Karl Swan, James? Why were you looking him up?" she asked.

"I saw him at the noon AA meeting yesterday. He was with his daughter, Sydnye. As he was pulling out of the driveway he looked over at me and said, 'Have a nice day,' or something like that. But Swan doesn't know me. We've never seen each other before. There was no reason why he'd stop to talk to me—there's no reason why he would be eyeing me like a plate of pickled herring."

"You've said it to me yourself, several times, AA people can be effusive and annoyingly friendly."

Then Mom's expression darkened. Leaning across the table, she picked up a manila envelope from a stack of four or five, then held it up. On the front, in black Sharpie lettering, was a name I couldn't read upside down.

"Remember," she said, "when you were visiting us last week, I was working on a chart?"

"You're always working on somebody's chart, Ma."

"He's sending his valet or secretary over at noon to pick

it up and drop off my check. What I'm telling you now is
confidential information, James. As you know, I never reveal
the identity of my clients."

"You mean, Karl Swan? That's Karl Swan's chart!"

"Yes, Karl Swan."

"Jesus!"

"You may remember that your father once had business
dealings with him."

"I didn't know that! What kind of business dealings?"

"It was many years ago. You were a boy. It was some
kind of studio dispute. I'm unsure of the substance of it but,
at the time, I do know it bothered your father. As you know,
your dad rarely discussed that kind of thing with me."

Gongs and whistles began going off in my head.

Now Mom was staring at me. "Are you all right, James?"

"Tell me about Swan's chart."

"Well, as I mentioned to you before, he has some rather
dark and unusual aspects, natally. Bluntly put, the man is
odd, perhaps even sick or pathological. But that's not the
worst of it. Currently, he has an alarming Saturn conjunction that began three days ago and may denote violence and
possibly indicate someone's injury or death. I'd keep my distance from him if I were you, James."

"That's in his chart?"

"The stars are ruthlessly honest, James."

I stood up from the table. "I don't like you doing this guy's
chart, Ma. I don't like it at all. He's a sick whacko fuck!"

"For God's sake, James, Coco and I are right here in the
room!"

"When did Swan order the chart? Give me the exact
date!"

"I'm not sure. A week or so ago. What's wrong?"

"Can you look it up?"

"I don't keep that kind of information. I simply tell my clients to call me in a week to ten days. Then, when I'm done I make arrangements for them to come by for a consultation and to pick up their horoscopes."

"Swan's coming by to pick it up? To this house?"

"His secretary told me that he doesn't require the consultation. He's sending someone over."

"What time is this someone coming by?"

"Today at noon."

AN HOUR LATER, after a shower, I was drinking from a fresh pot of coffee and smoking out on Mom's patio, with the door open, when the outside front-door buzzer went off.

I flipped my cigarette away, went into the kitchen, then waved Coco away after grabbing the brown manila envelope off the kitchen table on my way to the front door.

Standing there on Mom's porch was one of Swan's people, a well-muscled Latino wearing jeans, a polo shirt, and a sports jacket. He looked like a second-tier TV actor from a cop show.

He took off his sunglasses and we were eye to eye. His face was blank. "My name's Rudolpho," he said in perfect English. "I'm here to see Mrs. Nancy Fiorella—to pick up a package for Mr. Swan."

"I've got it right here," I said, swinging the door all the way open so he could see the envelope in my hand.

"You have a check made out to my mother, right?" I asked.

"Yes, I have the check. But I was told to speak to Mrs. Fiorella personally."

"Not today," I said. "I'll take the check now."

"My instructions are to give the check directly to Nancy Fiorella."

I closed the door behind me and stepped down the two concrete steps to be on the same level as the guy.

Before he could react, I snatched the check from his hand.

"What's your problem!" Rudolpho snarled.

"You're at my mother's house! That's my problem. And now I'm *your* problem!"

I spun him around. As I did so, he attempted a quick reverse kick and even tried a forearm to my chin. The kid had good moves but I blocked them both.

Now I had his arm in a hammerlock and his face pressed hard against the rough white stucco siding of my mom's house. He was no more than twenty-two or twenty-three and a hundred and seventy-five pounds, but his physical intensity felt powerful—martial-arts training.

I snatched the Beretta out of my waistband and pressed it as hard as I could against his tight jeans, placing the muzzle between the cheeks of his ass at an upward angle.

I quickly patted him down, found nothing, then leaned close to his ear. "Listen carefully, messenger boy," I hissed. "For some reason your boss is stalking my family. And he sent you here to ID my mother."

"Let me go now or you'll get hurt! That's a promise."

"You work for a man who has made a serious mistake and no amount of money and no kung-fu punk and no team of lawyers are going to stop me if I see one of you guys here again. Tell Swan I know how to find him and when I do the gun barrel that you're feeling up your ass will be aimed between his eyes. Can you remember all that, Rudolpho?"

"I advise you to release me," he said in a voice that was flat—and too calm.

I spun him around and quickly moved the Beretta to a position under his chin, then pressed it hard against his throat. "Did Swan teach you how to torture wetbacks, Rudolpho? Is my mother on his menu?"

His eyes were boring into mine. They were vacant and ice cold. "Are you done?"

I gave him a forward thrust to the stomach. Hard.

He went down and began gasping for air but instinctively knew how to cover up.

I had him by the hair and slammed his head against the stucco wall. Once. Twice. Then I leaned close to his ear.

"If you or anyone who works for Karl Swan makes any more moves against my mother—no matter what they are— they're dead. I'll kill you and I'll kill Swan. I'll kill his bodyguards and I'll kill his dogs. I'll kill everybody I see. From today on, your life is different, Rudolpho. Never come near this house again."

I spun him around, then scooped up the manila envelope and dragged him by the collar of his sports jacket—my gun under his neck—down the walkway toward Mom's front gate.

Swan's Bentley convertible was parked on the gravel cutout.

I opened the driver's door, then pushed Rudolpho onto the front seat. I tossed the manila envelope onto his lap.

"Mission accomplished, Rudolpho. You got what you came for and what you deserve. Tell Swan that he'll see the horoscope of a very sick fuck when he opens this up. Tell him that he has death in his chart."

Then, with the barrel of my gun, I slammed a hole in the Bentley's driver's-side window.

BACK INSIDE THE house, Mom was shaking and breathing hard. She and Coco had watched me handle the kid from the living-room window.

"What's the meaning of this, James? What just happened?" she said, gasping.

"I'm going to make a call, Mom. You and Coco and the cats are moving to a hotel—away from Malibu. You'll have someone there to look after you. I'll arrange everything."

An hour later, after talking to Mendoza, Carr's pal—the gun dealer in Canyon Country—I had what I needed: two ex-cops armed with shotguns who knew how to keep their mouths shut. They were on their way to Mom's house. The arrangements were set.

Out back, in my mother's garage, I moved Woody's Honda into the spare bay, removed my stuff from the trunk, pulled the license plates, then covered the car with a stinky old tarp left over from my father's sports-car days.

A few minutes later I helped Mom and Coco load their luggage and their remaining four cats into her white Escalade.

As I was closing the second garage door and was preparing to lock it, I heard a thud and looked down at the pavement near my feet. The stiff bodies of two cats were inches away from the end of my shoes. They had fallen as the garage door closed.

Both Mom's pets had mangled torsos. Their legs and heads were facing the wrong direction.

Mom and Coco were in Mom's car and busily arranging themselves. They hadn't seen the bodies.

Wordlessly, I got into the driver's seat, then slid the Escalade's shifting knob into reverse, and we were on our way.

TWENTY-THREE

When she woke up it was still dark outside. The girl rubbed her eyes and saw him standing by the side of her bed, tall and fully dressed in a dark jumpsuit and matching baseball cap. The coveralls looked like the work clothes some of his staff wore and, for a moment, she thought he might be one of the fellows that helped out during the day around the property. But then he clicked on her table light and she saw his face. "Up, child! Now!" her father said. "We have important things to do. Very important things."

He handed her a dark, thick sweatshirt and a pair of sweatpants of the same color. "Put these clothes on," he ordered.

Later, she would remember how cold it was, especially as they walked from the main house to the stables, where her horse, Stampede, and the others, were kept. As they walked, she even thought for a second that he might be taking her riding, though he had never done so before at this time of the morning and, of course, she wasn't wearing her riding boots, so she dropped the idea of riding. *Don't be a baby*, she thought. *Show him how grown-up you are.* She reminded herself that he'd told her more than once what a smart girl he thought she was. She had a way of figuring things out on her own, he'd said. No, of course they weren't going riding! They were doing something else. But maybe later, after this, she'd be able to go to the stables with Isabella, her nanny, and they'd let her brush Stampede again. That would be sooo cool.

He wasn't talking, her tall father, they were just walking. As he marched ahead of her she noticed that he was carrying something in his hand. It looked like a pole or a short, thick pipe. No, dummy! It was a flashlight. But it probably had something to do with the horses after all, she thought, because they were heading in the direction of the stables. Father went there a lot by himself and often stayed there for a long time.

Her dad unlocked the long door to the stable with a metal key, then slid it open. It made almost no sound as it glided along its tracks.

After they'd stepped inside, he slid the door closed again. Then he clicked on a switch. But no light went on. That was weird. He knew she didn't like the dark. Then he clicked on the flashlight.

He took her by the hand so she wouldn't be afraid, and they walked the length of the stalls, past Stampede and Sheba and the new horse that her father had bought only last week. He'd named him Attila, and Attila was the biggest horse she had ever seen. A stallion.

The horses were all still asleep now and Father aimed the flashlight on the floor to help them both see as they walked.

At the very end of the long row of dark stalls they came to another door. It was really a gate and not a door.

On the wall by the gate was a silver phone pad, like for a telephone, but there was no telephone. Father punched in some numbers and the gate made a clanking sound, then popped open.

The light was already on and they went down some stairs.

It didn't smell right on the stairs. It was stuffy, and later she would remember being afraid of the odor, but knowing that he was there with her, she thought it'd probably be okay.

At the bottom of the stairs he opened another door with the same kind of key pad that had no phone. A light came on inside the room.

This room was like nothing she had seen before. It had some kind of padding on the walls and ceiling. Gray padding. Like pillows but not really. They were puffy and stuck out from the walls.

Then she saw that there was a man there in the center of the room. He had no clothes on and he seemed to be asleep and there were straps on his wrists and feet and another one around his neck. He was lying on a long table, like a doctor's-office table or an operating table on TV, only this table was made of wood and not metal.

There were no pictures or windows in the room and the smell was stronger now, stronger than it had been on the stairs. It was like old, dirty clothes mixed with something else and it was making her start to feel sick. It smelled like poop.

Her father closed the door and then pushed some more numbers on the keypad next to it on the wall. She heard the clunking noise again.

Then he walked to the table where the man lay asleep.

"Over here, child," he ordered. "Stand on the other side of the table and face toward your father."

When she got to the table she thought that she recognized the man who was on it. The table was high, at the level of her shoulders, so she could only really see the side of the man's face. He had black hair and his stomach bulged up.

"Do you remember this fellow?" her father asked. "Look at him. Look at his face."

Then she remembered. She'd seen the man. On TV. He looked older now and fatter than the last time she had seen him, but she did remember him. "That's Matt something," she said. "I remember him. He used to be on that show. He used to come here with his friend, the bald man, and you all used to go to the screening room and watch movies. Right?"

"That's right, Sydnye. It's Matt Hauser," her father said.

Then she laughed. "I remember! I remember that he fell asleep that time while we were eating pizza at the restaurant by Paradise Cove. That was strange, Father."

Her father nodded. "Good. Excellent memory. Very commendable. Yes, I recall that incident as well. Matt made a fool of himself that day. Did you know that Matt's real name isn't really Matt, child. It is Miguel. Miguel Herrera. I once produced his TV series. It was several years ago, when you were small. He was an actor on TV at that time. I helped him make a lot of money, but then he spent it all. Now all Miguel does is get drunk and smoke crack cocaine and go to jail for assault. Last night he came here in his car. To our home. He was intoxicated. He wanted money. I gave Anthony, at the gate, permission to allow him in. Then Matt fell asleep in his car, in front of our home. Before he fell asleep he rang the bell several times but I gave instructions for no one to admit him. Matt is what I call a misanthrope, Sydnye. That means he's a fool. A mistake made by nature. Matt is human rubbish. Wastepipe rubbish. He is useless human rubbish. He's asked your father for important favors before and then falsely claimed that he didn't recall making the requests. So Matt is rubbish and Matt is also a liar of the worst kind. But today Matt will remember. He'll remember everything because I'm going to show him how to remember. Today is a special day for you, my child. It's a beginning. Today you will learn some of the things that your father has known for a long time—since he was your age. Special secrets, Sydnye. You are ten years old now and it is time that you learned."

Her father picked up a blue bottle from the table and poured some of what was in it on to a piece of cotton, then he held the cotton over Matt Hauser's nose.

Matt woke up right away. He looked confused and then, pretty soon, he looked afraid.

Father took a piece of thick cloth out of the pocket of his overalls and pushed the cloth into Matt's mouth as Matt was trying to say something. Matt pulled on the straps at his hands and feet, but then he knew—he understood—that he couldn't move. He was strapped down tight. Her father was smiling.

"Now Matt's ready, Sydnye. Now it's up to us to show Matt the things he must learn. Matt must learn pain, my child. He must learn to beg for his life. He must be taught the elegance of suffering. Your father knows the ways of suffering and how to administer pain. Soon Matt will beg your father. He will scream that he is sorry. He will scream and scream. But I will not hear him, because he is weak. And weakness is sickness, Sydnye. You see, my child, today you will begin to learn the special things that I know. I make that a promise to you. I will teach you my secrets, special things. Important things. We, you and I, will share those things together. There was once a great man named Nietzsche. He once wrote, 'To live is to suffer—to survive is to find some meaning in the suffering.' Today, you will begin to understand the meaning in suffering. The suffering of others."

Then her father motioned for her to come to his side of the wooden table. He unbuttoned his work suit, then pulled it down below his waist. He was smiling.

"Before we begin, Sydnye, you have to show Father how much you like him. You remember, just like we did the other times. Only this time I'm standing up. Remember?"

"I remember, Father."

"I want Matt to watch, Sydnye. I want him to see how you do it. Now get down on your knees, child."

"I don't like the smell in here, Father. It stinks in here."

"I know. I know it stinks. The smell is entirely unpleasant. But you'll adjust to it. In time, child, it won't bother you at all."

TWENTY-FOUR

After meeting Mendoza's men, Davis and Majuski, at the Raddison in Santa Barbara and giving them enough information to handle their assignment, I registered Mom and Coco at the desk under Coco's name—it was safer.

Then, leaving through the hotel's rear entrance, I moved on to the Canary Hotel nearby.

After everything was set up, I got back in Mom's Escalade and headed south, alone, toward L.A.

MY FIRST STOP back on the West Side was at the surplus store on Venice Boulevard near Motor Avenue. I picked up what I needed there, then decided to phone Archer. I told the detective what had happened earlier at Mom's house with Swan's man and the moves I'd made to protect her and Coco. Archer agreed to meet me near police headquarters in Santa Monica, at the bar Chez Jay on Ocean Avenue. He said he'd bring Sydnye's package and whatever else he had that was current on Swan. When I asked for his help with Mom and Coco, he said his hands were tied. There was no way he could get authorization for police protection in Santa Barbara. No crime had been committed.

AN HOUR LATER I was drinking my Diet Coke and Archer his shooter at Chez Jay's planked bar. Archer was not a subtle guy. He looked over both his shoulders, saw we were okay, then passed me what I needed. "You're in over your head on this," he whispered. "Just do me a favor and keep me up to speed as you go."

"You told me you'd been bumped on this. Is that why you can't get me help with my mother? Is that it?"

Archer nodded. "I might surprise you. I can still make a few moves if push comes to shove. I'm working on your Santa Barbara problem. I've got a friend or two left—whacked-out celebrity stalker cop that I am. If I ask the right way I can sometimes get what I need. I'll let you know. But it isn't me or your mother I'm worried about. You just poked a nasty gorilla with a sharp stick."

"Yeah," I said. "I got the old boy's attention. The best way I know to get a gorilla to sit up and start snorting is to use that stick."

"I never got the chance. Swan had his lawyers in the way every time I got close. My question to you is, are you sure about this? You can still back away. Your family's on the line now."

"I'm ready," I said. "And I'm not backing off."

Archer was sneering. "Swan recognized me at his AA birthday bash the other day. Between that and what happened at your mom's house, he's spooked and he's looking over both shoulders. Any update on Sydnye?"

"Not yet. But if Swan knows, then his kid knows too. I'm drawing them out of their hole."

"She's probably close by. Closer than you think. And get rid of everything I just gave you, especially the information about the witness I had. No paper traces, okay?"

"Okay."

AFTER I LEFT Archer, I walked to Mom's Escalade, which was parked at a meter on Ocean Avenue, twenty yards away. I removed my now authentic Handicapped placard from the inside rearview mirror and started the engine. On the seat next to me was the thin file on Sydnye and more backup documentation on Karl Swan. My eyes were stinging from tiredness and I decided to close them for a couple of minutes.

WAKING UP, I looked down at the instrument panel and saw that I'd been asleep for ninety minutes. I'd also burned a quarter of a tank in Mom's gas-guzzling Escalade.

I lit a cigarette and sucked in a deep hit, remembering to put the front windows down so Mom wouldn't be too pissed off about the residual stink of tobacco. After that I pulled Archer's files from the envelope on the seat next to me.

The stuff on Sydnye was contained in a clear plastic folder. While I was opening it, one of the sharp edges on the side cut a nasty little slash in my finger. Blood immediately appeared and began running down into my hand and dripping onto the leather seat. I had to dig in Mom's glove box for several tissues to contain the mess.

The pages I read on Swan all had the Santa Monica Police

Department masthead taped over, obscured. Archer had been careful. Almost everything we'd discussed before about Sydnye Swan and the witness Archer had found was there in his notes, along with the mention of Sydnye's past involvement in martial arts and yoga and two websites and the list of possible known acquaintances. A workout studio in Brentwood on San Vicente Boulevard named Maha Combat was named as the place she may have trained.

After looking the file over again, I made some detail notes on the pocket pad I carried inside my jacket and then, as agreed with Archer, I got ready to destroy what he had given me.

Getting out of the Escalade, I walked to a street garbage can near Chez Jay's entrance, removed the plastic report cover so I wouldn't cut my hand again, then tore half of the actual paperwork into quarters, tossing the upper and lower quarter of the pages into the trash.

Then I crossed Ocean Avenue and did the same thing with the remainder of the file at another street can. After that I threw the plastic report cover on top.

I WAS CLOSE enough to Sherman Toyota that I decided to drive by and maybe get Vikki's attention from outside the showroom without going in. I'd had two calls from her cell number in the last twenty-four hours that I hadn't responded to, plus another I didn't recognize. I wanted to check in with her, in person.

It was Wednesday. I remembered that Wednesday was Max's scheduled day off.

I rolled slowly past the dealership on my way to park

the Escalade, looking along Lincoln Boulevard and Santa Monica Boulevard for tan Crown Vics as I went. I also glanced across the open sales lot, trying to spot Max's SUV. It wasn't there.

I WAS SITTING in the Escalade with the passenger window down at the far end of the property, trying to spot Vikki, when Fernando stepped out from between two late-model Hybrids on the row of cars facing Ninth Street. He wasn't smiling. "Jou push jou lukk, majn."

"What's up, amigo?"

"Cops been hejr too timz again in the lass couple days lookin' por jou. Jou muss be hot as chit, Chay-Dee."

I smiled at him while glancing over his shoulder at the showroom doors. "I try to keep moving, my friend. Hey," I said, "where's Vikki? I don't see her demo. Is she inside?"

"No majn, cheesa quit. Jus walk in do Max's offiz and tsay cheesa quit. Yserdae."

"No kidding, that was sudden. What happened?"

"Done kno, majn. Cheeza juss go. No goo bye, no kiss my hass, no nocin. Den I hask Max. He juss sae min jour own bizniz. Maricon preek."

VIKKI'S APARTMENT WAS only four blocks away. I parked mom's Escalade near the corner of California and Sixth and walked down the block to her building.

I was about to ring her front-door buzzer when a couple came out of the elevator next to the entrance door. The guy swung the door open for his lady, then held it open for me

to enter. West Side yuppies out for a night on the town. I
nodded thanks to the guy as I entered the building.

When I got to Vikki's floor I felt a knot in my stomach.
As I walked down the hall my brain began flashing on doing
the same thing at my friend Woody's place only days before.
The feeling rattled me and my head began thumping harder
than ususal.

Above me, as I got to her door, the hallway ceiling bulb
was out. I was standing in cold semidarkness.

I sloughed off the bad thoughts. This was going to be a
glad-to-see-you greeting. I liked this girl.

I knocked three times, then waited.

A few seconds later, when I heard no movement inside, I
tried again.

Then I heard flip-flop footsteps against the parquet
flooring of her interior front hallway. "Yes," a voice called
through the door.

"It's JD, Vikki. I was in the neighborhood."

It took ten seconds until she answered. "Oh. Hey, look,
I've been sick. Call me, okay?"

"I'm just dropping by to say hi. Open the door."

Another long pause, then: "Okay. Okay. Give me a
minute."

"Sure," I said, "take your time. I'm not going anywhere."

It took a couple more minutes until I heard the double-
locks flip and the door came open.

Vikki was without makeup and was wearing a dark
robe cinched tight at the waist. Her hair was unwashed
and she looked tired, older, sadder. "Yes," she said, looking
past me down the hall.

"Well, hey, howya doing?" I said. "You've been sick, huh?"

"Look, do you mind—some other time, okay?"

I was still smiling, trying to keep it going, still working off of the good vibes at our last meeting. "Well, can I at least come in for a minute?"

Her eyes wouldn't connect with mine. "I just said I was sick."

I rested my hand against the door frame next to her head. "What's wrong here? What's going on, Vikki?"

She wouldn't look at me. "I just told you. Didn't you listen?"

As I lowered my hand from the door frame, its metal sealer lining scraped against my cut finger and I said, "Ouch."

I looked at the hand. It was bleeding again.

"I'm coming in," I said, and started to push past her.

She reluctantly backed away and let me move inside. "What's wrong," she half-whispered.

"Nothing. I cut my finger. It's bleeding."

The living-room curtains were drawn and the only interior light came from the TV. The sound had been muted. On the coffee table was a near-empty bottle of the expensive-looking wine I'd seen the last time I was here. Next to it was a tall, smudged glass with nothing in it. I remembered Vikki telling me that she didn't like TV.

"Hey," I said, "you're watching the tube. You must be really sick."

Vikki flicked on a lamp. Her eyes were flat. "What do you want here? What do you want with me?"

"Look, Fernando told me that you quit at Sherman. Just walked into Max's office and quit. What was that about?"

Now her eyes darkened. "Okay, I quit. So what? Why is that your business?"

Blood was running down my finger and into my hand. I held it up. "I need to use your bathroom. I need to wash this off."

She pointed to a door ten feet away. "It's there."

INSIDE THE BATHROOM I closed the door, then turned on the hot water. Next to the faucet was a holder for Vikki's toothbrushes and a pink soap dish, and next to that I saw a white, flat plastic cap.

While I was waiting for the water to heat up, I glanced at my face in the mirror. Something was very wrong here. It was like this woman didn't know me. My face in the mirror confirmed the feeling.

Holding the white plastic cap in my hand, I quietly pulled the medicine cabinet open. The top two shelves were full of prescription vials, as many as a dozen of them. Grouped together were four containers of sleeping pills. One of the vials was labeled Zaleplon. I'd been given Zaleplon before in the nuthouse for my insomnia. It was quick and effective but had only worked well for me short-term. I popped the vial open, dropped two of them into my hand, then slid the rest back into the vial. One night soon I would use them to get a decent night's sleep.

On the bottom shelf, by itself, was an open container with only a couple of pills left inside. The cap in my hand fit the top of that vial.

I pulled the unlabeled bottle out and looked at the small pills inside. They were orange.

Then, remembering, I reached into my left front pants pocket and scrounged at the bottom. I came up with the orange pill I had asked the pharmacist about. I set it on the sink, away from the faucet, then removed one of Vikki's tablets from the vial. Hers were an exact match in shade and size. I had found that pill between the seats of Woody's Honda, and I knew that Woody never took meds. Those weren't his. Suddenly—today—my friend Vikki had abruptly shape-shifted herself into another person. A person who took the same kind of meds I had found.

My mind began clicking. Vikki? Jesus!

AFTER WASHING MY finger I patted the cut dry with toilet paper, tossed the wad into the crapper, then flushed it. Replacing the pill in the vial, I tucked it into the coat of my leather bomber jacket.

Standing there staring at my image in the mirror, I went back over what I knew about the woman in the living room—about what had happened over the last several weeks.

She had come to work for Sherman Toyota a few days after I'd started, almost as if on cue—just appearing on the sales floor one day. Then, shortly after—very shortly after—she'd begun showing interest in me. A coincidence? Was Vikki's coming to work at the Toyota dealership part of some kind of plot? Her hostility and indifference just now had been the tell, a red flag. I had to know and I had to know now.

Quietly leaving the bathroom I made my way back into the dimly lit living room.

Vikki was standing next to her couch several feet away

with one hand in her robe's pocket and the other holding a corded phone, whispering. She hadn't heard me. "I know," she was saying in a low voice. "So what now?"

"Hang up, Vikki!" I boomed.

Turning toward me, she spit the words in my direction: "Get out of here! Get away from me!"

In one motion I pulled the phone from her hand, then yanked its wiring out of the wall.

Our bodies were now two feet apart.

Removing the pill vial from my jacket pocket, I held it up for her to see. "How long have you been taking these?" I demanded.

"None of your goddamn business!"

"These are the same pills that I found in my friend Woody's car after he was killed."

"Get out of my apartment! Now!"

"Tell me about Sydnye Swan, Vikki."

I saw the muzzle of the gun for only a second as it came up in her left hand.

My reflex was to turn my body. Then I heard the sound and felt the impact at the same time.

Before she could fire a second time I used a crisscross slapping move to knock the gun to the floor. It was a small-caliber automatic.

Grabbing her by the hair I pulled her to the couch and shoved my knee into her stomach. Hard. While she was gasping for breath I yanked the belt from my pants loops and wrapped it around her wrists.

Then I leaned back and pulled my coat open.

The bullet that had penetrated the left side of my leather bomber jacket had ripped through the inside pocket. The notebook I carried there had a hole in it. Then the slug had exited at the back of the jacket. Point-blank range. Her bullet had missed me by no more than an inch.

Now she was kicking and spitting curses and trying to bite me. I needed answers.

On her coffee table was a copy of the *L.A. Times*. I tore a page away, wadded it up, then stuffed it in Vikki's mouth.

Pulling her off the couch, I began dragging her to the rear of the apartment—to her bedroom.

I pushed the door open, flipped the light switch, and saw a four-poster bed.

With my Beretta in one hand I hauled Vikki across to the bed and dumped her onto it.

"It's time for us to talk," I said evenly, tightening the belt around her hands. Then I slammed my knee into her stomach again.

While she lay there gasping I got up and went to the closet door and slid it open. There I found a rack of belts and yanked the entire apparatus out of the wall mount and onto the carpeted floor.

It took a few minutes to bind her up with several of her own belts. I strapped her down, spread-eagled, faceup, on the bed.

Near us on the floor was a pink T-shirt. I stuffed it in her mouth, replacing the wad of newspaper.

Now that she was secure I decided to do a quick toss of the room. Next to the bed was her two-drawer nightstand. I started there, opening the top drawer and checking for more weapons.

What was inside gave me everything I needed to know about my girlfriend Vikki. There was a box of bullets for a

Colt .25 automatic. Beneath it was a stack of magazines, all with the same title: *Cuffed*. The same magazine that was in Woody's apartment near his murdered body. Bingo!

Reaching across the bed I pulled the T-shirt from her mouth, then whispered in Vikki's ear: "I see that you're a *Cuffed* fan."

She rolled her eyes, then cleared her throat. "You have no idea who you're messing with."

I had to smile. "Actually, I now know exactly who you are."

Vikki looked at me and sneered.

When I yanked her robe open she yelled, "What the fuck do you think you're doing!"

After stuffing the T-shirt back into her mouth I began cutting away her robe, using the sharp, six-inch folding knife that I'd bought at the pawn shop. After each piece was cut away I tossed it on the floor.

For the first time I saw fear register in her eyes. I now had her attention.

Climbing on top of Vikki, I straddled her upper body with my legs. "Now, lady," I said in an even voice, "it's question and answer time. The game we'll play is called truth or torture. Here's how it goes: I ask you a question, and if you lie to me, then I begin hurting you. Are you ready?"

I pulled the gag from her mouth.

She coughed, then shook her head. "You can't do this," she hissed. "You'd better let me go. You don't scare me."

"Remember something, Vikki," I said. "What happens here is your pal Sydnye's MO. If they find a body in this bedroom—your bedroom—they won't be looking at me. They'll be looking somewhere else. So, here we go.

Question one: How were you involved with Sydnye in the killing of my friend Woody?"

"You don't know what the fuck you're talking about!"

I restuffed the gag in her mouth. "Wrong answer!"

I put all my weight on her stomach again.

Her face contorted in pain. It took her half a minute to catch her breath.

"Okay," I said, "you get one more chance. Here's question number two. If you answer incorrectly I'm going to start hurting you. Really hurting you. So let's start again from the here and now. It's easier that way. The orange pills I found in Woody's car were your pills—correct?"

I removed the gag.

"What if they were? So what."

"Good. Very good. And were you at Woody's apartment?"

"Fuck you! I just told you all I know!"

"Jesus, dumb answer!"

She was leering up at me now. "You'd better understand something," she hissed. "All it takes is one call from me. I'm warning you."

I stuffed the T-shirt back into her mouth. "Okay," I said, "you were warned. Now we play the game your way."

I jammed my knee into her stomach again—harder this time.

As she lay gasping and squirming on the bed, I leaned down and put my mouth to her ear. "I'll be right back," I said.

In the master bathroom's cabinet's drawers I found everything I needed: a lady's safety razor, scissors, and a bar of soap. I then located a washcloth, soaked it, and returned to the bedroom with my supplies.

When she saw what I had in my hands Vikki began thrashing on the bed. Another knee to her solar plexus and she stopped resisting.

A couple of minutes later, now back on top of her, straddling her chest again, I began clipping away chunks of her hair, near the roots. When that was done I wet her head with the damp wash rag and coated it with soap, then began shaving.

Five minutes later, now done with her head, I moved down to her crotch and shaved that too. I hadn't done a very good job in either place but I had made my point: I had followed Sydnye's MO.

I pulled the gag from her mouth. "Now, do you think I'm serious?" I whispered into her ear. "Did that haircut remind you of anything?"

Vikki glared up at me. "Do you know what a pig you are?"

"Were you at Woody's apartment? Were you with Sydnye?"

"You're a pig. Fuck you, pig!"

I stuffed the gag back into her mouth, then moved off of her and down to the end of the bed.

"This may not be exactly the way my friend was tortured," I said, "but it'll be close."

Grabbing her right ankle with both hands, I twisted it hard until I heard the joint snap.

Vikki screamed into the gag for several minutes.

Back on top of her again, I could see her eyes bulging in pain. "Okay, here we go again. I'll rephrase my last question: "Did you help Sydnye kill my friend?"

I pulled the rag out again. Her face was set in a grimace

and she had trouble getting the words out. "Okay, God damn you! Don't hurt me again! Yes. Okay, yes! I was there! But I didn't know what was going on. That's the fucking truth."

"You were in the apartment and you didn't know Woody was going to be killed?"

"No."

"I don't believe you. I'm calling that another wrong answer."

"Stop! Please! I never saw her hurt anyone before. I thought it was a sick game—a bluff. I didn't know she was going to do him. I was just there. She ordered me to come along."

"Why don't I believe that?" I said.

Then I began sliding back down her body toward her other foot. Her right ankle was already swollen and turning purple.

"Okay!" she screamed. "I was there to watch! I was ordered to be there. I saw her break his arms and legs. I saw her kill him!"

"You watched my friend being murdered?"

"It was my job! She paid me to be there."

"Okay, next question. We're doing better. We're working together now."

"Look, she gets crazy. She just gets weird and crazy!"

"And who cut up his clothes in the closet and then poured whiskey down his throat as he was having his bones broken? Who did that?"

"Sydnye!"

"You're a liar! The two of you were there for hours. Maybe six or seven hours. All night. Sydnye was working—busy torturing Woody. She needed help. There was a lot to do."

"She wanted it to look freaky in the closet, so I cut the clothes up. She told me to smear his puke in the closet, so I did that too. That's it. That's all I did!"

"As she was breaking his bones, who gave him the whiskey?"

"She told me to do it."

"That was you?"

"Yes."

"Did you watch as she cut his cock off? Did you help?"

"No! I watched. Okay? I watched her do it. But he was dead by then."

"You stood by after he was dead and watched my friend get his penis cut off? And you stood there and watched him be tortured—all his bones broken. And you did nothing?"

"Look, she made me. You don't know her. She's scary."

I had to take several deep breaths. This piece of shit of a human being had assisted in my friend's death. She'd looked on as a decent man was being killed—and did nothing.

I had to change the subject or kill Vikki now with my bare hands.

"So, how did you come to meet Sydnye?" I finally asked.

"A year ago," she gasped. "We met a year ago. We both had the same shrink. We met in her office."

"Good answer."

"Then I went to work for her at the dating service in Hollywood. After that she started paying me to do side jobs."

"Side jobs? What kinds of side jobs?"

"She took me to clubs—places like that. She wanted to meet people but she didn't want to do it herself. She's weird and quiet around people. I would meet them for her and then introduce them to her."

"Men or women?"

"Both. But she's into women. She just uses men for sex sometimes."

"And she paid you to do that?"

"Yes. She paid me."

"Did she take you to an AA meeting to meet my friend Woody?"

"I introduced her to him at a meeting in Brentwood. It was a big meeting at a synagogue with a few hundred people. On a Wednesday night."

"And Sydnye was the one who told you to go to work for Sherman Toyota? Sydnye was the one who gave the orders for you to come on to me and to have sex with me?"

"*Yes!*" she screamed, "it was her idea, okay! All of it."

"Sydnye paid you to help her kill Woody?"

"Sydnye's rich. She's very rich. She's crazy too. I couldn't say no."

"How much did she pay you for your work with me, Vikki?"

"Twenty-five thousand dollars."

I leaned close to her. "That's a lot of money," I whispered. "Your services don't come cheap."

"Her trust fund pays a couple of million a year. Sometimes more. She does what she wants. Anything she wants."

"The day we had sex in my car—did she tell you to bring me back here to your place to fuck me so she could kill me?"

"I'm afraid of her. None of that was my idea!"

Now Vikki began howling, dripping snot and tears as she spoke. "C'mon, listen, I was afraid for my life! I had no choice."

"She planned to break my legs and arms and neck and

cut my cock off, too, right? And I bet that she had something even more special in mind for me. I bet you know what it was too."

"She has a drug. It can be injected into someone where they're conscious all the time while you cut them up. She wanted to use it on you."

"I believe that, Vikki."

"I told you she was a freak."

"Then tell me something else: Do you know her father? Do you know Karl Swan?"

"I only met him once."

"Only once?"

"In Malibu. At his home. He has a big estate. I drove her there. She likes having me drive her places."

I shook my head. "Just once? Why don't I believe that?"

Vikki rolled her eyes. "Hey, she hates him. She doesn't spend that much time with him. They don't get along at all."

"Where is Sydnye now?"

"I don't know! She calls me. Then we meet."

"Of course you know, Vikki. Of course you do. I'm calling that another incorrect answer."

Reaching back down to the end of the bed, I grabbed her by her broken ankle, then shook it violently with my right hand. "I've got all night, Vikki."

More sweat and tears and snot were running down her face. "No! That's enough, goddamnit! I'm telling you. C'mon, please!"

"Where does Sydnye live?"

"She has an apartment at the Sorrento Towers at the end of Ocean Avenue. Number seven twenty-one. She'll kill me when she finds out I told you. Now I'm dead for sure."

"I want the rest of it! All of it! I want details! Sydnye's a ghost—off the radar. No ID, no traces. What name or names does she use?"

"Her name is Laighne. Laighne Lazarus. That's the name she uses now."

"And she's at the Sorrento Towers. Does she have other addresses?"

"She has the guest house at her father's place in Malibu. It has a private driveway."

"Where else?"

"A place in Mexico. Her lover Sandra lives at the Mexico place. Laighne spends some of her time there with Sandra."

"Did you and Sydnye-Laighne have sex? Are you her lover too? Is that how you got hooked into this sick shit?"

"Okay, I guess that's it. I don't know."

I could feel the blood rushing to my cheeks. We were an inch apart, face-to-face. "So you admit setting me up to be killed! And you admit being there when Woody was killed. And helping while he was being killed. What does that make you, Vikki?"

"I didn't personally kill anyone, man!"

"Bullshit! Do you want to die—right here—right now!"

She could see the rage building in my eyes and I saw the fear in hers. "Tell me the truth," I yelled.

"Okay," she gasped, "I helped! Okay! I helped kill him!"

"How?"

"Just enough so she wouldn't hurt me too. I helped her break his legs."

"What else?"

"I was the one who cut his cock off. She ordered me to do it. But he was dead by then. That was all, goddamnit!"

I leaned back away from her. "Last thing, Vikki: I need phone numbers. Sydnye's numbers. I also need the names and numbers of the people who work for Swan at his estate. His numbers too."

"I have some. I have Swan's cell. Sandra's number in Mexico and Sydnye's numbers too. I have that stuff."

FIVE MINUTES LATER we were done. I had everything I needed. Vikki was still strapped down and lying faceup and naked on the bed. Her right ankle was now thickly swollen and contorted.

Holding up her .25 automatic, I leaned toward her. "I'm going to do you a favor, Vikki. I'm giving you a choice. A choice that Woody didn't have."

She saw the gun in my hand. "No, for God's sake. NO! I told you everything. No! Jesus, NO!"

"Here's the deal. We both know that you and Sydnye were planning to do me right here in this apartment. And we both know that you helped kill my friend. Right?"

"Please! C'mon, Fiorella! Jesus! Please!"

I leaned close to her ear and whispered: "You're going to die as an accomplice in the murder of my friend. It can go one of two ways: I can break your fingers and arms and legs and keep it going for another three or four hours. Trust me, I'm willing to do that. Or you can hold this gun in your hand and put a bullet in your brain. That's the deal."

"NO! Jesus, NO!"

"I'll start now. I'll start with the fingers on your right hand, then move to the left hand. Then I'll go to work on your other ankle. You remember how it goes, right?"

"C'mon! This is me, Fiorella! C'mon, we had something going together, remember?"

I loosened the restraint on her left hand. "You choose, Vikki. It's up to you."

She struggled, arching her body on the bed as her naked, thick breasts began flopping from side to side. Then she stopped squirming and glared at me, but said nothing.

After switching the gun to my opposite hand I forced the T-shirt gag back into her mouth. Now her eyes were like a wild animal's. I grabbed her index finger in my fist and, in one motion, forced it back until I heard a snapping sound.

It took several minutes for her to stop screaming.

NOW I LEANED close to her ear and pulled the gag out. "Tell me when you're ready to shoot yourself, Vikki. Your other fingers and the thumb are next. One at a time. I'm not going to rush this."

"Kill me! Just shoot me in the head. Just do it!"

"No no no. You're the one who'll do that. I'll aim the gun under your chin for you but you're the one who's going to squeeze the trigger and hopefully blow the top of your head off. I'll be the one who helps. Just like you helped Woody die. It's your call. You can die fast or you can die slow."

She glared at me but didn't speak.

I began forcing the gag back into her mouth but she resisted by clamping her jaw shut. Reaching down I slapped her swollen ankle with my hand, twice. Hard. That caused her to begin howling again and I jammed the T-shirt back into her mouth.

The broken finger was already swollen to twice its normal

size. I held another finger in my fist, then looked into her eyes. "Okay, here we go again, Vikki," I whispered. "Get ready."

She began screaming into the gag. Then she nodded her head up and down.

I pulled the gag out.

"Okay. Okay. No more. I'll do it! I'll fuckin' do it!"

Rolling her to her side, I freed her left hand from the belt restraint. Spit and tears were streaming down her face. I heard a sound, then looked down between her legs. She had pissed herself.

Grabbing her left hand tightly, I put the gun in it. My free hand was around her wrist, my finger blocking the trigger guard.

"Ready?" I said.

"Fuck you, man!"

"Right."

I put her finger on the trigger.

"Okay," I said, "here we go. Bye-bye, Vikki."

Her eyes were fixed on the ceiling as she squeezed the trigger.

I WASHED UP her bathroom and cleaned myself up. That done, I wet the hand towel, wrung it out, then wiped off any traces of my prints in the bathroom and in the bedroom.

A quick once-over of the remaining night-stand drawer revealed something new: a small black leather bag—a sort of miniature tool kit—behind a box of CDs. In it were leather thong restraints, three different sized pairs of pliers with black handles, along with two pairs of surgeon's gloves and a scalpel. Vikki's traveling torture kit. She only helped. Right!

Preparing to leave, I located her purse in the living room and removed her cell phone, tucking it into my jacket pocket. Then I returned to the bedroom for the last time, put on the surgeon's gloves from the torture kit, and wiped everything down again, including the belts I had used to bind her. Then I tore off the piss-soaked, blood-soaked sheets and put them in a pillowcase.

After picking up my Beretta I covered what was left of Vikki's head with the bedspread. Suddenly I felt the need to vomit and rushed back into the bathroom. It went on for five minutes.

LEAVING THE BUILDING with Vikki's sheets under my arm, on my way up Sixth Street to Mom's Escalade, I punched in the number to Archer's cell. Just as I was putting the phone to my ear, I saw a dark, four-door Benz hook a quick right onto California Avenue, then speed away.

Archer answered on the third ring. "Who's this?"

"It's JD. Look, I'm in business. With any luck this could all be over in twenty-four hours. Maybe less."

"You're on Sydnye? How'd you get to her?"

"What about my mother? Did you get help?"

"I tried. I made the calls. I'm still waiting."

"Okay, I'll call you when I'm done, Archer. Keep trying." Then I clicked off.

A few blocks away I threw Vikki's sheets into a Dumpster behind the Miramar Hotel.

TWENTY-FIVE

S wan knew he was not like other men. In fact he was highly aware that his own life was a rather unique one, and that, for whatever cosmic motive, he had been selected and had survived to emancipate himself to a far greater purpose. His existence on the planet represented what he considered to be, for lack of a better term, a sort of experiment—perhaps a kind of virtuoso celestial circus act. In his spare moments he had often mused on these things.

For over fifty years now the producer had risen to increasing riches and status in Hollywood to hold ever-expanding influence over others. On any number of occasions one call from his Century Park East office suite had changed the course of a person's life completely—for good or ill. In two situations that jogged his recollection, there had been suicides. In another, a pretty, full-breasted girl, whose movie-star career he has assisted for fifteen years (primarily to indulge his personal sexual whims) and whose life he now owned outright, at least on paper, had become engaged to a European head of state. She had neglected to call him for his permission. He had countered this slight simply by making two phone calls. In short order, an exposé of the woman's private life and drug use reached the tabloid press, complete with revealing photographs of her bisexual escapades. In no time, her betrothed changed his mind and the bitch's career in the film industry was over.

Swan knew that there had to be a reason he wielded so much power. For even as his star rose to new heights above the Santa Monica coastline, so did his personal zeal for his principal hobby: torture and murder. He had killed often as part of his unfolding mission and those uninterrupted events were profound evidence to him of his unique existence. To date, ninety-seven humans had met their end at his hands. He had preserved mementos of each occasion in a special underground room at his estate and reexamined these artifacts whenever he felt a bit out of sorts.

Over the last twenty or so years he had moved on from the more simplistic bone breaking to more advanced excisions and other, more complex surgical procedures. For instance, removing the intestines of one of his subjects while that person watched from a mirror mounted above their body, all without anesthetic, had become one of Swan's favorite diversions. The expression on his subject's face as he or she watched a nearly soccer-ball sized mound of their own steaming entrails unraveling on their sternum was, to say the least, entertaining to observe.

Swan was aware that his bent for the exotic had become more extreme as time passed. These days he often enjoyed feeding his clients their removed body parts, severed and with an array of condiments.

He could think of no other person of historical significance who had killed more people with his own hands simply for the purpose of amusement. The pleasure—the satisfaction from these acts— had continued to grow to ever-increasing heights. Re-watching an expression of terror in the eyes of his victims in his film archives gave him a full measure of pleasure. It fed his appetite—his need—for more. Seemingly, the more fear he harnessed, the greater his sense of power, and the more pleasurable his later sexual emissions became.

In Hollywood men trembled when he entered a room. The women he owned sought him out to provide certain kinds of pleasure in exchange for his favor and influence. Swan knew that men like himself had inhabited the planet as archetypes for millennia. What his personal quest, in the time accorded to him here, was to create a new record of human possibility for others like himself. Nothing less. And time had proven him unerringly correct. Karl Swan hadn't been stopped and he wouldn't be stopped.

Current scientific data informed Swan that light in the universe could be traced back in an unbroken stream 13.6 billion years. His own life had been designated as a punctuation mark in human history. The world was ready for something else—something with teeth. Something entirely unique. Something to make mankind first tremble, then gawk in awe.

On many occasions over the years, in leaning over his victim— intentionally inhaling their last breath just after delivering a fatal thrust of his blade—he had sensed that he had become part of the eternal. He had risen to experience unification with ultimate power. True transcendence.

Birth and death were the only constants, and to be present at the moment—*in* the moment—when another person surrendered his being was, Swan felt, a vocation of the highest calling. The weak deserved pain and death. Their fear was their purpose on the planet. Swan's task was to honor their uselessness by an act that emancipated them.

While the families of most men his age were interviewing board and care facilities for their aging and crippled loved ones, Swan's physical abilities had remained largely undiminished. He could still run two miles, full-out, three times a week, on the quarter-mile track at the rear of his estate. Thanks primarily to human growth hormone, over the last fifteen years he had remained a superb physical specimen. His blood pressure was a steady one-twenty-six over seventy-two and his weight a trim and ready one hundred ninety-seven pounds—certainly adequate for his seventy-five-inch frame.

His only physical deficit was his lifelong inability to sleep. The dreams that haunted him almost every time he closed his eyes had gone on unabated for over seventy years. Those dreams had been with him since he left Germany as a boy, and shed the cynical nickname Corporal Jewboy.

Swan took three or four one-hour naps daily to compensate and, over time, he'd made the necessary physical adjustments. After all, he was not like other men, was he?

Sexually, Swan considered himself to be still at his peak, and he held with the Chinese in their literature on men's sexuality in one important respect: Restricting one's ejaculation to one incident per week had great wisdom. The Chinese believed that a man's essence was contained in his reproductive fluid. His semen was the epicenter of his power. To disseminate that power carelessly and too frequently was, both Swan and the Chinese believed, to squander it.

All his life Swan had prided himself on his penis. Its length was eight inches by nearly four inches in circumference. For the last two years, he had confined his once-weekly orgasms to Friday afternoons, when his current attendee, pretty Catelena, a slender, twenty-year-old wetback girl from Jalisco who possessed unusually large brown nipples, willingly performed deep-throat fellatio on him.

Catelena would come to him half an hour after he'd punched in her cell number. She would enter his large and elegantly appointed library, which contained three thousand books and was known to be the largest collection of first editions west of Chicago. Swan delighted in having his cock sucked here. He would let his eyes scan

the shelves while Catelena serviced him. He felt he was sharing her
with the masters.

His remarkable collection had been purchased from the Estelle
Doheny estate. On his shelves were *Kapital*, edited by Friedrich
Engels, the *Aeneid* by Virgil, translated by Gavin Douglas, the original
Ulysses by James Joyce, published by Shakespeare & Company in
1922, *The Great Gatsby* by Fitzgerald, first state, in the rare dust
jacket, and *The General Theory of Employment, Interest and Money*—
Keynes, John Maynard, London. Also in the rare dust jacket and
inscribed by the author.

From time to time, while Catalena's head pulsated in an up and
down motion, he would even read to her.

On Fridays, his day to cum, he would not permit her to use her
hands at all. He would grasp her by the back of her neck and force
his piston down her throat again and again until the moment of
completion presented itself. His eruption never entered the girl's
mouth but rather traveled directly down her throat.

Catalena was a decidedly friendly girl who spoke no English, and
Swan made sure that she received three thousand dollars in cash every
week in a sealed white envelope. He also made it his business that
her mother and father were provided for nicely. The *patron* of Grey Fox
Estate prided himself on family values.

At the end of his Friday sessions with Catalena, she would always
look into his eyes and smile, then whisper, "Mucho gusto, señor."

Swan's daughter, Sydnye, had, for the five years prior, been the
only one to supply him oral sex regularly. Sydnye had quite simply
become a master at it. Then the girl, for her own reasons in her middle
teens, had declared that she was a lesbian and her sexual encounters
with her father had been terminated. A period of great turmoil between
the two of them had commenced and Karl Swan now considered his

daughter and the status of their relationship to be an irredeemable mess. He had made her wealthy and tried his best to stay out of her life, but the fact remained that his only offspring had become a psychiatric disaster. She consumed psychotropic drugs by the handful and carried with her any number of diagnoses that had necessitated her confinement for extended periods. The kid was, in the words of the street hoodlums in Los Angeles, a total whack job.

One of Swan's favorite pastimes for the last twenty-five years, when he was not experimenting in his work room or abroad working on a film, was adding to his estate on Grey Fox. The grounds now contained seven buildings. He had participated in the design of each structure and worked closely with the architects and engineers. Of particular interest to him were the apartments that had been specifically constructed for his newly recruited staff. The main building contained eight units. The day when fresh arrivals came north from Mexico, they would enter and occupy their attractively designed and furnished new quarters, and the estate would host a celebration. Swan always made sure to be there. He had been fluent in Spanish for years and he liked to wear his sombrero on those fiesta occasions.

Plump little Raoul, his estate manager, had been his right-hand man for almost three decades. It was with Raoul that Swan placed his requests for new people as the human requirements arose. Through a network of associates, in three major regions of central and lower Mexico, Raoul would recruit their new residents. These persons would be made offers of an eventual path to American citizenship, given a two-thousand-dollar cash bonus, and told to maintain complete confidentiality regarding any and all negotiations. On their initial meeting with Raoul they would be assured that if they did well at their first assignment in America, they would be taught a trade and then move on to another wealthy client in the United States. This, of course, was untrue.

All new arrivals were assigned kitchen duties, gardening, horse tending, and appropriate menial tasks around the grounds. None of them would leave the property alive. Swan exerted complete control at his estate and all those who were in his employ were bound by a strict code of silence, and paid handsomely. All infractions were dealt with quickly and firmly.

Of standing importance to Karl Swan and Raoul was that no new helper would be over thirty-five years old and that the females and males should be of equal populations.

The patron of Grey Fox liked to spend a good deal of his time in the basement of the apartment quarters, in the private video-monitoring room.

Each of the eight dwellings in the building had concealed cameras in all its rooms and in the closets, and the images and accompanying sound feed these generated amused Swan and had become his personal reality-TV show.

Over the last dozen years, what the owner of Grey Fox Estates was primarily looking for in the hours he spent alone in the basement in front of his video screens, were budding romantic involvements among his new residents. Swan had developed an interest in observing sexual interactions—mating rituals. These fresh unions would have a significant impact on his later activities in his hobby room, under the stables. Two-person deaths had begun to enhance his personal enjoyment immeasurably.

Having one lover, restrained on his wall unit, watch the other undergo increasing pain only feet away on the center table, made for highly captivating drama. The surprises that materialized were invariably fascinating.

Swan had personally overseen the installation of five video cameras in his hobby room. Naturally, only state-of-the-art equipment was used. By virtue of his position in Hollywood and his ongoing fascination with the mediums of film and video, Swan had dedicated himself to learning to become an accomplished editor. He derived pleasure from meticulously crafting each one-hour segment into a theatrical quality event. After years of primarily single-unit extinction, relationship deaths had given Swan, to borrow a phrase, new life.

When both subjects entered the hobby room and were confined to their assigned apparatus (both of course had secure restraints), the proximity of the standing-position table to the horizontal platform offered a profusion of possibilities.

Watching the reaction of subject no. two (the standing person, and almost always the female) after, for instance, an eye removal or a limb excision from their loved one at only inches beyond arms length, could be exhilarating.

Swan would typically begin his questioning of the naked participants in a casual vein. An opening like, "How long have you two known each other?" might be standard to the female on the upright table. Then he would comment on their evolving romance and produce his handheld camera to play back one of their more exciting sexual encounters.

On the other hand, if on that day Swan felt more like getting right down to business, he might simply begin with: "I've been watching you two have sex through a hidden camera in your room. I've enjoyed what I've seen. I've been thinking of fucking you in the ass before I kill you."

Swan might then explain the first of the session's procedures to the female. "I'm going to start now on your boyfriend. While you watch I'll insert these two twelve-inch needles into the shaft of his penis."

If, for whatever reason, that didn't produce the expected reaction, he might add: "But, you have a choice, my dear. I could use them on your breasts instead."

The second deaths in these dual sessions were what Swan found to be the most intriguing. His observer on the upright table, after watching half an hour of torture on her boyfriend, might be enticed into almost any act of degradation in order to spare herself from a fate similar to the one she was seeing. Acts like consuming blood mixed with fecal matter after the removal of a foot or hand, or the ingesting of a newly excised organ, were common in the hobby room. Nothing, no demand that Swan made, seemed too excessive to be gratified. The final result on film, after careful editing, was, to say the least, captivating.

On only one occasion had the female subject offered to be the first to die instead of her boyfriend. The girl's name was Felicia, a chubby child in her midteens.

Swan had just begun with a routine excision of all the toes on her boyfriend, Carlos's, left foot. He then decided to offer Felicia a compromise: if she ate two of these, with cream cheese, he would be more merciful when it came to her turn. Instead of his usual bilateral breast removal, he would simply drain her blood during the anal penetration procedure.

"Kill me now," the girl had screamed in her native tongue. "I cannot watch the death of the man I love."

Her tormentor was moved by this articulation of selflessness. Impressed, even. He set down his clippers, put a canvas bag over the girl's head, placed the muzzle of his .22 automatic between her eyes, then fired twice.

It was then that Swan did something he had never done before. He phoned the estate nurse and ordered her to come to the hobby room. When she arrived, Swan instructed the woman to take the boy to the infirmary and suture and bandage his wounds. Four weeks later the young man was flown to Honduras, then released on the streets with five thousand dollars in cash, a free man.

TWENTY-SIX

Half an hour after leaving Vikki's I parked on the street across the expanse of four-lane Ocean Avenue, opposite the Sorrento Towers, where Sydnye-Laighne lived. The luxury building, overlooking the ocean, was set back off the street. It was twelve stories tall with a circular driveway. Its front entrance was in my full view fifty yards away.

Just to be safe, keeping loose ends in mind, I used the Phillips screwdriver attachment to my fold-up knife to remove the license plates from a Buick convertible parked four cars away on the street. I then replaced Mom's plates with the Buick's and stowed her Escalade's plates under the mat in the cargo area.

My single motivation was to get to Sydnye, to find her and to kill her. If she wasn't there, I'd wait until she was, then do what I had come to do. Karl Swan was target B.

I locked Mom's car, then slipped on a pair of tinted glasses before crossing the street toward the glitzy glass façade. Entering the driveway I saw a large yellow lettered banner in the garden area centering the drive. It read: SHORT AND

LONG-TERM LEASES. INQUIRE ON PREMISES WITH RENTAL AGENT. It was an invitation. That sign was my way in.

Beyond the revolving door I saw a doorman in full uniform and cap sitting behind a long, wide desk. In back of his chair was a bank of monitors that flashed every few seconds, changing images. The guy's brass nametag read "Joe."

Pulling out my New York City detective's badge, I set it in front of the guy. "Joe, I'm Paul Foley, New York City Homicide. I need your help."

He picked up the badge and looked at it, then the ID that came with it, then handed them back to me. Then he leaned over for a last look at his laptop screen on the center of his desk. "Okay, Detective, I'm all ears. What can I do for you?"

"We've got a trial witness about to testify here in L.A. in Santa Monica Superior Court. I need safekeeping for him for a week, ten days max. I saw the short-term rent sign in front. Does the management here also rent by the day?"

Joe rolled his eyes. He sighed, took off his hat, then ran his hands through his hair. "Sure, that's possible. But I'm not the one you should be talking to. That'd be Adelaide. I know we have a few furnished units. But like I said, you'd have to talk in person to the rental agent. She gets in at ten in the morning."

Opening my notepad (with the bullet hole in it) to appear more coplike, I wrote down the name, "Adelaide," then the words "Sorrento Towers."

"Okay," I said, "that's helpful. Can I have Adelaide's number or her card?"

Joe looked down at his desktop. There were several plastic holders containing business cards. He found the right one, then handed it to me. "Call her in the morning, okay? And have a good night, Detective."

"Police business, Joe. Look, if it's not too much trouble, I'd like you to show me a floor plan of the building."

Joe immediately took on his best oh-Jesus-leave-me-alone-for-chrissakes face. "Look, Detective, you're going to have to talk to the rental agent."

"I've done this before, Joe. I do it all the time. The building floor plan is usually right here at the front desk. Help me out, okay, it's been a long day. A man's life is on the line, here."

Joe grimaced, then opened a drawer. It'd been just as I guessed. He removed a large laminated drawing that dia-grammed the building's interior and all its apartments. He handed it across to me. "Whataya know?" he said in fake amazement, "it was right here."

Before looking at the floor plan, my eye caught a side view of his computer screen. It showed a poker table. Appar-ently, Joe was an Internet gambler. Texas hold 'em.

I pointed at the screen. "How ya doin', Joe? Winning or losing?"

He shook his head. "Don't ask. I'm down a hundred and twenty-eight bucks for the day. That's how I'm doing."

"Bad habit," I said. "I had to give it up before it kicked my ass."

Joe made a face. "Man, I hear that."

I studied the building layout drawing for thirty seconds and saw what I thought I needed. But I had to be sure. "Hey, Joe," I said, "can you make me a copy of this?"

"Sorree. No can do. Not tonight, Detective. Like I said, the leasing office is closed. The copier's in there. Adelaide can help you out in the morning. So—is that all?"

Joe slid the diagram back into his desk drawer and returned to his computer screen.

"Okay, one last thing," I said. "I promise. I need to see the building's alarm system."

"That'd be Adelaide too. That's her job. I'm the doorman, Detective. I don't rent apartments or do extracurricular stuff. I greet people. I help load luggage into cars. I'm just a grunt wearing a uniform, okay? That's my job description."

"Joe, we're moving on this tomorrow. Just show me where the room is or point me to it. Five minutes. You don't even need to get up. I just have to check out the system. That's all I need. Then I'm gone."

Joe shook his head, minimized his Ultimate Bet Poker screen, then got to his feet. He pointed at a door a few feet down the wide hallway, then reached to the side of his belt and produced a thick key ring that held two dozen keys. "Here," he said, holding a single key in the air after unclamping it from the ring, "use this."

I took the key. "Thanks," I said, and began walking down the hall toward the door.

"Wait," he called from behind me. "Jesus, I gotta do it! I forgot, I gotta punch in the code. It's a new procedure. We're up to our nose hairs in new procedures around this place."

I followed him down the hall to a door marked ELEC-TRONICS / MAINTENANCE. Joe entered a combination on the key pad, then was able to key the door.

He flicked the light switch on. "Okay," he said standing aside for me to go in, "close it after you're finished. And don't forget the light, okay?"

Five minutes later I'd done what I needed to do.

"Hey Joe," I called, standing at the bank of elevators,

wanting to appear like I was ready to leave, "everything looks okay. One last thing: I'm going to check out the garage now. That okay with you?"

Joe didn't look up from his poker screen. "Whatever," he whispered under his breath. "Jesus. Whatever."

THE UNDERGROUND GARAGE was large and well lighted. It had three levels. I got off at one, then started checking the white painted numbers in front of the parking spaces. On two I found hyphenated numbers—tandem spaces. I walked to the two spaces that had the numerals 721A—721B. Seven twenty-one was Sydnye's apartment number.

The yellow Porsche was not there but a sport-top black Jeep Rubicon, set up with a roll bar, a winch, and half a dozen other off-road accessories, was parked in 721-A. It was covered with what looked like weeks of dust and I assumed it hadn't been driven in a while. A question I had neglected to put to Vikki before she'd exploded her brain was: how many cars does Sydnye own? Now I knew.

I WALKED UP the rounded driveway, two floors, to the exit. There was a side door at the end of the building façade, next to the automatic sliding parking gate. I went out the side door, but left it ajar behind me, and crossed the circular driveway on my way to Mom's Escalade.

Once out of the garage I was again in cell range, so I removed Vikki's phone from my pocket and punched in the first of Sydnye's numbers. Getting into Mom's Escalade I decided that it was time to stir the waters and coax the bottom feeders up through the swamp bottom—to be speared.

After several rings, the call went to voice mail. The message I left was five seconds of dead air. Then I clicked off.

Now I tried her second number. It too, eventually, went to voice mail. Again, I paused, breathing into the receiver for a few seconds, then clicked off.

I calculated that it would take time until my location, via cell tower, might be isolated by a computer-geek killer who kept track of such things. I knew that Sydnye was on me but I didn't know how close she might be.

Next, I dialed Swan's personal cell. When he picked up immediately, I was surprised. I could hear music and conversation in the background. A dinner party? "Yes, may I help you?" the smooth European accent intoned.

"Hello," I said, "Is that you, Karl?"

"Hello. Yes, this is Karl Swan. Please speak up! How may I help you?"

"Karl, I'm . . . sort of a friend of your daughter Sydnye's. I just wanted to check in and say hello."

"Who is this? Please tell me what you want."

"It's about the murder of my friend, Woody O'Rourke. Your daughter Sydnye killed my friend. I'm going to kill Sydnye and then I'm going to kill you for sending your man after my mother."

There was a long pause on the other end, so I kept going.

"Remember those bodies you dumped at the burial grounds out near Point Dume? You and I are going to meet face-to-face so I can deliver a message from them.

You're a sick, murdering, butchering piece of shit, Karl, and your time on the planet is now in countdown mode."

Another long pause at the other end of the line. Then: "Please forgive my abruptness. I'm with friends at the moment. May I call you back at this number? I would like to continue this conversation—in a more private setting."

"I'm coming. I'm coming very soon, Karl."

Then I hung up.

STARTING MOM'S ESCALADE, I drove to a side street, parked, and turned off the engine. My head was throbbing badly after my visit to Sydnye's apartment building and the conversation with her father. I could feel my body getting close to maxed out. I needed to close my eyes, if only for a few minutes.

The dream that came was odd and prophetic. I was standing on the Coast Highway by the gas station at Coral Canyon in Malibu, talking to a guy who had just pulled up in his car, needing directions. I didn't recognize the man, though he looked familiar. He had a map spread out on his trunk. He said that he was delivering sandwiches to Trancas Beach—to the home of Spencer Tracy.

Looking at the guy with curiosity, I said, "Spencer Tracy's been dead for fifty years."

"That's okay," the guy said, "the sandwiches are all cold by now."

Then a huge boulder, the size of a house, began tumbling down from the steeply graded hills above the gas station. When I saw it coming I stepped back and yelled "Look out!" But the boulder crushed the guy, then kept rolling across the highway into the ocean.

．．．．

WHEN I WOKE up I looked at my watch. I'd been asleep
for thirty minutes. My head wasn't banging as badly as
before.

I drove back to the Sorrento Towers and parked near
the circular driveway. Through the glass entrance window
I could make out doorman Joe, still battling online poker at
his desk. I could be fairly certain that, owing to Joe's passion for gambling, the video monitors behind him would be
neglected while I did what I needed to do.

Down the drive by the garage door entrance I waited in
the shadows while a green sports car, using a remote opener,
pulled in. After the car passed through the gate and was out
of my view, I stepped inside.

Walking down the sloping circular drive to the second
floor of the underground lot, I made my way along the
cars to the black sports Jeep parked in slot 721-A. Sydnye's
Porsche still hadn't returned.

Looking through the plastic, zip-down window into the
rear passenger area, I saw some things that would come in
handy. On the rear floor were a pair of ski boots, an orange
stocking cap, and a pair of orange ski goggles.

The Jeep's door was easy enough to open after slicing a
hole in the plastic window. I reached in and got the goggles
and the cap, then went to the glove compartment to make
sure I was robbing the right car. The vehicle was registered
in the name of Laighne Lazarus.

At the elevator I pressed "7" and went up to Sydnye's
floor. I let the doors slide open, then waited.

Not hearing any sounds, I pulled the stocking cap down

over my ears. Then I put on the goggles and turned my bomber jacket inside out and put it back on.

I stepped out into the carpeted hallway. Above me I saw the camera, then the other ones at both ends of the hall.

I knew from the building diagram that 721 was the first door on the right. With the apartment alarm now disabled, it took me less than a minute with my picks and WD-40 to work both locks.

I was about to push the door open when I heard a sound like a faint sniffing noise. A few seconds later there was more sniffing, then what I took to be the scratching of paws against a flat wooden surface. I stepped back immediately. I knew exactly what was behind the door—from experience. An attack dog, silence-trained. Maybe more than one. Animals disciplined not to bark—not to make excessive noise—but to dismember and kill. I'd met one of the fuckers in Hell's Kitchen one night, face-to-face, years ago. I knew immediately that I would have to come up with an alternate plan.

CLOSING THE DOOR to 721 I left it unlocked and moved back down the hall to the indented elevator doors, taking myself out of view of the hall cameras. Time to come up with plan B.

I took the elevator back down to the garage, removing my cap and goggles before I arrived at the lower level.

Stepping out, a few feet from the elevator bank, I saw a green Dumpster. I stowed my goggles and hat behind it.

NOW, LEAVING THE garage, I made my way across Ocean Avenue, back to where I'd parked the Escalade.

In a shopping bag in the cargo area of Mom's car, I found what would come in handy. The first item was a can of wasp spray. I'd bought the spray from the surplus store on Venice Boulevard, thinking about the Dobies at Karl Swan's estate. I needed it now. Wasp spray, unlike mace, is accurate up to twenty feet. Also, unlike mace, there are no legal restrictions for amounts of more than two ounces.

Next to the wasp spray in the shopping bag were the green khakis and a roll of duct tape. After putting the wasp spray in my jacket pocket I grabbed the roll of duct tape.

NOW, OPENING THE rear passenger door of the Escalade, I grabbed one of the mats. I would wrap the mat around my Beretta and use it to silence any gunshots if the wasp spray didn't work.

On top of the rear seat, left over from the weekend, was an unread copy of the Sunday *L.A. Times*. It was wrapped with a thick rubber band. I slid the rubber band off the newspaper and put it, too, in my pocket. I'd need the rubber band to hold the floor mat closed around my gun hand.

BACK INSIDE THE garage at the Sorrento Towers I picked up my supplies from behind the Dumpster. On the second level there was still no Porsche convertible next to the Jeep in space 721.

Returning to seven in the elevator, I paused again outside the car, listening for sounds, then slipped on the cap and goggles and reversed my jacket before again stepping into the hallway.

The door to 721 had remained closed but unlocked. I set my can of spray down on the hallway floor and waited and listened. My back was to the hall camera as I wrapped the rear floor mat from Mom's Escalade around my Beretta, creating a tube on my hand, then fastened it closed with the heavy rubber band.

Opening the door slightly, I picked up the wasp spray can. I immediately heard the faint sniffing inside and, eventually, the scraping of paws.

As I pushed the door open an inch into the darkness with the wasp spray in my hand, the black nose of a dog appeared for an instant, then backed away. I sprayed a thick stream from my can through the crack of the door and then on to the floor.

The reaction I got was immediate. There was whining and convulsive snorting from the dog.

Pushing the door open about twelve inches, I stepped inside. I immediately sensed the presence of another dog. Number two was whining in a low tone only a few feet away in the darkness.

My spray had done its job. Rottie number one was down and out of commission, rubbing his nose against the floor, writhing in pain.

Now I slipped the floor mat and the gun off my other arm and dropped it on the floor.

I knew that Rottie number two was very close, so I gave number one a final blast, then backed away.

In the dimness of a hallway light I was suddenly able to make out the large dark head of the second dog. He was baring his fangs.

Just as he moved toward me I let loose a stream from the

can, concentrating in the direction of his eyes. I missed the
eyes but did make connect with his mouth and chest. The
skin contact alone caused the monster to first hesitate, then
stumble back to regain himself.

My second blast hit the mark and got him across the eyes.
Immediately disabled, he went down, whining.

NOW, STANDING COMPLETELY still, I found the light switch,
turned it on, then set myself, looking for a third dog. A full
thirty seconds went by before I lowered my can of spray.
There's been only two dogs. Only two! Jesus!

Back at the front door, I opened it and stuck my head out
as far as the frame, then began listening. Apparently I had
attracted no attention.

TWENTY-SEVEN

With the dogs subdued, I decided not to take any chances. Removing the two sleeping pills that I had taken from Vikki's medicine cabinet from my pocket, I peeled the cheek skin back from each dog's mouth and inserted one of the pills. Nightie-night.

Now I was free to have a look around while I waited to kill Sydnye Swan.

I hadn't known what to expect inside the apartment. I had assumed the place would be a mess, mirroring the psyche of a crazed, computer-geek murderer. It wasn't. In fact it was just the opposite.

But before I could begin looking around, I had to take more security measures with the dogs. I stepped over to Rottie number 1 and duct-taped both his front and back legs, then his snout. I did the same with the second dog.

NOW I WENT to the kitchen, where I found the cabinet with the glasses. I removed several, then returned to the front door. I stacked the glasses unevenly against the door at the seam of the opening. If anyone came in, I'd hear the glasses falling on the hard surface and know I wasn't alone.

Stepping back around the disabled dogs, my eyes took in what looked more like an art gallery exhibit than a home. This room was wide and long, probably twenty by fifty feet. The curtains were open and solid sheets of floor-to-ceiling windows faced the street and overlooked the Pacific beyond.

The walls to my right and left were arrayed with black-and-white photographs, lined up one row above the other, beginning at eye level. All the photographs were in twenty-by thirty-inch black frames. There were, I guessed, forty photographs total.

As my eyes went from one frame to the next I could see that each photograph had something to do with the ocean as its theme. Many of them appeared to be shot from a high, rocky vantage point, in what could have been Carmel or Big Sur. All were professional-photographer quality.

In front of the photographs to my right, or, more accurately, between them, were a dozen pieces of bronze sculpture set on four-foot-high marble pedestals.

I walked to the one nearest to me and looked at the wording inscribed on the brass label. Then I moved to the next sculpture and read that inscription too. They were all the work of the same person: Camille Claudel. Claudel had been the young, obsessed nineteenth-century lover and protégé of the artist and sculptor Auguste Rodin. She had driven herself to insanity over the guy.

I had once seen an exhibit of Rodin's bronze sculptures at the Met in New York. Camille Claudel's own pieces were displayed in a side room of that show. She was good—talented. The detail, agony, and boldness in her forms was visually stunning. Was my murderer Sydnye a mutated version of Claudel? Was there a Rodin in her life? Maybe a Rodin-a. All of the sculptures appeared to be originals and worth, I was sure, several million dollars.

IN THE CENTER of the room, on top of a large, expensive-looking sand-colored throw rug, was the living room furniture: two high brown leather couches set at right angles to each other. There was an oversized glass coffee table in front of them. On the table were three black metal bowls of different sizes. All held unwrapped chocolates—expensive-looking chocolates.

The apartment was large. It had apparently once been two dwellings; then the walls were knocked out and the interior completely redone to accommodate the additional square footage.

I crossed the planked and buffed oak floor back to the open kitchen. It was glass and steel and immaculate. The cupboard where I'd removed the glasses was still open.

The countertops were empty except for a gleaming stainless steel coffeemaker. Everything was too perfect. Antiseptic. It occurred to me that no one used this kitchen.

I began opening more cabinet doors. Everything—utensils, glasses, pots and pans and silverware—all of it was gleaming, stacked neatly, and looked brand new.

The last cabinet I opened made me stop. It once had been a broom closet. Now it had shelves and was full, top to bottom, with Happy Meal toys: Batman, Buzz Lightyear, Spiderman, Avatar, Iron Man, Lego cars and Nerf football. Dozen of the damn things, as yet unwrapped.

. . . .

DOWN THE HALL I came to the bedrooms. The first one was empty save for what looked to be a rough handmade wooden table in the center of the room. It had leather hand, foot, and neck restraints attached to its sides and bottom. Sydnye's torture room. It was twenty by twenty. All the windows in the room had been covered and sealed over with soundproof padding, the type I'd seen in recording studios around Los Angeles when I was in the business of renting exotic cars to rock stars and their pals.

The next, smaller bedroom, fifteen by fifteen, was filled with workout equipment and training machines. The walls were mirrored. Nothing much there.

THE MASTER BEDROOM at the end of the hallway was the payoff. Opening the door I could tell that this room was the only one in the place used by anyone.

There were clothes thrown around everywhere; on the floor and on several overstuffed purple chairs. Skirts and jeans and sexy lingerie covered the extra-large custom-made bed. A widescreen TV was set diagonally in one corner of the room. Two large dog cushions were on either side of the bathroom door. In one corner was a rolling service table. On it was a microwave, a large coffee brewer, and coffee supplies.

The wall on both sides of the TV contained another set of large black-and-white photographs. A dozen of them. These studies were all of Sydnye. All nudes in different poses. The woman in the pictures was strikingly beautiful but more like an idealized replica of the one I'd seen in the flesh on the two previous occasions. Her wavy black hair fell to just above her waist and was parted in the middle. Her mouth and eyes were large and inviting. Her breasts were full and looked too perfect to be real. It was as if I were looking at a different girl. Like her pal Vikki: two separate personalities.

Another area of the big room was dedicated to two dozen stuffed animals, all horses of various sizes.

On a low bureau beneath a wide mirror were several expensive-looking figure-study photographic books. Stepping over to them, I thumbed a few pages. All nudes, all in black and white. All females.

Opening the drawer beneath the bureau, I discovered DVDs of children's movies. All the *Toy Story* movies, all the *Shrek* movies, *Finding Nemo*, *Barbie's Christmas Carol*, and a hundred others. Both bureau drawers were packed with the goddamn things. These were a weird extension of the Happy Meal toys I'd found in the kitchen. Somewhere here was the mind of a deviant psycho-killer.

The bathroom was a mess. It was tiled in black and white with stark, empty walls. All the puffy, oversized towels from the chrome racks were scattered on the gleaming, hard-polished black marble floor.

Across the bathroom, open makeup bottles and lipstick cases were strewn over a white vanity table. Above it was an ornate, out of place Victorian-looking gilded mirror.

At the sink, the medicine cabinet door was ajar and its outward-facing mirror smudged with cream or makeup and finger marks.

I pulled the cabinet open with my gloved hand. Inside, on the shelves, I found what did not surprise me: bottles and bottles of prescription pills: Prozac, Zoloft, Abilify, Xanax, among many others, and several varieties of still-sealed script sleeping meds. The lithium was on the top shelf by itself—four bottles of the stuff.

Opening one, I saw that the pills inside matched the ones I'd found in Vikki's medicine cabinet—same size and color.

I began popping the tops of all the plastic containers, then dumping the contents of each into the toilet.

When I was done I looked down into the water. It was completely covered in multi-colored pill casings. I hit the flusher. All the pills didn't go down with the first flush so I waited, then flushed again.

BACK AT THE front door, I moved the stacked glasses aside, then checked my watch. I'd been here almost an hour—still no Sydnye. My last act before leaving was to cut away the duct tape from the sleeping Rotties' legs and mouth.

A cell phone began buzzing in my pocket. Pulling it out I saw it was Vikki's cell that was going off. I looked at the printout: Karl Swan's private number.

"Go ahead, Swan," I said. "I'm right here. I'm listening."

"I hope your mother's rooms at the Raddison in Santa Barbara are satisfactory. I'm told the restaurant in that hotel features an excellent Southwest chicken curry."

"Fuck you, Swan. You're a dead man."

"You should know that several of my staff are stationed outside and in the lobby, awaiting my further instructions. It's my impression that your hired men are no match for Russian automatic pistols."

I whispered my response. "I was going to shoot you but

now I've decided that I'm going to kill you with my bare hands instead."

"Allow me to state my intentions clearly: Vaginal penetration, for a woman of your mother's years, can be very uncomfortable—especially with a pointed, sharp object. May I suggest that you stop by my Malibu home? There are issues between us that require resolution. You have one hour, Mr. Fiorella."

Then Swan clicked off.

What the psycho movie producer hopefully didn't know yet was that Mom and Coco were not at the Raddison. I was one step ahead of Swan. I didn't need Archer's cops. When we were leaving Mom's house on Point Dume, when I saw that I'd picked up a tail, I'd made the call. Then, when we arrived at the Raddison, I'd let Mendoza's ex-cops book the room before I escorted Mom and Coco out the back way to one of the guy's cars. I had then driven them to the Canary Inn, a few minutes away. I was betting and hoping they were still safe.

IN THE ELEVATOR I removed the jacket, ski cap, and goggles.

As the car arrived at the garage level and the doors opened, I felt a wave of something . . . I hesitated.

I waited until the doors began closing behind me, then moved out in a crouch, duck-walking beneath eye level of the parked cars, my Beretta in my hand.

LOOKING DOWN THE long row of front bumpers I saw the high front fender of the black Jeep standing out from the rest of the cars.

I continued shuffling toward it until I caught a glimpse of something bright yellow. The Porsche!

When I was two cars away from Sydnye's convertible I looked up over the top of a tall SUV. Rudolpho, the boy-toy thug from my mother's house, was in the passenger seat of the Porsche. Sydnye was behind the wheel.

Rudolpho leaned his head out the passenger window. "We know you're here, Fiorella. Step out where we can see you—and hold your gun up."

I waited.

"One call and your mother's dead, Fiorella! Last time! I said, step out!" Rudolpho barked.

It would have been easy enough to splatter them both right there with one squeeze on the trigger of my 93R. That was my first and best thought, but instead I decided to let the scene play out in a different way, knowing that Karl Swan might yet be holding the best hand. I didn't want to take any chances with my Mom's life.

I held my Beretta above my head, then stood upright.

RUDOLPHO MUST'VE REMEMBERED that he owed me because the kicks and blows to my face and stomach came fast and were delivered with the vengeance and skill of a guy holding a grudge. As I lay on the pavement I felt a rib or two give way.

Now Sydnye was above me, too, with something sharp and shining in her hand. "Did you kill my puppies, fucker?" she whispered.

It took me half a minute to spit out the blood and then hold enough breath inside my chest to say the words. "They're in dreamland, Syd. Not like sweet little Vikki," I whispered. "She died slowly. You won't be so lucky."

Now Sydnye was on her knees beside me. Her face was calm and expressionless. She might have been ordering a double latte at Starbucks. "I'm going to cut you now, Fiorella. I'm going to cut one of your eyes out. Right here. But just one—I don't want them both. I want you to be able to see the rest of what's going to happen. I want you to see it all. I want us to enjoy it together."

Rudolpho's hand pushed her stiletto away, then he made two quick moves and the blade skidded across the parking lot's concrete floor. "No way!" he snapped. "Please back off, Miss Swan! That's not the deal! Your father's instructions to me were to bring him back in one piece. He was very specific about that."

TWENTY-EIGHT

There wasn't enough room in the Porsche for the three of us so Rudolpho cuffed me behind my back and then punched me a few more times until he felt I was peaceful enough to travel.

When we were all in the dusty Jeep and Rudolpho had me covered with my Beretta from the passenger seat, Sydnye put her key in the ignition.

The car's battery was dead. There wasn't even a clicking noise from the solenoid.

"Okay," Rudolpho offered, "Plan B, Miss Swan. We'll have to improvise. I'll call and get more instructions."

Sydnye rolled her eyes. "Jesus, Rudy. Wake up! Get Fiorella's keys. We'll use his car."

He turned toward me. "Where's your vehicle, Fiorella? Your mother's Escalade? Where is it parked?"

"It's down the block. You're not very good at this, are you, Rudy?"

COMING UP THE steep ramp toward the electric garage gate, Rudolpho grabbed me with both hands from behind, by the cuffs, then cranked them hard in a circular motion.

"I'm taking these off now," he hissed. "If you move quickly or say anything, I'll kill you. Do we understand each other?"

I was smiling. "Okay, numbnuts," I whispered. "But you're improvising again. Tell me, does Swan hold your pee-pee for you when you take a squirt too?"

Rudolpho wasn't amused. I got a nasty toe kick to the upper thigh that sent me to the concrete, on my knees.

After he pulled me to my feet, he handed Sydnye the gun, then unlocked my cuffs. Then he slid the keys back into his shirt pocket.

WHEN THE THREE of us had made our way to Mom's Escalade, Swan's man tossed my front pockets only and came up with the keys to her car. "In the back, Fiorella," he ordered. "Miss Swan, I need you to drive again. I'll keep an eye on him. I'm following your father's orders."

Sydnye made a face at the kid, then snatched the keys from his hand. "You're a putz, Rudy."

Rudolpho remained stonefaced. He spun me around, then clamped the cuffs back on my wrists with my arms behind me, then shoved me into the rear passenger compartment behind the driver's seat.

ON OUR WAY up the Coast Highway toward Point Dume, the traffic was light. As we neared Gladstone's at Sunset Boulevard, I'd finally managed to work the can of wasp spray out of my back pants pocket. I'd been lucky with Rudy. The hothead had been so distracted, carried away with getting his payback in the garage, that he'd forgotten to look past the Beretta in my hand and into the rear pockets of my slacks.

My gun was still in his right hand as he sat in the front passenger seat across from Sydnye. He used his left hand to pull his cell phone from his jacket pocket, preparing to make a call.

I was directly behind Sydnye as she drove. I knew it was now or never. I had just enough leeway with my cuffed hands behind me to contort my body and aim the nozzle of the wasp spray at the side of Rudolpho's head. I took a deep breath.

The stream from the can caught part of his face and his left eye. My gun and his cell phone tumbled to the floor of the car as he grabbed at his face.

It took three or four seconds before Sydnye could fully react to what was happening and felt the first collateral sting of the pest spray.

Holding my breath I moved to the center space between the front seats and aimed blindly from behind my back. I began blasting away with the can, in her direction.

The spray missed her head but the ricochet off the inside windshield and the sun visor did immediate damage to her face and eyes.

Sydnye swerved the Escalade toward the shoulder, waving her right hand, trying to block the continuing blast.

When the car finally bumped to a stop against the embankment, I forced my right leg between the console and the driver's seat.

Now facing Sydnye, then bracing my back against the side of the passenger seat and Rudolpho's convulsing body, I began kicking at her: four, five, six times.

She was pinned by the driver's door and had no option but to absorb the punishment I was dealing. Two of my heel thrusts caught her on the side of the head. She slumped against the steering wheel, unconscious.

My eyes and face were burning like crazy from the secondhand contact of the spray. Having to breathe in the evil shit wasn't helping either.

Climbing across Rudolpho, my hands still shackled behind me, I fumbled to get to the door handle, pulled it, then tumbled to the street.

I immediately began gasping in as much fresh air I as could.

This was L.A. Here was a car in an accident with its front bumper against an embankment—what to any respectable citizen anywhere else in America would clearly be seen as an emergency situation—yet the cars on PCH continued rolling by and ignored our vehicle.

Once on my feet again, I saw that the kid, his eyes still clamped shut, had pulled himself together enough to start groping on the floor mat for my gun.

I leaned back inside the car, near his swollen face, and began using my head as a battering ram against his.

By the time I stopped, blood was streaming down his face and my forehead. The kid's nose was crushed and his two upper front teeth were dangling from his bleeding mouth.

Bending him sideways toward me in the seat, then turning around, I tore the cuff keys from his shirt pocket with my shackled hands.

TWENTY MINUTES LATER, with all the windows in the car open and the A/C blasting, I was at Cross Creek Road, the location where, only weeks before, my life had irrevocably taken a dump at Guido's Restaurant. The two of them were cramped into the front passenger area, Sydnye on the floor.

I wheeled the Escalade around to the back of the shopping center, then parked out of sight in back of Guido's.

I dumped both Sydnye and Rudy into the backseat. He was bleeding a lot, holding his head, and barely conscious. She was out cold. The large bulging contusion on the right side of her face and drooping jaw made it clear that bones were broken—probably in more than one place.

Looking around for spectators, making sure I wasn't being watched, I used my belt and Rudy's belt to bind Sydnye. Then I used the handcuffs on him.

It took me a few minutes to bring her around. I accomplished this by jabbing her in the thigh with my knife blade until her swollen eyes began to blink.

She couldn't move her mouth but she was able to garble a few words. "Ooo-re deeeead, Fi-ella," was her best effort.

I had to smile. "Easy for you to say, dollface. Now look, in a little while you and me and Rudy are going to pay a visit to your father's place. But before that, we're going to call Papa. I'll do most of the talking but I want to make sure that Karl knows that you two are still among the living. You'll have to speak to him."

"Ukkk huuuuuu."

"Right. Not bad. Keep working on it."

Drool and foam were forming at the corners of her mouth. "So here's the deal," I said. "If you don't talk to Karl and help me out, I'm going to hurt you again. Badly. Pretty simple. Understand?"

"Ukkk huuuuuu."

. . . .

USING RUDOLPHO'S PHONE, I scrolled down to the last out-
bound number, then pressed send.

The call was answered on the first ring. "Karl Swan
speaking."

"Okay Karl, Sydnye's here with me. Rudy too, only he's
sort of out of it. I'm the one holding the gun now. I've asked
Sydnye to say a few words to let you know that I haven't
killed her yet. It's time for you and me to have a little come-
to-Jesus reunion, Karl."

There was a long pause on the other end. "I have some
disappointing news for you as well," he said in his studied
whisper. "The situation here has altered somewhat—albeit
to my benefit. I have your mother, Mr. Fiorella. She's here in
front of me, unconscious. Your ruse and the evasions at the
Raddison hotel have failed. People were shot, but that was to
be expected under the circumstances. So please listen carefully: My primary imperative is for you to bring my daughter
and Rudolpho here to my estate, alive."

Swan's news hit me hard. The fucker had outsmarted me.
"I'll kill Sydnye," I said. "I won't even blink."

"I believe you. And that would be exceedingly sad for
me. I care deeply for my daughter. But, in truth, she has been
lost to me for a long time. Young Rudolpho would actually
be a far greater loss. He has great potential. So here is my
proposal: Deliver Sydnye and Rudolpho to me with yourself
in exchange. That's my proposition. Take it or leave it. You
should also know that I've made plans for your mum. Unlike
her, I am not an astrologer but my personal prediction is that
she will succumb slowly after an invasive surgical procedure.

My greatest skill, if I may boast a bit, is in keeping my subjects alert until I have accomplished what I set out to do. Naturally, there will be a great deal of pain. The delivery of high levels of discomfort is what enhances my pleasure. It is my finest talent."

"Instant death is my skill, motherfucker! I'll shoot Rudy through the head and not even blink! Want to try me now?"

"Quite simply, your mother will live unharmed in the trade for my daughter and Rudolpho. You, of course, will remain here with me. Mrs. Fiorella and her unconscious lady friend will go free. Do we have a deal?"

"Yeah, asshole, we have a deal."

"Now, I must assume that Rudolpho is injured. Is that the case?"

"He's a little lumpy but your young protégé is still alive. He'll need some dental work and other stuff."

"Mrs. Fiorella has no knowledge of being here. She and her companion were sedated in Santa Barbara before their drive down the coast. I can deliver the two ladies unharmed, if you and I can come to a suitable accommodation. Wait! How fortuitous, Mom is apparently beginning to come to! Excellent timing. Please, now I would like to speak to my daughter."

"Okay, asshole. Here's Sydnye. Then put Mom on the phone."

I stuck the cell to Sydnye's ear. "Talk now, bitch, or I'll punch your face," I whispered.

"Fah-ver," she groaned into the phone, "ish meee. Ahm ah-live."

I snatched the phone away. "Okay, Karl," I said, "now my mother."

There was another long pause on the line. Then: "Please hold on. This will take a few moments."

Half a minute later, through the receiver, I heard Nancy Fiorella's faint eighty-one-year-old voice. She sounded confused, not fully conscious. "Coco," she said haltingly, " . . . where are my glasses? What time is it?"

Then Swan was back on the phone. "I will expect you at my home within the half-hour."

With no options left, I said, "Okay, Swan, I'm on my way. But no watchdogs! And no cars at the gate at the Coast Highway, no armed assholes on the walls outside—none of it. Or one or both of them die. Rudy first. Got that?"

"Agreed."

I clicked the phone off.

I FOUND A bottle of spring water in the SUV's console, tore Sydnye's blouse off, then soaked it before cleaning the gashes on my forehead and over my eye with the thing.

I decided that if I was on Swan's death menu, I would make damn sure that Sydnye would permanently pay for her crime against my friend Woody. As Swan might say, it was my primary imperative. Rudy, as far as I knew, was a gofer, Swan's tool and a boy-toy, but not a murderer. He would have a nice long recovery ahead of him.

I opened the rear door and climbed into the backseat with my two captives. Rudy was still defenseless but trying to get it together, so I gave him a hard knee to the stomach. Then I flattened Sydnye's body against the seat cushion on her back, stuffed a scrap of a ripped shirtsleeve into her mouth, and extended her legs out of the rear passenger door. I slammed the door against her shins three or four times to make sure there were multiple fractures.

She was now only semiconscious. I loaded her back inside the rear seat compartment and put my knee on her chest and stomach, then grabbed my wasp spray can. Remembering the can's warning label—"May cause permanent blindness if not immediately treated"—I held Sydnye's eyelids open with my thumb and forefinger, then sprayed a four-second stream of the poison into each eye socket.

TWENTY MINUTES LATER, as we were approaching Grey Fox, I pulled over. I picked up my Beretta and made sure the safety was off.

The mansion's lights, which normally illuminated the wall and the perimeter of the grounds, were out. Pulling up to the gate, I got out of the Escalade, my gun in my hand behind me, then reached back inside to the steering wheel and honked the horn.

A few seconds later the shiny automatic brass gates began to swing open.

A man was standing there wearing the green work uniform I had seen before. He was short and stocky and looked immediately familiar. Then I nailed who the little shit was. It was Tomas Valenzuela, the husband of the couple who had committed identity fraud when they'd purchased the used SUV from me at Sherman Toyota. I felt like putting one in his kneecap to renew our acquaintance but decided against it. Sydnye was a malevolent, scheming little bitch.

Tomas held up both hands. "No choot," he said, looking at the arm I was holding behind my back.

"Don't worry, Tomas, I'm not here for you. Just take me to Swan."

He motioned for me to pull the car in, so I returned to the Escalade and got back behind the wheel.

"No litz," Tomas ordered. "No litz enside."

I turned the beams off.

After the brass gates closed behind Mom's car, Tomas, shining a flashlight on the cobblestoned roadway in front of him, began walking toward a long, flat building I could just make out a hundred yards away. It looked like a bunkhouse or stable.

When we arrived at the building another man wearing the same green outfit stepped away from the long metal door. He nodded to Tomas, who clicked off his flashlight, then turned and walked away.

At the side of the building, in the shadows, were two other guys with what looked like automatic pistols in their hands.

THE SHORT FAT guy at the stable door was in his late fifties and had long gray sideburns beneath his cap. "My name is Raoul," he said in perfect English. "Mr. Swan is expecting you. You are Mr. Fiorella, correct?"

I kept my gun next to me on the front seat and looked the little guy in the eye. "I come bearing gifts, asshole. Call me Santa Claus. Go get your boss out here!"

"I order you to remain exactly where you are."

"I'm not moving, Raoul, I'm waiting. See?" Then I lifted my hands above the steering wheel to show they were empty.

"My instructions are to make sure that Miss Swan and Rudolpho are alive."

"Then do it."

Raoul moved up next to the Escalade, then looked inside through the rear passenger window.

Then he popped the door open. Sydnye's contorted face got his attention in the bright light from the car's interior. She was whimpering.

"Miss Swan is seriously injured," he barked.

"And permanently blind, too, I hope. My deal was to bring them here, still breathing. I kept my end of that deal."

Raoul walked around to the other side of the car and opened that door. Rudolpho tumbled out onto the cobblestones, his arms still clamped behind him, banging his head hard as he hit.

"Is he alive?" Raoul barked. "He looks dead."

"See the blood coming from his face? Dead men don't bleed, Raoul. This one's alive. Now I'll need to see proof of life on my mother and Coco."

Reaching into his jacket pocket, Raoul took out his cell phone. He clicked a button on the phone's face and a photograph came up on the screen. "This picture is ten minutes old," he said.

I looked at the screen, then quickly lifted my Beretta and pointed it between Raoul's eyes. "Are you interested in dying right here, asshole? Because tonight the angel of fucking death is traveling with Santa Claus."

"I—I will telephone your mother now," he sputtered. "If you harm me in any way, Mr. Swan's men will shoot you."

The guys in the shadows at the side of the stables stepped out into the light from the open doorway.

"Not before you die, pal. Just make the call!"

Raoul punched in the number on the speaker-phone

option to his cell. It rang but there was no answer. Then he
tried again with the same result. Finally, he looked at me.
"I assure you that your mother is at home. Apparently she
is not answering her phone. I'll try again in a few minutes.
Now I will telephone Mr. Swan."

"No deal," I said, still with my gun pointed at his head.
"In the car. Now! Mom's house is five minutes away. I'm
going to see for myself. Tell your guys that they can keep
Rudolpho. Sydnye comes with us."

Raoul contorted his face. "I cannot act without permission, and Miss Swan is in need of immediate medical attention. Please, let me get someone."

"She'll live. Let's go."

"Sir, I promise you that your mother is well and unharmed. I escorted her to her home myself. Mr. Swan's instructions were to leave her unharmed. Mr. Swan is a man of
his word. Now please, let me get help for Miss Swan."

"Last time Raoul—in the car!"

He waved his men off, then got into the Escalade.

A black BMW sedan tailed us as we left the property.

AS I WALKED up Mom's thirty-foot entrance pathway with
Raoul two feet ahead of me, my gun pressed against his
spine, the front door swung open and I was surprised to
see one of Mendoza's men—one who hadn't been killed in
Santa Barbara—aiming a Browning shotgun at us. "Halt, or
you're dead!" Majuski yelled. "Halt or I open up!"

"It's me," I yelled, "Fiorella . . . Is my mom okay?"

He lowered the Browning, "Yeah, she's okay—you okay?"

"Still in one piece. Anybody else in there with her?"

"Your mom's friend, Coco. They're both unharmed. Your guy there says he made a deal with you, that he gave you his word and that they will not move on anyone here. Was that the deal?"

"That was the deal."

Majuski made a face. "Okay, but what about you?"

"Stay here with Mom," I said. "I've got business."

"No problem," he said. "I'm here until I hear from you otherwise."

TWENTY-NINE

On our way back to Swan's house, Raoul used his cell to have a staff nurse meet us at the entrance gate. As the gate was swinging open the woman rushed out, popped the rear door to the Escalade, and pulled Sydnye out. Swan's murdering daughter was mumbling and delirious. She was a blind gimp now and not dead, as I'd wanted, but I was pretty sure she'd never hurt anyone again. The nurse and two smaller Latino helpers carried her off into the darkness.

Tomas was back with his flashlight. He walked ahead of the Escalade, once more shining his flashlight on the cobblestones, until we reached the stables. Then he disappeared back into the darkness.

Karl Swan was standing in the doorway fifteen feet away facing my driver's side window; in front of him were two helpers acting as body shields. His expression was emotionless. "Welcome to Grey Fox, Mr. Fiorella. Now, as you have seen, I kept my word to you about your mother."

"So far," I said, leaning my head out the passenger window.

"As agreed, your life for hers. She will remain unharmed,

I assure you. She has not seen my face and does not know she's been on my property. Rudolpho is badly injured and unconscious," he half whispered. "I'm told that my daughter is in even more serious condition."

I smiled. "It was her own doing, Karl. I've just been playing catch-up. Our deal was for me to bring them here alive. I kept my deal."

"You and I will be playing catch-up, too, I give you my word on that."

"You're going to die, old man. I don't care what happens to me."

"Oh, but you will care. You will soon care quite deeply."

MY MIND DID the math quickly. I saw that I might be covered on all sides. The two guys with the Russian automatics had stepped into the light from the stable door and were coming toward me, and Raoul was now two feet away, holding what looked like a small caliber Smith in his sweaty little hand. In the distance next to Swan I could see the two men blocking him. I had to assume they had guns too. That meant six targets.

It was now or never. I had nothing to lose except my headaches and my shitheap of a life—but I did have an edge: the two with the automatics, and Raoul, had orders not to kill me but to give me alive to Swan. They just might hesitate for half a second when I opened up.

My decision was made an instant later: kill everyone. Do it now! I was close enough with my 93R and had a full clip to take them all out, starting with the guys with the Russian guns. Swan would be among my last targets. Just keep squeezing the trigger. Then, with any luck, I'd also find Sydnye and kill what was left of her.

Fuck it!!

I held the gun out toward Raoul as I feigned standing down from the Escalade in surrender. When he reached for it I mule-kicked him in the gut and he staggered back, off balance.

Now standing fully upright I spun the little shit to face the two goons with the Russian guns, using him as my shield. They were a few feet away and closing. In that instant they could have fired, but they didn't. I'd been right! I squeezed the trigger: pop pop pop pop pop! I was at can't-miss range. The taller of the two was not a center hit and he reeled and was able to raise his gun again just as I squeezed off four more rounds. Five seconds had elapsed. Maybe six.

Now I turned on Swan and his body-blockers. I knew I had to make my shots count. The old shit had been quick—my moves had given him time enough to slide farther behind his two guys. I had no clear shot at my main target. Again my solution was simple: keep firing. Kill whatever you can. Pop pop pop pop pop pop!

One of my slugs caught the first man in front of Swan in the arm and stomach. He spun to the left, firing at the ground. My next burst jerked the head of the second man backward. A center hit. He collapsed on the cobblestones.

Now I was able to aim directly at his unobstructed boss, who had begun firing at me from a small-caliber automatic— and missing.

Then, from behind me, came Raoul. I sensed him there an instant before I saw only black.

. . . .

IT MUST HAVE been after dawn when I came to. My brain was hammering inside my skull and what vision I had was blurred. I began blinking and realized that my right eye was swollen completely shut, probably from the head butting I had done with Rudolpho.

Trying to move, I discovered that I was shackled to a bed. Spread-eagled. Then I realized that I had little or no muscle control.

Still blinking my only working eye, I could finally see a little better. I understood that I must have been injected with something to calm me and make me cooperative.

Shifting my head with effort I begin to make out the room I was in. It looked like some kind of upscale Motel 6 in Texas or Mexico. It had two beds and oil paintings on the stucco walls: cheesy Mexican art—bullfighters in the one and twirling señoritas in the other. I stared at the bullfighter painting and kept blinking my good eye until my vision finally corrected itself fully.

Now I lifted my head again and looked toward my feet. I discovered that I was dressed in white, loose-fitting cotton clothes—the shirt and pants of a Mexican peasant. There were bloodstains down the front of my shirt. Then I realized that I badly had to take a piss.

Several minutes later I began to hear footsteps and shuffling in the hallway outside the door. Karl Swan came in first, wearing a tan cowboy hat. He looked taller than I remembered and he looked like he hadn't slept. Then a nurse in a white uniform entered too. The one from last night. I was surprised to see that she was pushing Sydnye Swan in a wheelchair. Sydnye had splints on both her legs and a bandage wrapped around her head with bars on each side to keep her jaw in place. Her eyes were taped shut with large cotton swabs.

It was hard to believe. Blindness, a crushed jaw, and several leg fractures would add up to immediate surgery and put anyone else in the ICU for at least six weeks.

Then I added it up: Sydnye, of course, had access to immediate medical care and primo pain meds. She had willed herself to be in the room.

Swan gestured toward the door and the nurse silently left the room. It was now me, Sydnye in the wheelchair, and her dad. To celebrate the occasion I decided to relieve myself— and a large spot of piss began to stain the front of my white pants.

Seeing what I'd done, Swan made a face. "Had you inquired, Mr. Fiorella, our staff would have been able to accommodate your needs."

"No problem, asshole," I said. "I feel right at home."

Then Swan moved Sydnye's head in my direction. "He's right in front of you," the old guy whispered. "Two feet away. Go ahead, my dear."

She leaned toward me, then spoke through a taped jaw without moving her lips. "Hii ashed my fazzer fur a favvr. Hii ashed hiiim to let me dooo uuu. Kno whaaa he saaad? Heee saad ho-kay."

I had to smile. "Too bad my legs are cuffed to the bed, Syd. I'd really like to kick you again—just for old times' sake."

"Too guyz . . . spezalizts . . . har on dar way prom Seeeeeders. Day gona fizz me hup."

"Nope," I said. "I don't think so. That bug spray is

pretty good shit. Your corneas are fried, bitch. I saw that for myself. And your jaw is busted in at least two places. You're disfigured, Sydnye. Your face'll never be pretty, or close to it, again. Better think about changing your photo on crazy-wats.com. You're a hopeless, blind geek now."

Her muffled hissing continued. "Urrr gonna diii slo-lee, Fi-rella. Hi promisss."

"No more pretty Hollywood starlets on daddy's tab, no more cutting your escorts' cocks off. That is, unless you're into Braille surgery. I'd call whatever happens to me after this a fair tradeoff."

KARL SWAN HAD been staring at me, smiling. He finally spoke. "You know your father was quite an unusual little man, Mr. Fiorella. He worked on a film for me many years ago."

"That's crap! He never worked for you, Swan."

"Unfortunately, he did. Unfortunately for me. I recall Jimmy Fiorella as a pompous, annoying fraud—much like a recalcitrant child who welcomes a good thrashing."

"That's bullshit, old man!"

"May I continue?"

"Do what you want."

"As you may have heard, I have long had a reputation for being a stern taskmaster when I produce a film. The maintenance of that perception has always been important to me and it has held me in good stead during my career in the movie industry. Those who have failed me invariably suffer harsh consequences. Jimmy Fiorella was no exception."

"Take a good look at your daughter's profile, Karl. Then tell me about harsh consequences."

"At the time, I was producing the film *Jailhouse* and I called your father into my office to terminate his employment. He had fumbled and stalled on an important rewrite assignment I had given him and his unprofessional behavior had put my film a month behind schedule. The director and my secretary were there as well that day. They witnessed it all.

"Before Jimmy Fiorella could seat himself I dropped the moronic and preposterous screenplay revisions he'd completed on my desk in front of him. 'Mr. Fiorella,' I said, 'what possessed you to write this drivel? Your take on the main character's motivation is absurd. And the dialogue between he and his girlfriend is amateurish and decidedly off the mark. What you've submitted is hopeless trash. You're fired, sir.' Naturally, the pathetic little troll begged me for another chance. It was quite awkward, actually. He wrung his hands and even wept as he apologized for his shoddy work. Of course it was well known at the time that little Jimmy was a skirt-chaser and a gambler and a drunk and I had learned that he had spent the previous weekend in Las Vegas.

" 'Jimmy,' I said, 'as you know, I am not without influence in Hollywood. I'm going to make it my business to make sure that you never sell another screenplay. By tomorrow the word will be out. Anyone who makes the miscalculation of hiring you will never work for me or this studio again. Full stop.'

"What followed was several more minutes of groveling and self-humiliation. The incompetent little fool even vowed to rewrite the entire first act by the following Monday. But, as you might suppose, I'm a rather busy man and finally— when I could tolerate no more—I stood from my desk. More tears were in your father's eyes. I actually believe that if I had demanded it, the little coward would have sucked my cock in front of everyone present. The scene was quite embarrassing, actually."

"The cops know I'm here, Karl. They're on their way."

"My only regret is that time passed and it turned out that I had not done enough to sufficiently extinguish your father's screenwriting aspirations in Los Angeles. Ironically, a few years later, one of my competitors did give him an assignment and the film he wrote managed to receive Academy Award consideration. I was left to suffer a long and unpleasant professional and public embarrassment, one that has remained vivid in my memory.

"So now we move forward in time to the day you encountered my daughter, Sydnye. You vandalized her sports car and humiliated her in a restaurant in front of two dozen patrons. My daughter! My only child. After she described the incident to me and we did some checking, we quickly discovered that you were, in fact, Jimmy Fiorella's wayward son. Naturally that discovery triggered my recollection of your midget father and his long past-due debt."

"Screw you, Karl. You're a butcher and a dead man!"

"You are here to account for what you did to my daughter and, in your own way, to compensate me for the embarrassment I suffered at the hands of your father. After today the slate, as they say, will be wiped clean."

Swan then tossed his cowboy hat on the bed and folded his arms across his chest. "So tell me, JD," he whispered, leaning closer, "the dreams you have—your overcompensating personality and those violent headaches—it all seems a bit bizarre. Apparently self-humiliation and mental illness run in your family? Like father, like son, as they say."

I had to smile. "Go fuck yourself, Pops! You're the one with the price on his head."

"The information that I've had my people compile on you, although somewhat abbreviated, speaks directly to a singular personality disturbance. I've done a good deal of reading and have had some limited personal experience in the area. May I say candidly that your violent nature and consistent substance abuse reveals what any schooled clinician would refer to as a baseline pathology. Self-hatred is the real key here. Perhaps you are even more like your father than you realized. I'm a steadfast believer in genetics. And in your case, apparently, the apple hasn't fallen far from the tree."

"Tell that to your kid. She's as crazy as you are."

Swan's hands were folded on his lap. He looked directly into my good eye. "I feel I must make an admission to you now," he said. "Frankly, I have misled you. I did guarantee the safety of your mother and her caregiver, Coco, but given the damage you inflicted on Sydnye and on our young Rudy, I'm sure you'll appreciate my circumstances. I can no longer honor our agreement. They will also die soon. And I assure you that their deaths will be as painful as possible."

Swan reached over and pressed a buzzer on the night stand. A second later the nurse reentered the room. She was holding a syringe in her hand. "You may inject our subject now," he ordered. "It's time to begin."

The woman missed the first two times because I was rocking from side to side and twisting my body. But on her third try, I felt the needle go in.

The last thing I remembered thinking was: *Well, okay, here I go. Fuck it!*

. . . .

THE LIGHTS IN the room I was in were bright and shining in my face as I started to come around. I saw Swan inject me with something and I watched as he put his syringe away.

Thirty seconds later I was totally alert, wide awake.

He was standing next to me dressed in form-fitting white overalls and wearing blue surgical gloves. There was a small metal table next to the larger one I was lying on. It contained surgical tools—scalpels and pliers and a couple of shiny saws.

Looking past the table I could see that the walls of the room were soundproofed, like the walls in Sydnye's murder room at her apartment. There were no windows.

About three feet above me, on either side of the bright lights, suspended from the ceiling, was a bank of two-foot-wide mirrors that ran the length of the table. When I looked up I could see myself fully in the reflection. Other than Swan and his instrument table and one wooden chair, there was no other furniture in the room.

I began to hear music playing, coming from speakers somewhere. He must have hit a switch.

It was Cole Porter again. Tony Bennett vocals this time. "It was just one of those nights . . . just one of those fabulous flights . . . a trip to the moon on gossamer wings, just one of those things."

Swan was leering down at me. "Welcome back, Mr. Fiorella. Time to get started. My daughter will be here in a few moments. I'll be assisting Sydnye and guiding her hands as she clips, or cuts, or saws, depending on her preference.

You'll have to forgive us but, given the circumstances, her work may not be as precise as we'd all like. I have just injected you with bupivacaine to ensure your full participation and I will use epinephrine to stop your bleeding. And, on my instrument table, I have a handy battery-operated cautery that will seal your wounds as we go.

"But before Sydnye arrives I'm going to administer a second mild injection. The dizziness and physical effects wear off rather rapidly but it will allow you to remain in a calm state of consciousness during your procedures. It's important for you to be with us every step of the way. My goal is for you to be completely aware of what is happening until the moment before you beg for death."

"That's nice, Karl. Got a cigarette?"

WHEN SYDNYE ARRIVED a couple of minutes later I had a nice buzz going. I couldn't see her through my overhead mirror but I could hear her wheelchair as it thumped down some stairs. Finally the nurse wheeled her close enough to the table that she came into my line of vision.

Swan helped steer his bandaged daughter against the table where I was lying. Then he spoke over his shoulder to the nurse: "Sydnye looks uncomfortable. I assume you gave her another injection? Will she be able to participate?"

"Yes, Mr. Swan. She's out of pain but please, not more than a few minutes. The Dilaudid will most likely cause dizziness off and on."

"Then that will be all, Maria," Swan snapped. "Sydnye and I will make do. We'll take it from here."

"Please call for me immediately if she appears to have any negative reactions."

"I said, that will be all, Maria. Leave the room!"

"Yes, *patron*."

SWAN SLOWLY HELPED his daughter into a pair of latex gloves. When that was done he smiled broadly at the bandaged geek beside him in the wheelchair. "Now, how would you like to begin, my dear?" he asked quietly.

"Figgers furs. I wann to doo hisss figgers," she said, hissing the words through frozen lips. "I wann hit to beee sloooo."

"The saw or the clippers, my dear?"

"I sad slooo, fadda! I wann da saw."

"Excellent choice."

I watched through the mirror as the tall, gray-haired man reached down under my table and turned up the volume on his Cole Porter CD.

" . . . so good-bye dear and amen
here's hoping we'll meet now and then . . .
It was great fun
but it was just one of those things . . . "

Swan then picked up a short stainless steel saw from his side table. He placed it in his daughter's hand, guiding her to the end of my arm. Then he put the blade on top of my little finger and said, "Make your first cut here, Sydnye. Now?"

There was no pain as the crazy bitch began grinding the blade into me. I felt throbbing, then watched my blood spurting upward. Thirty seconds later Swan held up my little finger.

"Excellent. A good excision. Excellent, Sydnye!"

Papa was smiling broadly as I bit down hard on my cheek and lower lip.

Then he reached for a syringe. "Mr. Fiorella, I'll be injecting coagulant as we go. We don't want blood everywhere, now, do we?"

At first I couldn't answer. I couldn't concentrate. Then I could finally get the words out: "Blow me, Karl."

"Fazzer," Sydnye mumbled through her taped jaw, "shob tha figger up Fi-rella's rectum."

"Of course, my dear. Should we do it one at a time or do you want to wait and do them all at once?"

"Noooo, onn hat a timmmm."

Swan spread my legs with one hand. He'd dipped my severed appendage into something greasy. Then I felt the thing as it entered my ass.

"Shall we continue?" Swan said to his daughter.

WHEN THEY HAD finished and all the fingers on my left hand were cut off, I could see what was left of my bloody stump in the mirror above me.

Swan tapped his daughter on the arm. "That was the last one," he said. "Now we're ready for the left foot, Sydnye."

A few minutes later the toes of that foot were wiped clean and lined up in a steel pan at the end of the table.

I could feel myself going in and out of consciousness.

"Mak hum heat zemm, fazzer," she whispered. "Whon hat a dime."

Just as the bitch said the words she was suddenly out cold. I saw her drop the saw to the floor and then teeter and slump at the end of the table.

Swan went to her and set her upright in the chair, but she was gone—unconscious.

A minute later I could smell ammonia, or something as strong. He stuck whatever it was under her nose and she seemed to be coming around.

Then I began hearing banging at the door. The noise seemed to be coming from far away but thudding loudly in my ears at the same time. I took a deep breath. I could feel myself letting go. After that there was only the relief of blackness.

THIRTY

I woke up slowly and began to try to clear my mind.

My first thought was that I was dead. But that had to be wrong. I was thinking, so being dead didn't make sense. Or maybe it did. Maybe dead people think too.

Trying to open my eye—the one that wasn't still swollen shut—I could sense light in the room. Then I tried lifting my head, hoping it would clear my vision, but nothing happened. I was unable to move or see.

Finally the good eye opened and I could make out that this wasn't Swan's operating room. There was no mirror above me. The walls weren't dark and there were other beds. There were people in the other beds and there was a TV playing somewhere. A basketball game.

Then I smelled the stink of stale reefer. No, this wasn't hell or Jesus-land or anywhere else. Somebody was howling. Then I realized that the howling was what had woken me up.

I couldn't sit up and I felt weak, so I tried to talk. Only a whisper came out. "Where am I?" I said to the ceiling.

"What?" a voice answered above the howling and the TV. Then another voice said, "Hey, he's awake."

Then the first voice again—laughing above the howling. "Where da fuck you think you is, muthafucka?"

"Just tell me, okay?" I said in a louder voice so as to be heard. "Is this a hospital?"

"Bullseye," the voice came back. "County USC. The bess firstes class shithole in L.A. You got here day before yestaday. You all fucked up, my man. Chopped up 'n'shit."

Then the howling subsided and I was able to close my eye again.

WHEN I NEXT came around, the head of my bed was elevated and Detective Archer was standing a foot away, talking to someone. I blinked a few times to make out who that was. It was Afrika.

Then, with a lot of effort, I tried to boost myself up so I could see them better. A sharp pain in my left hand caused me to change my mind. All I could do was to try to raise my head.

Looking across the room I saw that the other beds were now empty.

Seeing I was awake, Archer leaned toward me and pushed a straw into my mouth. "Take a drink," he said.

I took a drink, then slid my head back down on the pillow.

He was smiling. "You made it, tough guy. Just hang in. Relax. It's all okay."

It took another minute but I finally boosted myself up to take another hit from the bent straw. My thirst was overwhelming. My throat was raw. "Tell me something I don't know," I croaked.

"Like what?"

"Like what's wrong with me. My eye. Why the bandage? Am I blind?"

"No. Like I said, you're okay—mostly. The doctor told us you broke the bone above your eye. But that'll heal okay."

"Nice to know."

"You're getting better. You've still got two eyes."

"I keep thinking I'm dead. I'm all fucked up. My mind's playing tricks. I keep thinking that this conversation isn't happening."

"We got to you. We found you. That's the bottom line."

"Found me? Found me where?"

"Karl Swan and his daughter, Sydnye. Remember that?"

Then it started coming together. "Wait! Is my mother okay?"

"Yeah, she's fine. Never better. Her friend's okay too."

"What else? Did I get Swan? I remember shooting at him."

"Do you remember being in the room in the basement with Swan and his daughter?"

I had to think. "No. But I remember a big mirror."

"People died that day. A lot of people died."

With effort I held up my thickly bandaged left hand, then looked at it for several seconds. "Jesus! Sydnye was chopping me up. Now I remember!"

"Correcto," said Afrika.

Finally it was all back. The reality of what happened hit me fully. "Jesus Christ! Fuck! So what have I got left? What didn't they hack off?"

Archer made a face and fell silent. Then looked away.

"C'mon, for chrissakes!" I yelled.

"Well, okay," Afrika said, "they got your fingers and your thumb on your left hand."

"What else? Gimme more water!"

Archer put the straw back into my mouth, then spoke. "Your toes. The ones on your left foot. All your toes."

"What else? Don't fuck with me, Detective. Just tell me. I need to hear it."

"That's it. That's when we broke in."

"Jesus!"

"They sewed them back on. The doctors. We found them on a table at the scene. Your foot will probably be okay after the rehab. You'll be able to walk."

With effort I held up my bandaged hand. "And this? What about this? Did they save my fingers? What happened to my fingers?"

"Look, you're alive, Fiorella. If I were you I'd let that count for something."

"Meaning I don't have a hand anymore?"

"No man, you've got a hand—that's still there. Just no fingers or thumb on it."

"Jesus!"

"We couldn't find the fingers, at least not right away. Too much confusion. We didn't know."

"But you found the toes! So where were my fingers? They weren't with my toes?"

"If we could've found them, the surgeon would've sewn them back on, like the toes. But they didn't turn up until the next day."

"Turn up?"

"Think, Fiorella! Put it together."

Then I remembered. "Wait! You're saying they were still up my ass? Is that it?"

"Hey, the docs had no way of knowing. When they didn't

show up, we figured they were thrown out or washed down a drain somewhere. Then, after you took a dump—it was too late. They'd been off the hand too long."

IT TOOK ARCHER and Afrika the next hour to put the events together and explain the rest.

There was a food tray next to my bed and while we talked Afrika was apparently getting hungry. He began taking stuff off the tray, a piece at a time, and eating it.

According to Archer's theory, the banging I had heard after Sydnye collapsed—before I'd passed out—was probably Raoul, Swan's man. He had come to warn them, and was pounding on the door when I went unconscious. The transmitter that one of Archer's guys had stuck under Mom's Escalade's bumper while it was parked outside Chez Jay's in Santa Monica had led them to me. They'd tracked me to the Malibu estate.

It had taken a SWAT team over two hours and a lot of ammunition to invade Swan's compound, then the stable, and then the torture room. The cellar I was in had been defended by Raoul and three more bodyguards with automatic weapons.

Archer told me that there had been a delay of several hours because it was Swan's estate that was the target and no one—no high-level cop—wanted to stick his neck out. Permission for an assault had been rejected at the highest level.

That's when I interrupted. "So, okay, just tell me—did they get them both? What about Sydnye?"

Afrika was smiling. "Oh yeah, we got Sydnye. She won't be doing any more killin', that's for sure. She was in a coma at the scene from a blood clot from her head injuries. She's still in ICU at county lockdown. We had her DNA on the radio knob in the bedroom and on the bathroom mirror in O'Rourke's apartment. She'll get the needle, or life without. And, of course, she'll never walk again, without help. Both her shins are crushed. Plus her lamps are out—permanently—thanks to you. And Swan's man Raoul took one in the head. We won't know for a couple of more days who fired that shot. Oh, and we also found Swan's freaky video library where he'd filmed several dozen of his torture killings. His personal little cable reality show. They were all in a box in a safe in the basement of the apartment complex. Sick son of a bitch."

That information made me cringe. But I had more questions. A lot more. "Okay," I said, "so how did you guys take Swan down? What happened there?"

Archer went silent. He walked three steps over to the window and began looking down at the parking lot. The guy's every gesture was a tell.

Taboo was now peeling the wrapper on a granola bar from my tray.

"C'mon, guys. Who got Swan!" I yelled. "I want to hear about that."

Archer wouldn't turn back or look at me.

Finally Afrika took up the slack. But before speaking he stuffed most of the bar in his mouth. "They nailed the S.O.B.—finally."

"Good. Let me hear it. Tell me."

Afrika rolled his eyes. "Well, it took us another twenty-four hours, but we caught up to him—in Mexico."

"Put my fucking candy bar down! Mexico? How the hell did he get to Mexico?"

Ignoring me, Afrika consumed the last of the bar in one bite. "The tunnel," he said. "It took us almost four hours to find the tunnel."

"Tunnel! What goddamn tunnel?"

"There was a false wall down there in that cellar. When the fireworks started, Swan was in the wind."

"You're kidding!"

"We had two teams going over the grounds until we finally found it. But that took too long. The door, I mean the place where we think he came out, was under one of his sports cars in the stable; a fifties Ferrari. He must've had help to move the car out of the way and leave the tunnel, then pushed it back on top of the hole, after he'd climbed out. At least that's how we think he did it. That's what we assume."

I wanted to boost myself up higher but I couldn't. I'd just slammed my bandaged foot on the rail at the side of the bed. The pain was instant and brutal. I fell back down on the pillows.

"Relax," Afrika said. "Like I said: done deal. The point is, we got our guy."

I glared over at Archer standing by the window. He was mute, a nonparticipant.

It took a full minute for me to be able to talk again. "What happened in Mexico, Archer? Exactly?" I yelled. "*You* tell me! I want to hear it from *you!*"

Archer wouldn't look back at me.

Taboo was now picking his teeth with the cellophane

from the granola bar. "Okay," Afrika said, realizing Archer's decision to not answer me. "Here's how it went down: Swan landed at the private airport in Cabo. We'd tracked his plane from LAX. A Gulfstream 550. His private jet."

"And then what?" I said.

"When they set down, the Mexican cops were there on the tarmac. There was gunfire. Automatic weapons discharge was coming from the plane. The Mexican guys defended themselves. They returned fire. The plane exploded. End of story."

"And Swan, goddamnit?"

"Dead in the fire. Like I said—a done deal."

Archer suddenly turned from the window and spoke slowly, precisely. "Burned. Burned beyond recognition! Flames from the jet fuel. No bodies recovered."

"No bodies?"

"No bodies. Charred remains."

"But they got a shoe and a DNA match," Afrika said. "From the suitcases in the luggage bay. Eleven and a half C. Same size as the shoes in his closet at Grey Fox. And his house keys, verified by photographs shown to his housekeeper as belonging to Swan."

"Wait! Are you saying that you weren't there? You guys weren't at the scene? You took the word of the Mexican police and his fucking maid?"

Afrika glared at me, his arms folded across his chest. "The ID was made and verified. Solid police work. The only luggage on the plane belonged to Swam. It's a done deal. The man is dead."

"What about it, Archer?" I yelled. "You believe that? Did you buy that?"

He'd turned his back to me. "They wrapped it," he finally whispered, looking back at me from his reflection in the window. "It's over."

"No kidding? Then I guess that means it's also over for your eleven bodies buried out on the flats under Point Dume, too, and the others that he cut up and killed. It's over for them, too, right?"

"It's over! The fat lady sang."

"Fuck the fat lady, Archer!"

"When the fat lady says it's over, it's over. Remember us? Remember me? I work for that fat lady. It's wrapped. That's all there is."

THIRTY-ONE

It was almost three months later and I was sitting at the noon AA meeting room in the converted grammar school on Point Dume, sipping coffee in the back row, waiting for things to get started. After my hospital time I'd been living at Mom's house again. What was left of my left hand was healed and I had been working on turning my stump into a battering weapon, thanks to daily martial-arts training and the heavy bag at the gym. My balance with the left foot had continued to give me trouble and I still had a slight limp as I walked. It was 11:58 A.M.

Albert, from months before, continued to be the secretary of the meeting. He was making his way toward the podium at the front of the room with a cup of free coffee in his hand. I noticed that Al was dyeing his hair these days and his obvious lust for the newcomer women was still his most annoying personal characteristic.

In my spare time, away from the gym, I'd started to write again. Poetry mostly. My typing at the computer keyboard was improving. Knuckles and fingers now.

I hadn't seen pretty Meggie with the pink thonged panties

in months, until she walked in. She looked like shit. After she got her coffee—she had to hold the cup with both hands because of her shaking—she made her way to the row in front of mine, then dumped her purse down on the chair heavily, then looked up at me. "Oh, hi," she said, faking her best twelve-step grin. "How's it going? I forgot your name."

"JD. It's JD. Howya doing? It's been a while."

"Meggie."

"Yeah, I remember."

"I'm back again," she whispered. "I had a kinda bad slip. I just did a thirty-day mini bit for possession. So I'm back from the dead, I guess you could say."

I shook my head. "No, Meggie, the dead don't make it back to meetings. You and me are the lucky ones."

She smiled with effort, then sat down in the seat in front of me. I was pleased to note that she still wore thonged panties. Today they were black. "Hey, look," she said, turning back to me, "if you don't mind—I mean, do you mind—going for coffee after the meeting? I really could use somebody to talk to. A familiar face. I'm having a tough time."

"Sure. We can go to that place up on Dume Drive by the highway. The café."

Then Meggie's sad eyes wandered down to my stump of a hand with the missing thumb and fingers. "Hey, what happened to you? Oh geezzz! Shit, sorry—I mean, I hope you don't mind me asking?"

I chose the words before I answered. "Surgery. I had surgery," I said. "But it's better now."

Meggie made a face. "Jesus! That was some surgery."

"Yeah. It was."

There was stillness for several seconds on the once pretty

face. I could feel her brokenness—her exhaustion with words—with the brutal disease inside her.

Finally, she looked me in my eyes. "But you're okay? I mean, other than the hand?"

"Yeah, I'm okay. I'm good. And still sober."

"That's good, JD. That's cool."

"So, look," I said, "I'll meet you up at the café after we get done here. I gotta check my P. O. box but I'll be there by one-thirty, okay?"

"Thanks. I'll wait for you. Look, I mean it; thank you."

"Hey, no problem. We'll talk later."

I WAS SMOKING in the parking lot after the meeting, still favoring the foot as I made my way toward Mom's Escalade. The speaker for half an hour had been a knucklehead named Milt, some kind of former personal manager to a rich Malibu celebrity. During his share, Milt made a big point of not mentioning the guy by name, always calling him "Mr. B." Milt hated this Mr. B. Mr. B had made Milt work sixteen-hour days, and he had numerous crazy personal issues. Milt had been sober for three years until he'd gone to work for Mr. B. But then there had been endless nights of dope and teenage hookers and lots and lots of pressure, so Milt—to make himself feel better at a job he hated—began snorting some of Mr. B's dope and screwing a few of Mr. B's girls. He'd shit-canned his recovery. Then Milt's marriage had fallen apart and—surprise, surprise—Milt stole fifty thousand dollars worth of jewelry and cash from Mr. B and went off to Tahoe and got drunk for three weeks while he spent all the money. Milt was now a year clean and sober again and augmenting his recovery by going to therapy three times a week. He was also considering becoming a Scientologist. He'd just done three rounds of their auditing. Almost all of Milt's share had been about his hatred and resentment toward his celebrity ex-boss and how the guy had ruined Milt's life. He waved his arms a lot and used the word "motherfucker" as often as he could. These days Milt was interviewing for jobs, etc., etc., etc., and was determined to make it back on top and finally get his screenplay produced.

At the end of his recovery-free soliloquy, the thirty or so of us sitting in the chairs had not heard ten seconds about recovery, the Twelve Steps or a Higher Power, or anything worth remembering. There are over three thousand AA meetings in L.A. every week. Some of them represent Alcoholics Anonymous, but these days most have devolved into generic, canned recovery-speak that comes from inpatient programs that have little to do with any spiritual change. In treatment programs, after you pay your forty to seventy-five thousand, or whatever it is, they teach you that all addiction is the same—which is a lie. So the message of Alcoholics Anonymous has been permanently watered down and today the success rate is about one to two percent.

WHEN I REACHED Mom's car, I clicked the automatic door mechanism and was getting in when, out of the corner of my eye, I saw a beige four-door Crown Vic pull up, one space away. Detective Archer was behind the wheel. He leaned out his window and called, "I figured I'd find you here."

I didn't turn around; I threw the words over my shoulder. "Twelve to one every day, Detective."

"It's all over—the backwash on the Swan thing. I thought you'd want to know. All the pending stuff you had—the shootings and the B&E and the other thing with Sydnye's girlfriend, Vikki—it all went away. Sydnye plea-bargained for life without possibility of parole. You're in the clear. Funny how fast the smell of shit can disappear when the right names are mentioned in a courtroom by the right people."

I finally turned toward him and made a face. "Yeah, it disappeared. But it'll stay rotting and stinking under the rug for quite a while—along with the corpses that Karl Swan buried. Those people will never have grave markers."

"You gunned down four people, pal. I'd call that a win-win. All charges against you are dismissed. You bought your walk because me and Taboo went to bat for you all the way. I'd say an atta-boy was in order—maybe even a thank-you."

I glared at Archer. "I didn't do enough," I said. "I didn't get Swan. I'll have to live with that."

The detective was looking down at my hand. He grinned. "So, you still crapping out fingers, Fiorella?"

"Not anymore, lawman." I held up my now calloused stump. "Take a look for yourself. I've been working the heavy bag. In a couple of more months my trainer, a serious martial-arts kid I met named Kwan, tells me I'll have the lethal weapon I want."

"How about the headaches? How you doing there?"

"I'm down to only a couple a week. It's livable. Much better than before. So let me ask you one: Are you still jerking yourself off? Pretending Swan is dead and this deal is over?"

"This is reality, pal. It's part of my job description. Anyway, I thought you'd want to hear some good news."

Archer clicked the gearshift of the Crown Vic into reverse. I pointed down at the car's wheels I could see from my
side of the car. I'd noticed sand in both rims—sand that had
to have come from Swan's former body dump site on Point
Dume and nowhere else. Archer wasn't fooling anyone.

"So," I said, "you took the day off to play messenger and
come out here and tell me I'm in the clear? What about the
sand on your wheel rims? You didn't get that sand in this
parking lot."

"I had to make a stop. Must've picked it up when I
parked."

"Don't shit me, Detective. You could have dialed my cell.
That's not the only reason you're here. You were back out on
Point Dume again today. You were at Swan's dump site. I'll
bet you went through the house again too. I know it's still
taped off. Am I right or wrong? You'll never let this thing go.
And neither will I."

"The case is closed, Fiorella."

"Sure it is. Look," I said, "I'm meeting someone. I gotta
go."

"Hey, Fiorella, something's still bothering us—me and
Taboo: a dumb detail. We never found your friend Woody's
johnson. Feel like telling me about that?"

I made my best I-have-no-idea face. "Got me," I said.
"Maybe Sydnye or her sidekick Vikki flushed the thing down
the toilet."

Archer sneered. "And maybe you did."

Then he backed up and was shifting his Crown Vic into
drive. "So what are you up to these days?" he asked.

"I'm writing again—one-handed or one-handed with a

stump. Some poetry, and I'm getting myself better. That's it—until I'm ready to go again. You?"

"I'm going on vacation."

"You're not a vacation type of guy, Archer."

"Yeah, I'm taking my full three weeks this year. Going down to Mexico. Maybe do a little fishing."

"Fishing, huh? I didn't know you fished, Detective."

Archer smiled. "I have all my life—for one thing or another."

"Not me," I said. "I hunt. I'll be hunting again very soon. And when I catch what I'm after, I'll kill it. But I guess that's the difference between us."

THE END